DONALD E. WESTLAKE

Nobody's Perfect

M. Evans and Company, Inc.   New York, New York 10017

M. Evans and Company titles are distributed in the United States by the J. B. Lippincott Company, East Washington Square, Philadelphia, Pa. 19105; and in Canada by McClelland & Stewart Ltd., 25 Hollinger Road, Toronto M4B 3G2, Ontario

Library of Congress Cataloging in Publication Data

Westlake, Donald E.
    Nobody's perfect.

    I. Title.
PZ4.W53No [PS3573.E9]   813'.5'4   77-24180
ISBN 0-87131-249-2

Design by Al Cetta

Manufactured in the United States of America

9 8 7 6 5 4 3 2 1

This is for James Hale,
who comes close to belying the title.

THE VERSE

Dortmunder slumped on the hard wooden chair, watching his attorney try to open a black attaché case. Two little catches were supposed to release when two bright buttons were pressed, but neither of them worked. In other cubicles all around this one, defendants and their court-appointed attorneys murmured together, structuring threadbare alibis, useless mitigations, attenuated extenuations, mathematically questionable plea bargains, chimerical denials and hopeless appeals to the mercy of the court, but in *this* cubicle, with its institutional green walls, its black linoleum floor, the great hanging globe of light, the frosted-glass window in its door, its battered wooden table and two battered wooden chairs and one battered metal wastebasket, nothing was happening at all, except that the attorney assigned to Dortmunder by an uncaring court and a malevolent fate couldn't get his goddam attaché case open. "Just a—" he muttered. "It's always a— I don't know why it— I'll— It's just a—"

Dortmunder shouldn't have been here at all, of course, waiting for his preliminary hearing on several hundred counts of burglary and knowing he was merely the victim of another

accident of fate. Two weeks, two solid weeks, he'd cased that
TV repair shop—he'd even brought in a perfectly good Sony
table model and let them charge him for six new tubes and
nine hours' labor—and *not once* had any police patrol gone
down the alley behind the row of stores. A prowl car cruised
past the front from time to time, but that was all. And the
cops were definitely never there when the pornographic movie
house around the corner let out; at those moments they were
always parked across the street from the theater, glaring
through their windshield as the patrons came slinking past, as
though their moral disapproval would somehow make up for
their legal ineffectuality. "If we *could* arrest you," they tele-
pathed at the pussyfooting porn devotees, "'and if we *could*
turn you over to the proper authorities for castration and re-
habilitation, by the Blessed Virgin we'd do it." And the customers knew it, too; off they'd go, scurrying, hands deep in
pockets, shoulders hunched against society's disapproval, while
the theater marquee flashed its enticements at their backs:
SEX SORORITY sex sorority SEX SORORITY sex sorority. . . .

Dortmunder, well aware of his own history of bad luck,
had done his best to cover every possibility. A quick check of
the timesheet Scotch-taped to the movie cashier's window had
told him *Sex Sorority*'s schedule for the evening: 7:00, 8:45,
10:30. Meaning the last show would finish at 12:15. Therefore,
at 10:30 exactly on this crisp clear November night, Dortmunder had nosed his station wagon into the alley, had driven
slowly past the repair shop's rear door, and had parked two
or three shops farther on. Using two keys, a crowbar and the
heel of his left foot, he'd effected entry into the shop, and
during the next hour and a half he'd assembled most of the
TVs and radios and other appliances over by the rear door,
his work illuminated by a combination of the streetlight outside and an anti-crime nightlight over the empty cash register.
At 12:15 by his watch, by the clock over the rear-room work-
table, and by nine digital clock-radios he'd rejected as too
penny-ante for the effort, he had opened the rear door, picked

up two television sets—a Philco and an RCA—and stepped outside to the sudden dead-white glare of four headlights. (Leave it to cops to keep their high beams on in the city.)

Tonight—*tonight*—one of the cops all of a sudden had to take a leak. In fact, Dortmunder, handcuffed and advised of his rights and disencumbered of the TV sets, had had to wait in the back seat of the prowl car while the goddam cop went over to some garbage cans and proceeded to relieve himself. Relieve himself. "I could also use some relief," Dortmunder had muttered, but no one had heard him.

And now, this excuse for an attorney. He was young, possibly fourteen, with scruffy black hair, round cheeks, and pudgy fingers that poked and poked at the buttons on his attaché case. His tie was loud and lumpily knotted, his checked jacket clashed with his plaid shirt, and his belt buckle sported a bucking bronco. Dortmunder watched him for some little time in silence, and then finally he said, "Would you like me to help?"

The attorney looked up, pudgy face hopeful. "You think you could?"

This was the fellow supposed to keep Dortmunder out of jail. His face expressionless, Dortmunder reached over, took the attaché case by the handle, swung it in a great loop once around over his head, and slammed it down onto the table. The catches snapped, the lid popped up, and a hero sandwich fell out onto the floor.

The attorney hopped in his chair, his face becoming a lot of round O's—eyes mouth cheeks nostrils—and then he stared at his now-gaping case. Messy documents mingled in there with a folded-up *News,* amid several sealed plastic packets of ketchup and mustard and salt and pepper, a small bottle of nasal spray, a pocket pack of tissues, and a scattering of used movie ticket stubs. The attorney gazed at all this as though he'd never seen it in his life before, and then Dortmunder picked up the hero sandwich and plunked it back into the case, saying, "There. It's open."

The attorney now stared at Dortmunder, and Dortmunder

could see he was about to get on his high horse. Perfect. All he needed. Icing on the cake. Now his own attorney was sore at him.

"Well," said the attorney, as though still trying to decide exactly how to phrase what he had in mind. *"Well."*

Explain? Defend? Apologize? Dortmunder considered all the various things he might say, and could see already that none of them would do any good. This was one defense attorney who'd be bargaining with the prosecutor for a *longer* sentence. Dortmunder sighed, and the cubicle door was flung open. A person had arrived.

No, not a person: a Personage. He stood framed in the doorway, filling the cubicle with the effulgence of his presence, as though he had been borne to this place atop a golden cloud. His large head, like some Olympian mountaintop, was haloed in a great white cloud of hair, and his barrel body was smoothed and stroked with impeccable pinstripe tailoring, accentuated by crisp white shirt, precise dark tie, gleaming black shoes. Sparks flashed from his eyes, his well-padded cheeks promised peace and prosperity, and his pepper-and-salt moustache assured reliability, dignity, and the support of a long-established tradition. The faint echo of a fanfare of trumpets seemed to follow him through the doorway and hang in the air about him, as he stood with one hand dramatically grasping the knob.

He spoke: "John Archibald Dortmunder?" The voice was a remarkable baritone, mahogany and honey, a soft juggernaut.

Dortmunder had nothing more to lose. "Here," he said. "Present."

"I," announced the manifestation, moving forward, "am J. Radcliffe Stonewiler. I am your attorney."

THE FIRST CHORUS

1

Leonard Blick had been a member of the New York bench for twelve years, seven months and nine days, and the last time he'd been surprised by any occurrence in his court had been some twelve years, seventh months and three days ago, when a prostitute had dropped her pants in front of him in an effort to prove she couldn't have solicited the undercover police officer since it was the wrong time of the month. Having gaveled that enterprising young woman into her clothing and out of his courtroom, Judge Blick had settled down to year after year of ordinary drunks, thieves, wife beaters, non-supportive ex-husbands, traffic-ticket scofflaws and Army deserters, with nothing ever to attract his attention. A few murderers had come before him for their preliminary hearings, but they'd been of no interest; they were the sort of murderer who pulls a knife in the middle of a barroom argument. It was all so dull, so drab, so tediously predictable, that more than once Judge Blick had said to his wife Blanche, in their pleasant airy home in Riverdale, "If I ever get an *interesting* crook in front of me, I'll let the son of a bitch go." But it had never happened, and of course it never would.

15

"Thirty dollars or thirty days," he announced to a defendant of such low quality that the fellow actually started adding things up on his fingers. "*Next* case."

"Bail to be set at five hundred dollars. Remand in the custody of—"

"License suspended for ninety days."

—"to be enjoined from communication of any kind with the said ex-wife—"

"Bail to be set at four thousand dollars. Remand in the custody of—"

"—to be turned over to the military authorities at—"

"Bail to be set at seven hundred fifty dollars. Remand—"

"Bail to be set at forty-seven dollars." (Complaint from the public defender.) "You're quite right, Counselor, I wasn't thinking. Bail to be set at eight hundred dollars. *Next* case."

The next case, according to the papers on Judge Blick's desk, was a grand larceny. Not very grand; the fellow had been caught stealing television sets from a repair shop. John Archibald Dortmunder, unemployed, forty years of age, two convictions and prison terms for robbery, no other convictions, no known source of income, being represented by an attorney appointed by the court. A loser, obviously. Another dull fellow, another dull crime, another dull two and a half minutes in the judicial career of the Honorable Leonard Blick.

A stir in the courtroom, as of a sudden breeze across a cornfield, caused Judge Blick to look up from his papers at the two men approaching the bench. It was clear which was the defendant; that thin glum-looking fellow in the gray suit with the lumpy shoulders. But who was that striding next to him, causing shock waves of astounded recognition among the pews of drunks and whores and lawyers? Judge Blick frowned once more at the papers before him. "Attorney: Willard Beecom." He looked up again, and that was no Willard Beecom advancing on the bench, that was—

J. Radcliffe Stonewiler! By God, it really was! One of the most famous lawyers in the country, a man whose nose for the glamorous, the wealthy and the powerful was only matched by his instinct for publicity. If an enraged actress smashed a paparazzo on the head with his own camera, it was J. Radcliffe Stonewiler who defended her from the charge of assault. If a rock group was found smuggling heroin into the country, J. Radcliffe Stonewiler was certain to be there for the defense. And who would defend an Arab oil minister from a paternity suit lodged in a Los Angeles court? Who else but J. Radcliffe Stonewiler.

So what in Blackstone's name was the man doing *here?*

For the first time in his judicial career, Judge Blick was hornswoggled.

And so was almost everybody else in court. The spectators murmured to one another like a crowd scene in a Cecil B. De Mille movie. Never had Judge Blick's court seen such excitement, not even when that hooker dropped her drawers. About the only person not impressed by it all—except the defendant himself, who simply stood there like a ragman's horse, gloomy and fatalistic—was Judge Blick's bailiff, who arose and read out the charge in his usual sloppy-dictioned way, at the finish requesting the defendant's plea.

It was Stonewiler who answered, in a large, round, confident voice, announcing, *"Not guilty."*

Not guilty? *Not* guilty? Judge Blick stared. What an idea! The concept of somebody entering his courtroom who was *not* guilty was so startling as to verge on the physically impossible. Judge Blick frowned at the defendant—who was guilty as hell, you could tell it by looking at the man—and repeated, *"Not* guilty?"

"Completely not guilty, Your Honor," Stonewiler declared. "It is my hope," he continued, declaiming as though for multitudes, "to prevent, with Your Honor's assistance, a tragic miscarriage of justice."

"With my assistance eh?" Judge Blick narrowed his beady eyes. *No funny business in my courtroom,* he told himself, and said to the bailiff, "Is the arresting officer here?"

"Yes, Your Honor. Officer Fahey! Officer Fahey!"

Officer Fahey, a huge beefy Irishman in dark blue, came confidently forward, was sworn, and told a simple story. He had been on radio-car patrol with his partner, Officer Flynn, and they had started a routine check of an alley behind a row of stores when they saw the defendant—"That fella right there"—emerging from a doorway with a pair of TV sets in his hands. The fella had frozen in their lights, they had stepped out of the car to investigate, and they had found approximately thirty other TVs and similar appliances stacked just inside the door, apparently for easy removal to the defendant's automobile, parked nearby. The defendant had made no statement, and had been arrested, advised of his rights, brought to the precinct and booked.

Judge Blick listened to this tale with the soothing calm of long familiarity. How nicely policemen testified! Thud thud thud came the facts, each word following inexorably like the brogans of a cop walking his beat. Judge Blick nearly smiled as he listened to it, this gentle lullaby, and at the end said, "That seems very straightforward, Officer."

"Thank you, Your Honor."

Judge Blick turned a suspicious eye on defendant's counsel. "Does Counsel wish to cross-examine?"

J. Radcliffe Stonewiler, smiling and at his ease, bowed his gracious thanks. "If Your Honor pleases, I would reserve the right to question the officer a bit later. Not that I have any argument with his presentation of what he himself observed. I consider that an excellent recital of the facts, and I would like to congratulate Officer Fahey on the clarity and precision of his testimony. Perhaps a bit later we could clear up one or two minor points together, but for now I would like my client sworn, and with Your Honor's permission I would ask him to tell his story."

"Certainly, Counselor," Judge Blick replied and the defendant was duly sworn and seated, and proceeded to tell the following absurd story:

"My name is John Archibald Dortmunder, and I reside by myself at 217 East 19th Street. In my past life I led a life of crime, but after my second fall, when I was on parole, I gave all that up and became a square citizen. I got out the last time three years ago, and while I was on the inside everything changed in the movies. When I went inside, there were two kinds of movies, one kind that you went to a movie and you saw it and one kind that you went to a smoker or some guy's garage and you saw it, and it was people, uh, men and women. But when I got out, there weren't any more smokers, and that kind of movie was in the regular movie houses. I never saw one of them in a movie house, and I was curious about it, so last night I went to a different neighborhood where nobody knew me, and I parked my car in an alley so nobody would recognize it, and I went to look at a movie called *Sex Sorority*."

(At this point, defendant's counsel interrupted to enter into evidence the movie theater's schedule showing that the final performance of *Sex Sorority* last night had finished at 12:12, just five minutes before the 12:17 given on the arrest report as the time of the defendant's apprehension. Counsel also offered to have defendant recapitulate the story line and incidents of *Sex Sorority* to demonstrate that he had actually seen the film, but the bench felt that was unnecessary, and the defendant was instructed to go on with his ludicrous invention.)

"Well, Your Honor, when I got out from seeing *Sex Sorority,* I went back around to the alley where I left my car, and I saw these two guys with a car doing something at the back door of one of the stores there, and I shouted at them, like this: 'Hey!' And they looked at me, and jumped in their car and took off. So I went down to where I saw them, and it was the back door of this repair place, and they left two TV sets outside in the alley. So I figured, somebody's gonna steal these things if they stay out here, so I picked them up to put back inside the store when the officers came by and arrested me."

Judge Blick gazed with something like disappointment at the defendant, and said, "That's your story? That's it?"

"Yes, it is, Your Honor." But he himself didn't look all that happy with it.

Judge Blick sighed. "Very well," he said. "And would you mind explaining to the court why you didn't tell this very interesting story of yours to the police officers when they apprehended you?"

"Well, Your Honor," Dortmunder said, "like I mentioned before, I used to live a life of crime, and I'm a fellow with a record and all, and I could see the way it must of looked to the police officers, so I just didn't see any point in trying to convince them of anything. I thought I ought to just not say anything, and wait till I had a chance to tell my story to the judge."

"To me, in fact."

"Yes, Your Honor."

Judge Blick turned his attention to J. Radcliffe Stonewiler, saying, almost plaintively, "Is that it? That's what you're here for?"

"Essentially, Your Honor." Stonewiler didn't seem at all abashed. "I'm finished with Mr. Dortmunder," he went on, "and if Your Honor pleases, I would like now to cross-examine Officer Fahey."

The bench so ordered, and while the defendant slunk away to his seat—guilty as all *hell,* just look at him—Officer Fahey retook the stand, and Stonewiler approached him, smiling, saying, "Officer, I realize we're taking up your free time here, and I'll try to be as brief as possible."

Officer Fahey's heavy-jowled red face was impassive as he glowered at Stonewiler. He could clearly be seen thinking to himself, *You won't get around* me *with your shenanigans. You'll not pull the wool over* my *eyes.*

Stonewiler, undaunted, went on: "Officer, may I just ask you to describe the defendant as he was in the instant when you first saw him?"

"He was coming out the door," Officer Fahey said, "with a TV set in each hand."

"Coming *out?* Directly into your oncoming headlights?"

"He stopped when he saw us."

"And had he already stopped when you first caught sight of him?"

"He froze there. But he was coming out."

"*Before* you saw him."

"He was *facing* out," Officer Fahey announced in some irritation. "He was *coming* out because he was *facing* out."

"But he wasn't in motion when you first saw him, Officer, is

that right? I just want to have this absolutely clear. Whether he
was entering or leaving the store, he had already frozen in
place when you first saw him."

"Facing out."

"But frozen."

"Yes, frozen. Facing out."

"Thank you, Officer." Turning to the bench, Stonewiler said,
"With Your Honor's permission, I would like to try a small
experiment."

Judge Blick frowned on him. "Getting fancy, Counselor?"

"Not at all fancy, Your Honor. Very plain indeed. May I?"

"Proceed, Counselor," Judge Blick said, "but watch your
step."

"Thank you, Your Honor."

Stonewiler turned and walked to a side door, which the
judge knew led to a small waiting room. Opening that door,
Stonewiler gestured to someone inside, and two men appeared,
each carrying a television set. They placed these on the floor a
few steps into the room, then turned and departed again, leaving the door open behind them. The door, however, was on a
spring, and slowly it closed itself, until Stonewiler stopped it
with his palm just before it would snick shut. The door remained open half an inch, and Stonewiler returned to the bench
to smile impartially upon Officer Fahey and Judge Blick, and
to say, "With the court's permission, I would like to ask Officer
Fahey's cooperation. Officer?"

Officer Fahey glanced uncertainly at Judge Blick, but the
judge was still faintly hoping for something interesting to happen, so all he said was, "It's up to you, Officer. You may
assist Counsel if you want."

The officer brooded at Stonewiler, mistrust oozing from every
pore. "What am I supposed to do?"

Stonewiler pointed. "Merely pick up those two television
sets," he said, "and return them to the other room."

The officer's brow furrowed. "What's the point?"

"Perhaps there is none," Stonewiler acknowledged, with a
sudden humble smile. "We won't know till we've tried."

The officer frowned once more at Judge Blick, then at the television sets, and then at the door. He appeared indecisive. Then he looked at the defendant, Dortmunder, slumping hopelessly in his chair, and a sudden confident smile touched his lips. "Fine," he said. "Right."

"Thank you, Officer." Stonewiler stepped back as Officer Fahey rose and crossed the court to the television sets. Picking them up by their handles, and pretending the combined weight didn't bother him, he approached the door. He hesitated, facing the door, his hands full of TV sets. He put one of the sets down, pushed on the door, and it swung open. He picked the set up again, and the door swung closed. Quickly, before it could slam, Officer Fahey turned about and bunked the door with his behind.

"*Freeze!*" boomed J. Radcliffe Stonewiler, pointing his long manicured finger at Officer Fahey, who obediently froze, a TV set in each hand, his behind stuck out behind him. The door swung open, hesitated, and swung back, lightly spanking Officer Fahey on the bum.

Stonewiler, his pointing finger still calling attention to the frozen Officer Fahey, turned toward Judge Blick. "Your Honor," he cried, in a voice similar to that which Moses heard from the burning bush, "I leave it to the Court. *Is that man going out, or coming in?*"

2

May said, "And the judge believed it?"

Dortmunder shook his head, in slow bewilderment. The whole thing was still too baffling to think about.

May watched him shake his head, and shook her own, frowning, not sure she understood. "The judge *didn't* believe it," she suggested.

"I don't know what the judge believed," Dortmunder told her. "All I know for sure is, I figure I'm home about six years early."

"What you need is a beer," May decided, and went away to the kitchen to get one.

Dortmunder settled back into his easy chair, kicking off his shoes, relaxing in the scruffy familiarity of his own living room. This was not the address he'd given in court, nor did he live here alone—it was Dortmunder's policy never to tell authority the truth when a lie would do—but it was his home, his castle, his refuge from the buffets and abrasions of the world, and no way had he expected to finish his day in it, shoes off, feet up on the old maroon hassock, watching May carry a can of beer back from the kitchen. "Home sweet home," he said.

"Got a match?" She had a fresh cigarette flopping in the corner of her mouth.

He traded her a book of matches for the beer can, and swigged while she lit. May was a chain-smoker, but she never gave up on a cigarette until the stub was too small to hold, so she could never light the next cigarette from the last, and as a result the Dortmunder-May household was always in a match crisis. Dortmunder was the only burglar in the world who, having finished rifling some company's cash register or safe, would pause to fill his pockets with their promotional matchbooks.

May settled herself in the other easy chair, adjusted the ashtray to her left hand, puffed, enveloped her head in a cloud of smoke, leaned forward out of the smoke, and said, "Tell me all about it."

"It's crazy," he told her. "It makes no sense."

"Tell me anyway."

"This lawyer came by—"

"J. Radcliffe Stonewiler."

Dortmunder frowned, thinking it over. "I've seen him in the papers or something."

"He's famous!"

"Yeah, I figured. Anyway, he walked in, he threw this court-appointed jerk out on his ear, and he said, 'Okay, Mr. Dortmunder, we got about an hour and a half to cook up a story.'"

"And what did you say?"

"I said he could cook for a *year* and a half and it didn't matter what story he came up with, because what was cooked was my goose."

"Didn't you know who he was?"

"I could see he was some rich-type lawyer," Dortmunder admitted. "For a while, I figured he was in the wrong cubicle. I kept telling him, 'Look, my name's Dortmunder, I'm up for B&E.' And he kept saying, 'Tell me all about it.' So finally I told him all about it. The cops had me cold, and I told him so, and he nodded and said, 'That's okay. When the going gets tough, the tough get going.' And I said, 'Yeah, and I know *where* I'm going, and it's upstate.'"

"That wasn't any way to talk to J. Radcliffe Stonewiler."

"I wasn't feeling cheerful."

"Naturally," May agreed. "So what happened?"

"This Stonewiler," Dortmunder said, "he kept me going over and over the details of what happened, and then he went away to make a phone call, and when he came back he had a skinny little guy with him called George."

"Who's George?"

"Stonewiler said, 'Here's my movie expert. Tell him the story, George.' And George told me the whole story of this movie, *Sex Sorority,* so I could tell it to the judge in case I was asked. Only I don't think it's legal to even *tell* a story like that in court. Do they really make movies where a girl takes her—"

"Never mind movies," May said. "What happened next? Where does this door business come into it?"

"It was Stonewiler's whole idea, completely. He even wrote my story down for me, and then made me write it myself, copying from him, so I'd remember it. Not word for word, but so I could tell it smooth and easy when I got to court. I didn't believe in it, you know, because he didn't tell me the part where he was gonna make a monkey out of the cop. He just gave me

this song-and-dance about carrying TV sets *in* instead of *out*—
I mean, you couldn't get away with that one in Sunday school.
I kept saying, 'Why don't we make a deal? Why don't we trade
them a guilty plea for a lesser charge?' And Stonewiler kept
saying, 'Trust me.' "

"So you trusted him."

"Not exactly," Dortmunder said. "I thought he was crazy,
but on the other hand he looked rich and he acted sure of himself, and what the hell did I have to lose anyway? So finally I
said, 'All right, I'll do it. Things can't get worse.' And I did it,
and the judge looked at me like he figured maybe it was time
to bring back some cruel and unusual punishments, and then
Stonewiler did his little number with the cop and the door, and
all of a sudden you could see the judge wanted to laugh. He
looked at the cop, with his ass stuck out behind him and the TV
sets hanging off his hands, and he rubbed his hand over his
mouth like this, and he went, 'Rrrumph rrrumph,' and then he
said something like, 'Counselor, you have created reasonable
doubt, though I still have reason to doubt you. Case dismissed.'
And I come home."

May's expression, around the cigarette in the corner of her
mouth, combined equal portions of wonder and delight. "What
a defense," she said. "Not every lawyer in the world could have
pulled it off."

"I'll have to go along with that," Dortmunder admitted.

"But why? Why'd he do it?"

"I don't know."

"What's this gonna cost?"

"I don't know," Dortmunder said. "He didn't say."

"Didn't he say anything at *all*?"

Dortmunder took an embossed business card from his breast
pocket. "At the end there, after he shook my hand, he gave me
this, he told me call this guy." Dortmunder frowned at the
card, reading off the name as though the sound of the syllables
would give him a clue to what was going on: "Arnold Chauncey. What kind of a name is that?"

"Arnold Chauncey." It sounded just as mysterious when

May said it. Shaking her head, she asked, "Who's he supposed to be?"

"I don't know. Stonewiler gave me the card, told me to call, said good luck, and went away."

"When are you supposed to call?"

"Today."

"Why don't you do it now?"

"I don't want to," Dortmunder said.

May frowned. "Why not?"

"People don't do people favors just for the fun of it," Dortmunder said. "This guy Chauncey, he wants something."

"So?"

"The whole thing makes me nervous," Dortmunder said. "I'm not gonna call."

"But you've got to—"

"I don't want to," Dortmunder said, and set his jaw. Nobody could be quite as mulish as Dortmunder, when he put his mind to it.

"You took the man's assis—" May started to say, and the phone rang. She snapped it a quick irritated glance, then got up and crossed the room and answered on the second ring. Dortmunder lapped up some more beer, and then May told the phone, "Hold on," and turned to say, "It's for you."

Dortmunder hunched his shoulders, and pushed himself lower in his chair. He wasn't in the mood to talk to anybody on the telephone. He said, "Who is it?"

"J. Radcliffe Stonewiler."

"Oh," said Dortmunder. He hadn't given Stonewiler his phone number or his right home address. "So it's like that," he said, and got to his feet, and went over to take the phone, saying into it, "Stonewiler?"

But it was an English-accented female voice that answered, snippily, saying, "Hold on for *Mister* Stonewiler, please." And there was a click.

Dortmunder said into the phone, "Hello?" When there was no answer, he frowned at May, saying, "Who's that?"

May, elaborately whispering, told him, "His sec-re-ter-ry."

"Oh," Dortmunder said, and the phone said hello to him with Stonewiler's deep confident voice. "Yeah," Dortmunder answered. "Hello."

"I just spoke with Mr. Chauncey," Stonewiler said. He sounded cheerful, but in charge. "He says you haven't called yet."

"I been thinking about it," Dortmunder said.

Stonewiler said, "Mr. Dortmunder, why don't you drop by Mr. Chauncey's house now for a chat? It's on East 63rd Street, you could be there in half an hour."

Dortmunder sighed. "I suppose that's what I'll do," he said. "Right."

"The address is on the card."

"Yeah, I saw it."

"Goodbye, Mr. Dortmunder."

"Yeah, goodbye," Dortmunder said, and hung up, and turned a bleak eye toward May, who was back in her chair, watching him through cigarette smoke. "He didn't threaten me," Dortmunder said.

May didn't get it. "I don't get it," she said.

"He could have said, 'I got you off the hook, I can put you back on.' He could have said, 'I got weight I could throw around.' There's lots of things he could have said, and he didn't say any of them."

May continued to frown at him. "So?"

"His not threatening me," Dortmunder said, "was a lot more threatening than if he threatened me."

"What did he want?"

"I'm supposed to go see Chauncey at his house in half an hour."

"You'd better go."

"I don't like this, May."

"Still, you'd better go."

Dortmunder sighed. "Yeah, I know." And he sat down, to put his shoes back on.

May watched him, frowning, thinking her own thoughts, and when he stood up to leave she said, "One thing."

Dortmunder looked at her. "What?"

"That business about backing out a door if you're carrying things in both hands. That *is* true, people do that."

"Sure," Dortmunder said. "That's how I got off."

"Then how come you were facing the police car?"

"It was a different kind of door," Dortmunder explained. "It didn't have a spring closer. I just opened it and picked up the TV sets and walked out."

May's frown deepened. "That's all there was to it?"

"They didn't ask about the door," Dortmunder said. "They might have, if we just talked about it straight out, but the way Stonewiler worked things, he had everybody thinking about that cop's ass."

May nodded, thoughtfully. "You better watch your step with those people," she said.

"I figure to," Dortmunder told her.

3

The third time Dortmunder walked past the house, in the raw November afternoon, its front door opened and a guy with long yellow hair leaned out, calling, "Mr. Dortmunder?"

Dortmunder broke stride, but didn't quite stop walking. He quick looked across the street, as though he hadn't seen the man or heard what he'd said, but almost immediately gave all that up and stopped and looked back.

The house was one of a row of four-story brownstones on this tree-lined quiet street off Park Avenue; an expensive house, in an expensive neighborhood. The building was fairly wide, with a dozen broad concrete steps leading up to the front door, at the second level. Flowers and ivy and a couple of small evergreen shrubs were in concrete pots in the space to the right of the steps.

It had taken Dortmunder twenty minutes to get here by sub-way, and he'd spent the last quarter hour casing the joint and thinking things over. The house was anonymous, beyond the obvious indication that its inhabitants must have money, and no matter how long Dortmunder stared at it he still couldn't figure out why anybody who lived in there would strain himself to get John Dortmunder off the hook on a felony charge, and then invite him over for a chat. He'd walked around the block the first time to get the lay of the land, and the second time hoping to find a way to see the rear of the place—there wasn't any—and the third time he'd simply walked as an aid to thought.

And now some tall slender yellow-haired guy in a dark blue pinstripe suit, white shirt and dark blue patterned tie had come out of the house, called him by name, and was standing up there grinning at him.

Dortmunder took his time. Staying where he was on the sidewalk, he studied the guy the way he'd been studying the house, and what he saw wasn't reassuring. The fellow was about forty, deeply tanned and very fit, and everything about him suggested dignified secure wealth; his banker's clothing, his self-confident smile, the house in which he lived. Every-thing, that is, except the shoulder-length yellow hair, hanging in long waves around his head, neither sloppy nor pretty, but somehow totally masculine. Like a knight in the Crusades. No; better yet, like one of those Viking raiders who used to play such hell along the English coast. Some Viking barbarian, that's what he was, plus all the civilization money could buy.

He was also clearly willing to let Dortmunder look him over forever. He stood there grinning, studying Dortmunder in re-turn, and it was finally Dortmunder who ended it, calling up to him, "You're Chauncey?"

"Arnold Chauncey," the other one agreed. Stepping to one side, he gestured at his open doorway. "Come on up, why don't you?"

So Dortmunder shrugged and nodded and went on up, climbing the steps and preceding Chauncey into the house.

A wide carpeted hallway stretched to an open doorway at the far end, through which could be seen delicate wooden-armed chairs in a bare-floored gleaming room with tall windows. On the left side of the hallway, a staircase with a red runner and dark-wood banister extended upward. White light filtering down suggested a skylight at the top of the stairs. To the right of the hallway were two sets of dark-wood sliding doors, one near and one far, both shut. A few large paintings in heavy frames were on the pale walls, with a number of spindly occasional tables beneath. A hushed, padded quiet pervaded the house.

Chauncey followed Dortmunder inside, shutting the door behind himself and gestured at the staircase, saying, "We'll go up to the sitting room." He had one of those Midlantic accents that Americans think of as English and Englishmen think American. Dortmunder thought he sounded like a phony.

They went up to the sitting room, which turned out to be a living room without a television set, where Chauncey urged Dortmunder into a comfortable velvet-covered wing chair and asked him what he'd like to drink. "Bourbon," Dortmunder told him. "With ice."

"Good," Chauncey said. "I'll join you."

The bar—complete with small refrigerator—was in the cabinetry in the far wall, beneath an expanse of a well-filled bookcase. While Chauncey poured, Dortmunder looked at the rest of the room, the Persian rug and the antique-looking tables and chairs, the large ornate lamps, and the paintings on the walls. There were several of these, mostly small, except for one big one—about three feet wide, maybe not quite so high—which showed a medieval scene; a skinny fellow with a round belly, wearing varicolored jester's clothes and a cap and bells, was dancing along a road, playing a small flute. The road led down in darkness to the right. Following the jester along the road were a whole bunch of people, all of them with tense staring faces. They were apparently supposed to represent a great variety of human types: a fat monk, a tall knight in armor, a short fat woman with a market basket, and so on.

Chauncey brought Dortmunder's drink, saying, "You like that picture?"

Dortmunder neither liked nor disliked pictures. "Sure," he said.

"It's a Veenbes," Chauncey said, and he stood beside Dortmunder's chair, smiling thoughtfully at the painting, as though reconsidering its position on the wall, or his attitude toward it, or even the fact of his ownership of the thing. "You've heard of Veenbes?"

"No." The bourbon was delicious, a very smooth brand. Dortmunder hadn't recognized the shape of the bottle when Chauncey was pouring.

"An early Flemish master," Chauncey said. "A contemporary of Brueghel, possibly an influence, nobody's quite sure. This is *Folly Leads Man to Ruin*." Chauncey sipped bourbon, and chuckled, nodding at the painting. "Woman, too, of course."

"Sure," Dortmunder said.

"The painting has been valued at four hundred thousand dollars," Chauncey said, the way a man might say the weather was good, or that he'd just bought a pair of snow tires.

Dortmunder looked up at Chauncey's profile—tanned face, sharp nose, long yellow hair—and then he frowned again at the painting. Four hundred thousand dollars? For a picture to cover a water stain on the wall? There were parts of life, Dortmunder knew, that he would never understand, and most of those parts of life had something to do with people being cuckoo.

"I want you to steal it," Chauncey said.

Dortmunder looked up again. "Oh, yeah?"

Chauncey laughed, and moved off to seat himself in another chair, putting his glass on the drum table at his right hand. "I don't suppose," he said, "Stonewiler told you my instructions to him."

"No, he didn't."

"Good; he wasn't supposed to." Chauncey glanced at the picture of Folly again, then said, "Three months ago, I told him I wanted a crook." His bright eyes flickered toward Dortmunder's face. "I hope you don't object to that term."

Dortmunder shrugged. "It covers a lot of people."

Chauncey smiled. "Of course. But there was a very specific kind of crook I wanted. A professional thief, not too young, successful at his profession but not wealthy, who had served at least one term in prison, but had never been convicted or even charged with anything *other* than larceny. No mugging, murder, arson, kidnapping. Only theft. It took three months to find the man I wanted, and he turned out to be you." Chauncey stopped—for dramatic effect, probably—and sipped more bourbon, watching Dortmunder over the rim of his glass.

Dortmunder also sipped bourbon, watching Chauncey over the rim of *his* glass. They studied one another over the rims of their glasses for a while—Dortmunder was getting a bit cross-eyed—and then Chauncey put his glass back on the drum table, Dortmunder lowered his own glass into his lap, and Chauncey shrugged as though embarrassed, saying, "I need money."

Dortmunder said, "Who owns the painting?"

That surprised Chauncey. "I do, of course."

"That was legit? You want me to steal it?"

"Let me explain," Chauncey said. "I have a rather good collection of art, fifteenth and sixteenth century mostly, here and in my other places, and of course everything is completely insured."

"Ah," Dortmunder said.

Chauncey's smile now had lost that brief touch of embarrassment. "You see the plot already," he said. "Since I truly love paintings, it isn't necessary for me to display my possessions in public. If I arrange to have a painting 'stolen' from me, at some point when I am very short of cash, then I can collect from the insurance company, hang the painting in some private place, and enjoy both the picture and the cash."

"You don't need a thief," Dortmunder told him. "Put the thing away in a closet and say a burglar got in."

"Yes, of course," Chauncey said. "But there are problems."

Again the trace of embarrassment appeared in his smile, but this time Dortmunder could see the embarrassment was tempered by self-satisfaction, self-indulgence. Chauncey was like a boy who's just been caught making an obscene drawing in the school lavatory; he's embarrassed, but he's also pleased with the skill and the cleverness of the drawing.

Dortmunder said, "What problems?"

"I am very extravagant," Chauncey said. "I needn't give you my autobiography, but I inherited money and I'm afraid I never learned to be a good manager. My accountants are usually furious with me."

Dortmunder didn't even have one accountant. "Is that right," he said.

"The fact is," Chauncey said, "I've already done it twice."

"Done it? Faked a theft?"

"Twice," Chauncey said. "The second time, the insurance. company made their suspicions very plain, but they didn't really push the matter. However, if I do it a third time, I can see them becoming cross."

"They might," agreed Dortmunder.

"I imagine," Chauncey said, "they would do their level best to *prove* it was a fake theft."

"They might."

"So it has to be a *real* theft," Chauncey said. "Professional thieves actually do have to break into the house and steal the painting."

"While you're out of town."

"Good Lord, no." Chauncey shook his head, and then laughed again, saying, "That's the *worst* thing I could do."

Dortmunder drank bourbon. "So what's your idea?"

"I will give a dinner party," Chauncey said. "In this house. I will have two couples staying with me at the time, in rooms on the top floor. Very well-to-do people. There should be a lot of valuables in their rooms while they are down to dinner. Because my house guests, and the other guests invited for the dinner, will all be wealthy people, most of the women wearing jewelry and so on, I will have hired private guards for the evening. During dinner, with me very much in the house, and with private guards hired by me in the house, thieves will break in from the roof, rifle the guest bedrooms, rifle my own rooms —carefully, please—steal the Veenbes from this room, and make their getaway."

"With private guards in the house," Dortmunder said.

"Whose attention will be on the persons and jewelry of my guests, downstairs." Chauncey shrugged, smiling in a relaxed and self-approving way. "No insurance company in the world could suggest a fake robbery under the circumstances."

"Will your guests be in on it?"

"Of course not. Nor will the guards."

"What do we do with their stuff?"

"Keep it. Returning mine, of course. And giving me back the painting."

"You mean selling you back the painting," Dortmunder said.

Chauncey nodded, his self-satisfied smile now spreading to include Dortmunder; Chauncey thought they were *both* terrifically witty and clever. "Of course," he said. "You'll want your own profit out of the transaction."

"That's right."

"You'll get to keep whatever items you find in the guest bedrooms, of course," Chauncey said.

"That stuff doesn't matter."

"No, you're perfectly right. Very well; I told you the insurance valuation, and believe me I'm being accurate. The newspapers will carry the story of the theft, and they'll surely give the valuation themselves."

"Four hundred thousand," Dortmunder said.

"I'll give you twenty-five per cent."

"A hundred thousand."

"Yes."

"When?"

"When I collect from the insurance company, of course. If I had a hundred thousand dollars, I wouldn't need to get into an operation like this."

Dortmunder said, "Then you'd get the painting back when you paid us."

Chauncey looked startled. "But— My dear Mr. Dortmunder, I am a respectable citizen, very well established, I have this house, other properties, I'm not going to simply up and disappear. You can trust me for the money."

Dortmunder said, "You're robbing an insurance company. You're inviting your own friends to your house so I can steal their goods. I wouldn't trust you with a ham sandwich in a phone booth for five minutes."

Chauncey burst into loud laughter, apparently genuine. "Oh, my God," he said, "Stonewiler did himself proud! Mr. Dortmunder, we can do business, you and I, we understand one another very well."

"Maybe we can," Dortmunder said.

Chauncey finished his laughing jag, and became suddenly serious, pointing a stern finger at Dortmunder and saying, "Can you hold on to the painting that long? Without damage, without having it stolen from *you?*"

"How long?"

"In my previous experience, it takes the insurance company about six months to finish its investigation and process the claim."

"Six months? Fine. I'll hold on to the painting six months, then you'll give me the hundred thousand, I'll give you the painting." Dortmunder turned to look at the picture again, visualizing it over the sofa in May's living room. Sure, why not? Look good there.

"I'll have to think about that," Chauncey said. "Table that for the moment. Otherwise, do we have a partnership?"

Dortmunder said, "You want a complete legit theft. That means no inside help, no doors left open, nothing like that."

"Absolutely not," Chauncey said. "I can give you some help ahead of time, let you look the house over—casing the joint, isn't that it? I can show you where the burglar alarm wires are, things like that."

"Burglar alarm?"

"Oh, yes. All the doors and windows are hooked up to an alarm system. Watson Security Services. If a door or window is opened, or a wire is cut, it triggers an alarm in the Watson

offices down on 46th Street. They phone the police, and also
send a car of their own."

"That's great," Dortmunder said.

"Surely you know how to bypass alarms," Chauncey said.

"To break into a private house? If *I* was the insurance company, I'd smell a rat."

"No, I don't believe you would," Chauncey said, speaking
judiciously, as though he'd considered this point himself at
some length. "I'll have a few famous wealthy people here, you
know. A princess, an heiress, an oil sheikh and so on. The
gossip columns will mention the house party, and the dinner,
before they take place. All certainly enough to attract the
attention of an enterprising team of burglars."

"If it really does get in the paper," Dortmunder said, "then
okay."

"It will, I guarantee. Possibly only 'Suzy Says' in the *Daily
News,* but the public prints nevertheless."

Dortmunder sat back, swirling the remaining bourbon in his
glass, thinking it over. In a way it was a crazy deal, stealing a
man's goods and then giving them back, but in another way it
was just a simple straightforward B&E with inside help; except
that in this case the inside help wasn't a disgruntled maid or
hungry plumber, it was the mark himself. The burglar alarm
wouldn't be that much of a problem, not with Chauncey pointing out where the wires ran, and if the guards did actually stay
downstairs they'd be no trouble either. And a hundred thousand
dollars, plus whatever jewelry or other valuables were in the
guest bedrooms, would come in very handy right now. Dortmunder had been living on May's salary as a cashier down at
the Safeway supermarket for so long he was almost forgetting
to be embarrassed about it; the time had come to bring some
money of his own into the house.

And that painting really would look okay in the living room,
for the next six months.

Chauncey said, "Well, what do you think? Can we work
together?"

"Maybe," Dortmunder said. "I got to look the house over

first, and I got to see what kind of string I can put together."

"String?"

"The people to work with me. This isn't a one-man job."

"No, of course not. Have you ever stolen a painting before?"

"Not a big one like that."

"Then I'll have to show you how it's done," Chauncey said. "It's a delicate operation, really, you don't want to harm the painting in transporting it."

"We'll just carry it away," Dortmunder said.

"Indeed you will not," Chauncey told him. "You'll do a professional job of it. You'll cut the picture out of its frame—"

"We don't take the frame?"

"Certainly not. An art thief uses a razor blade, cuts the painting out of the frame, carefully rolls it into a cylinder, being sure not to crack or break the paint in the process, and finishes with something that can be readily transported and hidden."

"So the frame stays here." Dortmunder looked at the painting again, wondering if Woolworth's had frames that big. Or maybe they could just thumbtack it to the wall.

"I'll show you all that," Chauncey said. "But would you like to see the rest of the house first?"

"Yes."

"And can I freshen your drink?"

Dortmunder looked at his glass. Nothing but an amber echo around the bottom. "Yes," he said.

While Chauncey was pouring more bourbon, Dortmunder walked over to look at the painting closer up, seeing the lumps and streaks of paint on the canvas. That could be a little tricky to carry around.

Chauncey brought the fresh drink, and stood next to him a moment, smiling at the painting, finally saying, "It is good, isn't it?" His tone was fond, almost paternal.

Dortmunder hadn't been looking at the painting at all, just at the paint. "Yeah, it's fine," he said, and turned to frown at Chauncey. "You got to trust me, don't you?"

Raising an eyebrow, Chauncey grinned on one side of his mouth and said, "In what way?"

"That I won't just walk off with this, and not bring it back."

Chauncey smiled broadly, nodding. "That is a consideration, but there are two things that ease my mind. The first is, with a painting as well-known and valuable as this one, you couldn't possibly find another buyer to give you more than the twenty-five per cent I'm offering. And the other is, the list of requirements I gave our friend Stonewiler."

"Such as?"

"In fact, I asked Stonewiler to find me *two* men," Chauncey said. "The first, which turned up you, was for a professional thief *without a record of violence*. You are not a dangerous man, Mr. Dortmunder."

Nobody likes to be told he isn't dangerous. "Um," said Dortmunder.

"The other man I asked him to find," Chauncey went on, "was a professional killer." His smile was very bright, very sure of itself. "It was amazing," he said. "That part took practically no time at all."

4

When Dortmunder walked into the O. J. Bar and Grill on Amsterdam Avenue at eleven that night, three of the regulars were deep in discussion with Rollo the bartender about private versus public education. "I tell ya what's wrong widda private schools," one of the regulars was saying. "You put your kid in there, it's like a hothouse, ya know what I mean? The kid don't get to know all kinds a people, he don't get prepared for real life."

One of the others said, "Real life? You wanna know about real life? You put your kids in a public school they get themselves mugged and raped and all that shit. You call that real life?"

"Sure I do," the first one said. "Meeting all kinds, that's what real life is all about."

The second one reared back in disbelieving contempt. "You mean you'd put your kid in a school with a lotta niggers and kikes and wops and spics?"

"Just a minute there," the third regular said. "I happen to be of Irish extraction myself, and I think you oughta just give me an apology there."

The other two stared at him, utterly bewildered. The main offender said, "Huh?"

"Or maybe you'd like a swift left to the eye," said the Irishman.

"Not in here," Rollo the bartender said, and he left the discussion to stroll down the bar and say to Dortmunder, "How you doin?"

"Just fine," Dortmunder said.

"You're a double bourbon," Rollo told him, and made a generous drink, from a bottle labeled Amsterdam Liquor Store Bourbon—"Our Own Brand." Pushing it across to Dortmunder, he said, "Settle up on your way out."

"Right. Anybody here?"

"A vodka-and-red-wine." Rollo nodded his head toward the rear, saying, "He went on back."

"Fine," Dortmunder said. "There'll be two more. The sherry —you haven't seen him for a while—"

"Little skinny fella? Professor type?"

"That's the one. And the draft-beer-and-salt."

Rollo made a face. "He's terrific for business, that one."

"He doesn't like to drink too much," Dortmunder explained. "He's a driver."

"I'm an advocate of mass transit myself," Rollo said. "I'll send them back when they show."

"Thanks," Dortmunder said. Picking up his bourbon, he walked on by the discussion group—they had switched from education through ethnics to religion by now, and tempers were beginning to fray—and headed for the bar's back room. Going past the two doors with the dog silhouettes on them (POINTERS and SETTERS), and past the phone booth (which smelled as though some pointers had missed their turnoff), he went through the green door at the end and into a small square room lined to the ceiling all around with beer and liquor cases. On the concrete floor in the middle of the small open space stood a battered old table with a green felt top and half a dozen chairs. Over the table hung a bare bulb with a round tin reflector, the only light source in the room. And sitting at the table was a monster in semi-human form, his great hairy hand wrapped around a tall glass holding what looked like cherry soda.

Dortmunder, closing the door behind himself, nodded at this prodigy and said, "Whadaya say, Tiny?"

"Hello, Dortmunder." Tiny had the voice of a frog in an oil drum, but less musical. "Long time no see."

Dortmunder sat opposite him, saying, "You look good, Tiny," which was a palpable lie. Tiny, hulking on the little chair, his great meaty shoulders bulging inside his cheap brown suit, a shelf of forehead bone shadowing his eyes, looked mostly like something to scare children into going to bed.

But Tiny apparently agreed with Dortmunder that he looked good, because he nodded, thoughtfully and judiciously, and then said, "You look like shit, on the other hand. You looked better in stir."

"Things have been a little slow," Dortmunder admitted. "How long you on the street?"

"Ten days." Tiny wrinkled a fistful of his own suit lapel, saying in disgust, "I'm still in the state's threads."

"I think I've got a good one," Dortmunder told him. "But wait'll the others get here, so we'll go over it just once."

Tiny lifted his shoulders in a shrug—seismograph needles trembled all over the Northern Hemisphere—and said, "I got nothing but time." And he knocked back about a third of the red liquid in his glass.

"How have things been inside?" Dortmunder asked.

"Bout the same. You remember Baydlemann?"

"Yeah?"

Tiny chuckled, like far-off thunder. "Fell in a vat of lye."

"Yeah? Get hurt?"

"His left thumb come out pretty good."

"Well," Dortmunder said, "Baydlemann had a lot of enemies on the inside."

"Yeah," Tiny said. "I was one a them."

There was a little silence after that, while both men thought their own thoughts. Dortmunder sipped at his drink, which didn't taste even remotely like the nectar called bourbon that Chauncey had given him. Maybe there'd be a bottle or two of the stuff upstairs the night of the heist; not to drink on the job, but to take away for the celebration afterwards.

Dortmunder was tasting one kind of bourbon, and dreaming about another kind, when the door opened and a stocky open-faced fellow with carroty hair came jauntily in, carrying a glass of beer in one hand and a salt shaker in the other. "Hey, there, Dortmunder," he said. "Am I late?"

"No, you're right on time," Dortmunder told him. "Tiny Bulcher, this is—"

The newcomer said, "I took a different route. I wasn't sure how it'd work out."

"Your timing is good," Dortmunder assured him. "Tiny, this is Stan Murch—he'll be our—"

"You see," said Stan Murch, putting his glass and shaker on the table and taking a chair, "with the West Side Highway closed it changes everything. All the old patterns."

Tiny said to him, "You the driver?"

"The best," Murch said, matter-of-factly.

"It was a driver got me sent up my last stretch," Tiny said. "Took back roads around a roadblock, made a wrong turn, come up *behind* the roadblock, thought he was still in front of it. We blasted our way through, back into the search area."

Murch looked sympathetic. "That's tough," he said.

"Fella named Sigmond. You know him?"

"I don't believe so," Murch said.

"Looked a little like you," Tiny said.

"Is that right?"

"Before we got outa the car, when the cops surrounded us, I broke his neck. We all said it was whiplash from the sudden stop."

Another little silence fell. Stan Murch sipped thoughtfully at his beer. Dortmunder took a mouthful of bourbon. Tiny Bulcher slugged down the rest of his vodka-and-red-wine. Then Murch nodded, slowly, as though coming to a conclusion about something. "Whiplash," he commented. "Yeah, whiplash. That can be pretty mean."

"So can I," said Tiny, and the door opened again, this time to admit a short and skinny man wearing spectacles and a wool suit, and carrying a round bar tray containing the bottle of Amsterdam Liquor Store bourbon, plus a glass with something that looked like but was not cherry soda, and a small amber glass of sherry. "Hello," said the skinny man. "The barman asked me to bring all this."

"Hey, Roger!" Stan Murch said. "Where you been keeping yourself?"

"Oh," said the skinny man, vaguely. "Just around. Here and there." He put the tray on the table and seated himself, and Tiny reached at once for his new vodka-and-red-wine.

Dortmunder said, "Tiny Bulcher, this is Roger Chefwick."

Tiny nodded over his glass, and Roger said, "How do you do?"

Dortmunder explained to Tiny, "Roger is our lock-and-alarm man."

"Our *terrific* lock-and-alarm man!" Stan Murch said.

Roger Chefwick looked pleased and embarrassed. "I do my best," he said, and delicately lifted his sherry from the tray.

Tiny washed down some red stuff and said, "I'm the smash-and-carry man. The *terrific* smash-and-carry man."

"I'm sure you're very good at it," Chefwick said, politely. Then he pointed at the glass of red stuff and said, "Is that really vodka and red wine?"

"Sure," said Tiny. "Why not? Gives the vodka a little taste, gives the wine a little body."

"Ah," said Chefwick, and sipped sherry.

Murch said, "Roger, somebody told me you were in jail in Mexico."

Chefwick seemed both embarrassed and a bit annoyed at the subject having come up. "Oh, well," he said. "That was just a misunderstanding."

"I heard," Murch insisted, "you tried to hijack a subway car to Cuba."

Chefwick put his sherry glass on the felt surface of the table with some force. "I really don't see," he said, "how these silly rumors spread so far so fast."

"Well," Murch said, "what *did* happen?"

"Hardly anything," Chefwick said. "You know I'm a model-train enthusiast."

"Sure. I seen the layout in your cellar."

"Well," Chefwick said, "Maude and I were in Mexico on vacation, and in Vera Cruz there were some used New York City subway cars awaiting shipment to Cuba, and I— well— I actually merely intended to board one and look around a bit." A certain amount of discomfort was evident in Chefwick's face now. "One thing led to another," he said, "and I'm afraid the car began to move, and then it got out of control, and the first thing I knew I was on the main line to Guadalajara, having a great deal of difficulty staying ahead of the two-thirty express. But, so far from hijacking a subway car *to* Cuba, the Mexican police at first accused me of stealing the car *from* Cuba. However, with Maude's help we got it all straightened out in a day or two. Which," Chefwick concluded petulantly, "I'm afraid I can't say for the rumors and wild stories."

Tiny Bulcher abruptly said, "I did a bank job once with a lock man that thought he was a practical joker. Give me a dribble glass one time, exploding cigar one time."

Dortmunder and Murch both looked at Tiny a bit warily. Dortmunder said, "What happened?"

"After we emptied the vault," Tiny said, "I pushed him in and shut the door. He thought he was such hot stuff, let him get himself out from the inside."

Dortmunder said, "Did he?"

"The bank manager let him out, Monday morning. I hear he's still upstate."

"That wasn't very funny," Roger Chefwick said. His expression was very prim.

"Neither was the cigar," Tiny said, and turned to Dortmunder, saying, "We're all here now, right?"

"Right," Dortmunder said. He cleared his throat, sipped some more bourbon, and said, "What I got here is a simple breaking and entering. No fancy caper, no helicopters, no synchronize-your-watches, just come in through an upstairs window, take what we pick up along the way, and go after our main thing, which happens to be a painting."

Tiny said, "Valuable painting?"

"Four hundred thousand dollars."

"Do we have a buyer?"

"That we got," Dortmunder said, and went on to explain the whole story, finishing, "So our only problems are the burglar alarm and the private guards, but we got the best kind of inside help, *and* a guaranteed buyer."

"And twenty-five thousand a man," said Stan Murch.

"Plus," Dortmunder reminded him, "whatever we pick up on the upper floors."

Tiny said, "I don't know about that six-month wait. I like my money right away."

"The guy has to get it from the insurance company," Dortmunder said. "He said to me, and it makes sense, if he had a hundred thousand cash on him he wouldn't have to pull anything like this."

Tiny shrugged his huge shoulders. "I guess it's okay," he said. "I can make a living in the meantime. There's always heads to crack."

"Right," Dortmunder said, and turned to Roger Chefwick. "What about you?"

"I've seen Watson Security Services and their installations," Chefwick said, with some disdain. "The easiest thing in the world to get through."

"So you're with us?"

"With pleasure."

"Fine," Dortmunder said. He looked around at his string—an erratic genius lock-and-alarm man, a compulsive one-track-mind driver, and a beast from forty fathoms—and found it good. "Fine," he repeated. "I'll work out the timing with the owner, and get back to you."

5

Dortmunder was sitting on the sofa with his feet up on the coffee table, a beer in his right hand and a luncheon-loaf sandwich on white with mayo in his left hand, his sleepy eyes more or less focused on *Angels with Dirty Faces,* being screened this afternoon on WNEW-TV, channel five, when the doorbell rang. Dortmunder blinked slowly, but otherwise didn't move, and a minute later May walked through the living room, trailing a thin wavy line of smoke from the cigarette in the corner of her mouth as she dried her sudsy hands on a dishtowel. She crossed the line of vision between Dortmunder and the television set—he blinked again, as slowly as before—and went on out to the foyer to open the door.

A loud and rather angry voice cut through the background music of *Angels with Dirty Faces: "Where is he?"*

Dortmunder sighed. He filled his mouth with bread and mayo and luncheon loaf, sat up a bit straighter on the sofa, and waited for the inevitable.

Out in the foyer, May was saying something soothing, which was apparently not doing its job. "Just let me at him," insisted the loud angry voice, and then there were heavy footsteps, and in came a wiry sharp-nosed fellow with a chip on his shoulder. "You!" he said, pointing at Dortmunder.

May, looking worried, followed the sharp-nosed fellow into the room, saying, in a ghastly attempt at cheeriness, "Look who's here, John. It's Andy Kelp."

Dortmunder swallowed white bread and luncheon loaf and mayo. "I see him," he said. "He's between me and the TV set."

"You got a *job!*" Kelp yelled, in tones of utter outrage.

Dortmunder gestured with his sandwich, as though shooing a fly. "Would you move over a little? I can't see the picture."

"I will *not* move over." Kelp folded his arms firmly over his chest and stamped his shoes down onto the carpet, legs slightly spread, to emphasize his immobility. Dortmunder could now see about a third of the screen, just under Kelp's crotch. He scrunched down in the sofa, trying to see more, but then his own feet on the coffee table got in the way.

And Kelp was repeating, "You got a job, Dortmunder. You got a job, and you didn't tell me."

"That's right," Dortmunder said. He sipped beer.

"I brought you a *lotta* jobs," Kelp said, aggrieved. "And now you got one, and you cut me out?"

Stung from his lethargy, Dortmunder sat up straighter, spilled beer on his thumb, and said, "Oh, yeah, that's right. *You* brought me jobs. A kid that kidnaps *us*."

"He never did."

"A bank," Dortmunder said, "and we lose it in the goddam Atlantic Ocean."

"We took over two thousand apiece out of that bank," Kelp pointed out.

Dortmunder gave him a look of disgusted contempt. "Two thousand apiece," he repeated. "Remind me, was that dollars or pesos?"

Kelp abruptly shifted gears. Switching from antagonism to conciliation, he spread his hands and said, "Aw, come on, Dortmunder. That isn't fair."

"I'm not trying to be fair," Dortmunder told him. "I'm not a referee. I'm a thief, and I'm trying to make a living."

"Dortmunder, don't be like that," Kelp said, pleading now. "We're such a terrific team."

"If we were any more terrific," Dortmunder said, "we'd starve to death." He looked at the sandwich in his left hand. "If it wasn't for May, I *would* starve to death." And he took a big bite of sandwich.

Kelp stared in frustration, watching Dortmunder chew. "Dortmunder," he said, but then he just helplessly moved his hands around, and finally turned to May, saying, "Talk to him, May. Was it my fault the bank fell in the ocean?"

"Yes," said Dortmunder.

Kelp was thunderstruck: "B-b-b-b-b— How?"

"I don't know how," Dortmunder said, "but it was your fault. *And* it was your fault we had to steal the same emerald six times. *And* it was your fault we kidnapped some child genius that boosted the ransom off us. *And* it was your fault—"

Kelp reeled back, stunned by the number and variety of charges. Hands spread wide, he lifted his head and appealed to Heaven, saying, "I can't *believe* what I'm hearing in this room."

"Then go to some other room."

Having had no help from Heaven, Kelp appealed again to May, saying, "May, can't you *do* something?"

She couldn't, and she must have known she couldn't, but she tried anyway, saying, "John, you and Andy have been together so long—"

Dortmunder gave her a look. "Yeah," he said. "We just been reminiscing."

Then he stared at the television set, which was now showing a commercial in which ballerinas in tutus danced on top of a giant can of deodorant spray, to the music of *Prélude à l'après-midi d'un faune.*

May shook her head. "I'm sorry, Andy."

Kelp sighed. His manner now was stern and statesmanlike. He said, "Dortmunder, is this final?"

Dortmunder kept watching the ballerinas. "Yes," he said.

Kelp drew his tattered dignity about himself like a feather boa. "Goodbye, May," he said, with great formality. "I'm sorry it ended like this."

"We'll still see you around, Andy," May said, frowning unhappily.

"I don't think so, May. Thanks for everything. Bye."

"Bye, Andy," May said.

Kelp exited, without looking again at Dortmunder, and a few seconds later they heard the front door slam. May turned to Dortmunder, and now her frown showed more annoyance than unhappiness. "That wasn't right, John," she said.

The ballerinas had at least been replaced by the angels with dirty faces. Dortmunder said, "I'm *trying* to watch this movie here."

"You don't like movies," May told him.

"I don't like new movies in movie houses," Dortmunder said. "I like old movies on television."

"You also like Andy Kelp."

"When I was a kid," Dortmunder said, "I liked gherkins. I ate three bottles of gherkins one day."

May said, "Andy Kelp isn't a gherkin."

Dortmunder didn't reply, but he did turn away from the television screen to give her a look. When they'd both contemplated May's remark for a little while, he returned his attention to the movie.

May sat down next to him on the sofa, staring intently at his profile. "John," she said, "you need Andy Kelp, and you know you do."

His lips tightened.

"You *do*," she insisted.

"I need Andy Kelp," Dortmunder said, "the way I need ten-to-twenty upstate."

"Wait a minute, John," she said, resting a hand on his wrist. "It's true the big jobs you've tried in the last few years didn't go well—"

"And Kelp brought me every one of them."

"But that's the point," May told him. "He *didn't* bring you this one. This is yours, you got it yourself. Even if he is a jinx in his own jobs—and you know you don't really believe in jinxes, any more than I do—but even if—"

Dortmunder frowned at her. "What do you mean, I don't believe in jinxes?"

"Well, rational people—"

"I do believe in jinxes," Dortmunder told her. "And rabbit foots. And not walking under ladders. And thirteen. And—"

"Feet," May said.

"—black cats crossing your— What?"

"Rabbits' feet," May said. "I think it's feet, not foots."

"I don't care if it's elbows," Dortmunder said. "I believe in it whatever it is, and even if there aren't any jinxes Kelp is *still* one, and he's done me enough."

"Maybe *you're* the jinx," May said, very softly.

Dortmunder gave her a look of affronted amazement. "Maybe what?"

"After all," she said, "those were Kelp's jobs, and he brought them to you, and you can't really blame any one person for all the things that went wrong, so maybe *you're* the one that jinxes *his* jobs."

Dortmunder had never been so basely attacked in his life. "I am not a jinx," he said, slowly and distinctly, and stared at May as though he'd never seen her before.

"I know that," she said. "And neither is Andy. And besides, this isn't you coming in on a job he found, it's him coming in on a job you found."

"No," Dortmunder said. He glowered at the TV screen, but he didn't see any of the shadows moving on it.

"Damn it, John," May said, getting really annoyed now, "you'll *miss* Andy and you know it."

"Then I'll shoot again."

"Think about it," she said. "Think about having nobody to talk it over with. Think about having nobody on the job who really understands you."

Dortmunder grumped. He sat lower and lower in the chair, staring at the volume button instead of the screen, and his jaw was so clenched his mouth was disappearing up his nose.

"Work with him," May said. "It's better for both of you."

Silence. Dortmunder stared through a lowered curtain of eyebrow.

"Work with him, John," May repeated. "You and Andy, the same as ever. John?"

Dortmunder moved his shoulders, shifted his rump, recrossed his ankles, cleared his throat. "I'll think about it," he muttered.

"I *knew* you'd come around!" Kelp yelled, bounding in from the foyer.

Dortmunder sat bolt upright. He and May both stared at Kelp, who leaped around in front of them with a huge smile on his face. Dortmunder said, "I thought you left."

"I couldn't go," Kelp said. "Not with that misunderstanding between us." He grabbed a chair, towed it over to the sofa, sat at Dortmunder's left and leaned eagerly forward. "So what's the setup?" Then he suddenly sat back, looking concerned, glancing toward the TV. "No, not yet. Watch the rest of your movie first."

Dortmunder frowned almost wistfully at the screen. "No," he said. "Turn it off. I think it ends badly."

6

"Linda," murmured Arnold Chauncey, snuggling the girl closer to his side.

"Sarah," she responded, and bit him rather painfully on the cheek, then got out of bed.

"Sarah?" Rubbing his cheek, Chauncey gazed up over the jumbled sheets and blankets at the tapered bare back of the girl reaching now for her blue jeans draped on a Louis Quinze chair. Astonishing how much Sarah and Linda look alike, he thought, at least from a back view. But then, so many attractive women have that elongated-cello look from behind. "How beautiful you are," he said, and since lust had very recently been satiated it was purely the comment of a connoisseur.

"Whoever I am." She was really quite angry, as she showed by her clumsiness when stepping into her bikini panties; lavender, a very wrong color for her.

Chauncey was about to say "don't go" when he noticed the clock on the mantel: nearly ten-thirty at night. The appointment with Dortmunder was half an hour from now, and if it hadn't been for that slip of the tongue he might well have lazed himself right through it. As it was, his carelessness had saved him once again from his carelessness, and what he did say to poor Sarah was, "Must you go?"

She gave him a resentful glare over her shoulder, and he saw that her nose was much blunter than Linda's. Same forehead, though, same eyebrows. Same shoulder, if it came to that. Woman may have an infinite variety, but each man's taste is rather circumscribed. "You *are* a bastard," she said.

Chauncey laughed, hiking himself up to a sitting position amid the pillows. "Yes, I suppose I am," he said. With so many Lindas in the world, why placate the Sarahs? He watched her dress, her movements eloquent of outrage and humiliation as she paused at the mirror to touch her hair, touch up her face. Seeing that pouting face framed in the rococo gilt of the mirror, he suddenly realized how common she looked. That exquisite seventeenth-century looking glass, its darkly gleaming surface surrounded and supported by gilded twining rose bushes and cherubim, was meant to reflect more regal faces, more substantial brows, more stately eyes, but what had he placed before it? A series of pinched beauties, faces meant for reflection in commonplace mirrors in gas-station rest rooms, next to the hot-air blower. "I *am* a bad man," Chauncey said, mournfully.

Immediately she turned away from the mirror, misinterpreting what he'd said. "Yes, you really are, Arnie," she said, but already forgiveness was implicit in her voice.

"Oh, go away, Sarah," Chauncey said, abruptly irritable, angry at himself for being such an endless wastrel, angry at her for reminding him, angry in general because he knew he wouldn't change. Thrashing up out of the bed, he stalked past her astonished expression, and spent the next five minutes calming himself in a too-hot shower.

It was his Uncle Ramsey Liammoir who had defined Arnold Chauncey, years ago while Chauncey was still a boarding-school boy in softest Massachusetts. "Wealthy families begin with a sponge and end with a spigot," Ramsey had written to Chauncey's mother, in a letter Chauncey never saw till he was going through her papers after the wicked old woman's death. "Our sponge was Douglas MacDouglas Ramsey, who founded our fortune and made it possible for half a dozen generations of Ramseys and MacDouglases and Chaunceys to live in stately and respectable comfort, with here a life peerage and there a board chairmanship. Our spigot, who will piss away his patrimony before he's twenty if he's given his head, is your son Arnold."

Which was undoubtedly one of the reasons the old lady's will had ringed Chauncey's patrimony (*matri*mony? since it had come from his mother?) with so many strings of barbed wire. Three accountants and two attorneys had to be brought in for approval before he could tip more than fifteen per cent; an exaggeration, but not by much.

On the other hand, he was far from poor. Chauncey's actual income—as opposed to what it said along about page 63 of his tax return—was in fact quite substantial. The year he didn't clear three hundred thousand dollars was a bad year indeed, and usually he was comfortably above that. Or would have been comfortable were he not, in the words of his own interior monologue, such a wastrel. Piss away his patrimony he did, proving his now-departed uncle right by engaging in every kind of squander known to man. He had married badly, and paid too much for the divorce. He had supported an auto-racing stable, and had even done some driving himself until he realized he was mortal. He maintained fully staffed houses or apartments in New York, London, Paris, Antibes and Caracas. His love of beauty in furniture, paintings, sculpture, in all the fine arts, led him to purchases he could barely afford even if he were to scrimp elsewhere, and he had never been able to scrimp *anywhere*.

Thus it was that Chauncey was forced from time to time into risky alternative methods of balancing his books, of which false insurance claims—such as the plot currently in preparation—was only one. Arson, bribery, blackmail, procuring and simple unadorned theft had been other techniques by which over the years he had kept himself and his expensive tastes afloat. He had, for instance, stolen about forty per cent of the royalties supposed to be paid to Heavy Leather, the rock band he had managed back in the late sixties, when running with rock musicians was the thing to do. He hadn't *wanted* to steal those benighted Glaswegians' money, but at the time it had seemed to him his need was greater than theirs; certainly his arithmetic was. But how his conscience had pricked him, as it pricked him now, standing in the steamy heat of his shower cursing himself for a weakling and a wastrel and a spendthrift. A spigot, in fact, just as dear departed Uncle Ramsey had said, the old fart.

It took five minutes of hot spray to soothe Chauncey and make him forget again his disrespect for himself (he'd forgotten Sarah the instant he'd left her), and then he returned to the bedroom (Sarah was gone, of course), toweled himself dry, used the blower on his long blond hair—naturally yellow, and the envy of all his friends, male and female—and dressed himself completely in dark colors. Black suede moccasins and black socks. Black slacks and a navy blue cashmere sweater with a turtleneck. Then down the stairs (he almost never used the elevator) to the front-hall closet, where he put on a dark blue pea jacket and tucked his yellow hair inside a black knit cap, which made his tanned face look bonier, tougher. Black leather gloves completed his costume, and then he went down one more flight to the ground floor, which in front was actually somewhat below ground level but which in back opened onto a small neat flagstone-covered garden. Flowering shrubs and bushes and small trees, all planted in large ornamental concrete pots, stood about in formal array. Ivy climbed the rear of the house and covered the eight-foot-high brick walls surrounding the garden on the other three sides. Now, in November, the garden was all bare branches and black stumps, but in the summer, when Chauncey was almost never in New York, it was a place of beauty.

Chauncey was a darker shape against the dark as he crossed the garden to the knobless door in the corner of the rear wall. A key from the cluster in his pocket opened this door, and he slipped through into utter blackness. This was a passage through a thick wall separating two properties that fronted on the next street. The wall, apparently left over from some earlier construction, was actually double, two thicknesses of old chalky brick with less than three feet of space between. A trellis had been laid across the top at some later date, and a jumble of vines crawled over the trellis, making a thick and leafy roof.

The footing underneath was treacherous with broken bits of stone and brick, but Chauncey slid along on the balls of his feet, his shoulders brushing the walls on both sides, dangling ivy branches occasionally catching at his knit cap.

At the far end was another featureless wooden door, which Chauncey opened with the same key, stepping out to a brick-floored areaway in front of a townhouse very like his own. The door he'd emerged from looked as though it belonged to this house, was perhaps a basement entrance, though in fact there was no direct link between them.

It was two and a half blocks to the meeting place with Dort-munder and the alarm specialist, and as Chauncey neared it, coming south on Madison, he moved very slowly, determined to see Dortmunder and the other one before they saw him. It was just after eleven now, the streets were full of hurtling cabs and blundering buses and cowering private cars, and the side-walks were virtually empty. Chauncey's breath steamed in the air and he came to a complete halt partway up the block, frowning, looking forward at all four corners of the intersec-tion. Dortmunder wasn't there.

Had something gone wrong? Chauncey believed he under-stood Dortmunder, the man's low-key style, his low expecta-tions and defeatist outlook. A man like that was ripe for direc-tion from a stronger personality, which was the way Chauncey saw himself. He had been pleased with Stonewiler's choice, and convinced he could deal with Dortmunder without fear of being outfoxed.

Not that he intended to default. He would pay the man his hundred thousand, and welcome to it.

On the other hand, where was he? Not sure what was going on, Chauncey backed into the darkened entranceway of a nearby boutique, and his left heel came down on something soft, which moved. "Ouch!" yelled a voice in Chauncey's ear. "Get off my foot!"

Chauncey spun about, astonished. "Dortmunder! What are you doing in *here?*"

"The same thing you are," Dortmunder said, and limped out to the sidewalk, followed by a skinny scholarly looking man wearing large spectacles and carrying the kind of black leather bag doctors used when doctors made housecalls.

Dortmunder glared back over his shoulder at Chauncey, saying, "Well? You coming?"

7

Dortmunder and Chefwick nosed their way around the roof of Arnold Chauncey's house like a pair of hunting dogs in search of the scent. Illuminated by light angling up through the open trapdoor, Chauncey stood and observed, a faint expectant smile on his face.

Dortmunder wasn't sure about this fellow Chauncey. It was all right, for instance, for Dortmunder and Chefwick to hang around in dark corners, that was more or less part of their job, but Chauncey was supposed to be a straight citizen, and not only that, a wealthy one. What was *he* doing lurking in doorways?

It was Dortmunder's belief that in every trade with glamour attached to it—burglary, say, or politics, movies, piloting airplanes—there were the people who actually did the job and were professional about it, and then there were the people on the fringe who were too interested in the glamour and not enough interested in the job, and those were the people who loused it up for everybody else. If Chauncey was another clown leading a rich fantasy life, Dortmunder would have to rethink this entire proposition.

In the meantime, though, they were here and they might as well look the thing over. Even if the Chauncey deal fell through, it could be useful to know how to get into this place at some later date.

This was one of a row of ten attached houses built shortly before the turn of the century, when New York's well-to-do were just beginning to move north of 14th Street. Four stories high, twenty-five feet wide, with facades of stone and rear walls of brick, they shared one long continuous flat roof, with knee-high brick walls delineating each property line. Three of the houses, including Chauncey's, featured roof sheds housing elevator mechanisms, added later. Television antennae sprouted like an adolescent's beard on all the roofs, but many of them were tilted or bent or utterly collapsed, marks of the spread of cable TV. The roof construction was tar over black paper. The front parapet showed marks of a fire escape, since removed.

While Chefwick studied the wires that crossed to the roof from the nearby power and telephone poles, clucking and muttering and peering through his spectacles, Dortmunder took a stroll down the block, stepping over the low brick walls, crunching on one tarred roof after another until he reached the end of the row, where he stood facing a blank brick wall. Or, not entirely blank; here and there the outlines of bricked-in windows could be seen.

What was this building? Dortmunder went to the front, leaned over the parapet—trying not to see, from the corner of his eye, the sidewalk forty feet below—and saw that it was some kind of theater or concert hall, which faced onto Madison Avenue. What he could see from here was the side of the building, with its fire exits and posters of coming attractions.

Leaving the edge, Dortmunder backed off to study that blank wall, which rose another fifteen or twenty feet above the level of the row-house roofs. Near the top of the wall were several grilled vents, but none of them looked useful for a human being seeking passage.

Finished, Dortmunder retraced his steps, finding Chauncey still waiting by the open trapdoor and Chefwick now dangling off the rear of the building, head hanging down, humming happily to himself as he fingered the wiring. A line tester glowed briefly, showing Chefwick's earnest absorbed face.

Dortmunder continued on, walking to the other end of the row of houses, and there he found a ten-foot open space across a driveway, with an apartment building on the far side, its drapes and curtains and Venetian blinds and Roman shades and Japanese screens and New England shutters all firmly closed. The vision of a board stretched across that open space from one of those windows to where he was standing was followed immediately in Dortmunder's mind by a vision of himself crawling across that board. Turning his back on both vision and building, he returned to the Chauncey roof, where Chefwick was cleaning his hands on a Wash'n'Dri from his leather bag. "We'll come from down there," Dortmunder said, pointing toward the blank back of the concert hall.

"Our best bet would be the elevator shaft," Chefwick said. To Chauncey he said, "It would be easier if the elevator weren't on the top floor."

"It won't be," Chauncey promised.

"Then there's really no problem," Chefwick said. "Not from my point of view." And he looked a question at Dortmunder.

It was time to clear the air. Dortmunder said to Chauncey, "Tell me about that passage we came through, the one into your back yard."

"Oh, you won't be able to use *that*," Chauncey said. "You'd have to go right up through the house, all full of people."

"Tell me about it anyway."

"I'm sorry," Chauncey said, moving closer, away from the trapdoor illumination, "but I don't understand. Tell you *what* about it?"

"What's it for?"

"Originally?" Chauncey shrugged. "I really don't know, but I suspect it began merely as a space between walls. I understand my house was a speakeasy at one point during Prohibition, and that's when the new doors were added."

"What do *you* use it for?"

"Nothing, really," Chauncey said. "A few years ago, when there were some rock musicians hanging about, a certain amount of dope came in that way, but normally I have no use for the thing. Tonight was different, naturally. I don't think I should be seen with suspicious characters just before my house is robbed."

"Okay," Dortmunder said.

Chauncey said, "Now let *me* ask a question. What prompted the interest?"

"I wanted to know if you were a comic-book hero," Dortmunder told him.

Chauncey seemed surprised, then amused. "Ah, I see. No romantics need apply, is that it?"

"That's it."

Chauncey reached out to tap a finger against Dortmunder's upper arm, which Dortmunder hated. "Let me assure you, Mr. Dortmunder," he said, "I am no romantic."

"Good," said Dortmunder.

8

One of the regulars was flat on his back atop the bar at the O. J. Bar and Grill on Amsterdam Avenue when Dortmunder and Kelp walked in on Thursday evening. He was holding a damp filthy bar rag to his face, and three other regulars were discussing with Rollo the best way to treat a nosebleed. "You put an ice cube down the back of his neck," one said.

"You do and I'll flumfle your numble," the sufferer said, his threat lost in the folds of the bar rag.

"Give him a tourniquet," another regular suggested.

The first regular frowned. "Where?"

While the regulars surveyed the body of their stricken comrade for a place to put an anti-nosebleed tourniquet, Rollo came down the bar, nodded at Dortmunder and Kelp over his impaired customer's steel-toed work boots, and said, "How you doing?"

"Better than him," Dortmunder said.

"He'll be okay." Rollo dismissed the Death-of-Montcalm scene with a shrug. "Your vodka-and-red-wine is here, your sherry is here, your beer-and-salt is here."

"We're the last," Dortmunder said.

Rollo nodded hello to Kelp. "Nice to see you again."

"Nice to be back," Kelp told him.

Rollo went off to make their drinks, and Dortmunder and Kelp watched the first-aid team. One of the regulars was now trying to stuff paper bar coasters into the bleeder's nose, while

another one was trying to get the poor bastard to count backwards from one hundred. "That's for *hiccups*," said the third.
"No no," said the second, "you drink out of the wrong side
of the glass for hiccups."

"No, that's for when you faint."

"No no no, when you faint you put your head between your
knees."

"Wrong. If somebody faints, you slap their face."

"You do and you'll stumbun with me," said the patient, who
now had bar rag *and* paper coasters in his mouth.

"You're crazy," the second regular told the third. "You slap
somebody's face if they've got hysterics."

"No," said the third regular, "if somebody's got hysterics,
you have to keep them warm. Or is it cold?"

"Neither. That's for shock. You keep them warm for shock.
Or cold."

"No, I've got it," the third regular said. "You keep them
warm for hysterics, and you keep them cold if they've got a
burn."

"Don't you know anything?" asked the second regular. "For
a burn you put butter on it."

"*Now* I know!" the third regular cried. "Butter's for a nosebleed!"

Everybody stopped what they were doing to stare at him,
even the bleeder. The first regular, his hands full of paper
coasters, said, "Butter's for a nosebleed?"

"You stuff butter up the nose! Rollo, give us some butter!"

"You won't dumrumbin *my* nose!"

"Butter," said the second regular in disgust. "It's ice he
needs. Rollo!"

Rollo, ignoring the cries for butter and ice, carried a tray
past the invalid's feet and slid it across the bar toward Dortmunder. It contained a bottle of Amsterdam Liquor Store
bourbon, two empty glasses with ice, and a glass containing, no
doubt, vodka-and-red-wine. "See you later," he said.

"Right." Dortmunder reached for the tray, but Kelp got to
it first, picking it up with such eagerness to be of help that the

bourbon bottle rocked back and forth, and would have gone over if Dortmunder hadn't steadied it.

"Thanks," Kelp said.

"Yeah," Dortmunder said, and led the way toward the back room.

But not directly. They had to stop for a second so Kelp could throw in his own contribution with the medics. "What you do for a nosebleed," he told them, "is you take two silver coins and put them on both sides of his nose."

The regulars all stopped squabbling among themselves to frown at this outsider. One of them, with great dignity, pointed out, "There haven't been any silver coins in circulation in this country since 1965."

"Oh," said Kelp. "Well, that is a problem."

"Sixty-six," said another regular.

Dortmunder, several paces ahead, looked back at Kelp to say, "*Are* you coming?"

"Right." Kelp hurried in Dortmunder's wake.

As they went past POINTERS and SETTERS, Dortmunder said, "Now, remember what I told you. Tiny Bulcher won't be happy about you because you're costing him five grand, so just be quiet and let *me* do the talking."

"Definitely," Kelp said.

Dortmunder glanced at him, but said nothing more, and then went through the green door and into the back room, where Stan Murch and Roger Chefwick and Tiny Bulcher were all seated at the green-felt-topped table, with Tiny Bulcher saying, ". . . so I went to his hospital room and broke his other arm."

Chefwick and Murch, who had been gazing at Bulcher like sparrows at a snake, looked up with quick panicky smiles when Dortmunder and Kelp came in. "Well, there you are!" Chefwick cried, with a kind of mad glitter in his eyes, and Murch actually spread his arms in false camaraderie, announcing, "Hail, hail, the gang's all here!"

"That's right," Dortmunder said.

Talking more rapidly than usual, his words running together in his haste, Murch said, "I did a new route entirely, that's why

I'm so early, I was coming from Queens, I took the Grand Central almost to the Triborough—"

Meanwhile, Kelp was putting the tray on the table and placing Bulcher's fresh drink in front of him, cheerily saying, "There you go. You're Tiny Bulcher, aren't you?"

"Yeah," Bulcher said. "And who are you?"

"—then I got off, and turned left under the El, and, uh . . ."

And Murch ran down, becoming aware of the new tension in the room as Kelp, still cheery, answered Bulcher's question.

"I'm Andy Kelp. We met once seven or eight years ago, a little jewelry-store job up in New Hampshire."

Bulcher gave Kelp his flat look. "Did I like you?"

"Sure," Kelp said, taking the chair to Bulcher's left. "You called me pal."

"I did, huh?" Bulcher turned to Dortmunder. "What's my pal doing here?"

"He's in," Dortmunder said.

"Oh, yeah?" Bulcher looked around at Murch and Chefwick, then back at Dortmunder. "Then who's out?"

"Nobody. It's a five-man string now."

"It is, huh?" Bulcher nodded, glancing down at his fresh vodka-and-red-wine as though there might be some sort of explanation engraved on the glass. Looking at Dortmunder again, he said, "Where does his cut come from?"

Same as everybody else's. We'll get twenty thousand a man."

"Uh huh." Bulcher sat back—the chair squealed in fear—and brooded at Kelp, whose cheery expression was beginning to wilt. "So," said Bulcher, "you're my *five thousand dollar* pal, are you?"

"I guess so," Kelp said.

"I never liked anybody five grand worth before," Bulcher said. "Remind me; where were we pals?"

"New Hampshire. A jewelry—"

"Oh, yeah." Bulcher nodded, his big head going back and forth like a balancing rock on the mountain of his shoulders. "There was a second alarm system, and we never got into the place. All the way up to New Hampshire for nothing."

Dortmunder looked at Kelp, who did not look back. Instead, he kept smiling at Bulcher, saying, "That's the one. The finger screwed up. I remember you hit him a lot."

"Yeah, I would of." Bulcher took a long slow taste of his fresh drink, while Kelp continued to smile at him, and Dortmunder brooded at him, and Murch and Chefwick went on doing their hypnotized-sparrow number. Putting the glass down at last, Bulcher said to Dortmunder, "What do we need him for?"

"I already been at work," Kelp said, bright and eager, and ignoring Dortmunder's shut-up frown.

Bulcher observed him. "Oh, yeah? Doing what?"

"I checked out the theater. Hunter House, it's called. How we get in, how we get out."

Dortmunder, who was wishing Kelp would get laryngitis, explained, "We get to the roof through a theater nearby."

"Uh huh. And we're paying this guy twenty grand to go find out how we get in a theater." Bulcher leaned forward, resting one monstrous forearm on the table. He said, "*I'll* tell you the secret for *ten* grand. You buy a ticket."

"I bought tickets," Kelp assured him. "We're gonna see the Queen's Own Caledonian Orchestra."

Dortmunder sighed, shook his head a bit in irritation, and paused to pour some Our Own Brand bourbon into one of the glasses on the tray. He sipped, watched moodily as Kelp poured his own drink, and then said, "Tiny, I make the plan. That's my job. Your job is to carry heavy things and to knock people down that get in the way."

Bulcher jabbed a thumb the size of an ear of corn in Kelp's direction. "We're talking about *his* job."

"We need him," Dortmunder said. Under the table, he crossed his ankles.

"How come we didn't need him the first time we got together?"

"I was out of town," Kelp said brightly. "Dortmunder didn't know where to find me."

Bulcher gave him a look of disgust. (So did Dortmunder.)

"Bull," he said, and turned back to Dortmunder, saying, "You didn't mention him at all."

"I didn't know yet I needed him," Dortmunder said. "Listen, Tiny, I've been to the place now. We have to get in through the top of an elevator shaft, we got a fifteen- or twenty-foot brick wall to go down and then back up, and we don't have all night to do it. We need a fifth man. I'm the planner, and I say we need him."

Bulcher turned his full attention on Kelp again, as though trying to visualize a circumstance in which he would find himself needing this person. His eyes still on Kelp, he spoke to Dortmunder, saying, "So that's it, huh?"

"That's it," Dortmunder told him.

"Well, then." A ghastly smile turned Tiny's face into a cross between a bad bayonet wound and a six-month-old Halloween pumpkin. "Welcome aboard, *pal*," he said. "I'm sure you're gonna be very helpful."

Dortmunder released held breath, his shoulders sagging in relief. So *that* was over. "Now," he said, "about tomorrow night. Stan Murch will drive us to this Hunter House a little before eight-thirty. . . ."

9

The hall was full of Scotsmen. Hundreds of them gamboled in the aisles and thronged the lobby, with more arriving every minute. Some were in kilts, some were singing, some were marching arm in arm, most were clutching mugs, flasks, bottles, cups, glasses, jars, demijohns, goblets and jugs, and all were calling out to one another in strange and barbarous tongues. Around many necks and trailing down many backs were long scarves in the colors of favorite soccer or rugby teams. Tam o' Shanters with bright wool balls on top were jauntily cocked over many a flashing eye. Hunter House bulged with Highland bonhomie.

"Well, *now* what the hell?" said Dortmunder.

Tiny Bulcher said, "That guy's wearing a dress."

"It's a kilt," Roger Chefwick told him. A level crossing of English manufacture in one part of Chefwick's model-train layout featured a man in a kilt who would glide out and wave a red flag every time a train went by. Chefwick was very familiar with kilts. "These are all Scotsmen," he explained.

"I don't know," Dortmunder said. "I don't know about this."

"I've got the tickets," Kelp said, in a hurry to get them all upstairs and on about their business. "Follow me."

Except it wasn't quite that easy. Kelp tried to lead, but everywhere he turned there were another six Scotsmen in his path. Also, the two fifty-foot rolls of vinyl clothesline he had tucked inside his coat didn't increase his maneuverability. For all his efforts they remained becalmed, four innocent bystanders abroad on a roiling sea of Scotsmen.

And now some of them were fighting. Over there by the head of the second aisle, two or three lads were rounding and punching and clutching at one another, while another half dozen tried to either stop them or join in, hard to tell which. "What are they *fighting* about?" Kelp cried.

A passing Scot paused to answer: "Well, you know," he said, "if it's neither football nor politics, it's more than likely religion." And away he waded, to join the discussion.

Dortmunder, sounding ominously bad-tempered, said, "Kelp, give me those tickets."

What was he going to do, ask for his money back? Apprehensive, Kelp gave him the tickets, but Dortmunder immediately turned and handed them to Tiny Bulcher, saying, "*You* lead the way."

"Right," Bulcher said. Clutching the tickets in one enormous fist, he waded forward, moving his shoulders and elbows, tamping startled Scotsmen left and right, the other three in his wake.

When they reached the balcony, it was so full they couldn't possibly open the door leading to the roof stairs without being noticed. "We'll sit down and wait," Dortmunder decided, and

Bulcher ushered them through the throng to their seats. "You'd make a wonderful locomotive," Chefwick told him as they sat down.

10

In Wednesday's New York *Post*—in the section that in the unenlightened past was known as the Woman's Page, but which today operates under a discreet anonymity, offering Fashion, Social Notes, and Recipes to an audience presumably no more than fifty-two per cent female—the following item appeared:

> Spending a few days in town are the **Princess Orfizzi** (the former Mrs. Wayne Q. Trumbull) with her husband, **Prince Elector Otto** of Tuscan-Bavaria, here for the opening of the **Hal Foster** Retrospective at MOMA, staying at the townhouse of jet-setter **Arnold Chauncey,** just back from his whirlwind tour of Brasilia. Also houseguesting with Chauncey are **MuMu and Lotte deCharraiveuneuirauville,** here to confer with designer **Humphrey Le-Stanza** at his new salon on East 61st Street. A Friday bash is planned, with guests to include **Sheikh Rama el-Rama el-Rama El,** film star **Lance Sheath** and cosmetics heiress **Martha Whoopley.**

What a dinner party, what a ghastly affair. Arnold Chauncey sat at the head of the table, behind his false-face host's smile, and observed his guests with all the affability of Dortmunder observing the Scotsmen. Mavis and Otto Orfizzi, to begin with, hated one another so uncordially, so spitefully, and with such unremitting verbal venom, that no one could be said to be truly safe in their presence, while MuMu and Lotte de Charraiveuneuirauville were both too absorbed in themselves to be much help under the best of circumstances. As for the dinner guests, they approached the unbearable, except for Major General (Ret.) and Mrs. Homer Biggott, both of whom seemed merely to be dead. Sheikh Rama, on the other hand, was very much alive, cheerfully and suavely insulting everyone his glittering oily eye lit upon, making jokes about the West's incipient decline and the Arab world's upcoming dominance, name-dropping shamelessly and endlessly, and generally behaving like the well-educated (Cambridge) snotty little nouveau riche he was.

But the worst of all was Laura Bathing. "I don't mind a *bit*, sweetheart," she'd said upon arrival, when Chauncey had apologized for her inadvertent omission from the item in the *Post*, and in the last two hours she had made perfectly clear just how little she'd minded by breaking three glasses, two plates, an ashtray and a table lamp, all in small clumsy accidents, smearing whiskey, wine and gravy in her wake, and screaming almost without respite at Chauncey's staff, until he had very nearly been driven to point out that these days servants were much harder to find than dinner guests. It wasn't much help that both Lance Sheath and MuMu deCharraiveuneuirauville were quite obviously courting—no, probably *stalking* was the better word —cosmetics heiress Martha Whoopley, a stocky stodgy fortyish styleless frump with the face of a TV dinner and the personality of a humidifier and the ownership of eleven million dollars in her own right. MuMu was obviously interested in marrying up, but Chauncey had planned Lance for Laura Bathing, unaware that Lance was currently in search of backing for a film. Laura, placed at table between the insulting sheikh and the back of Lance Sheath (whose front was determinedly toward Martha Whoopley, on his other side), was not taking her situation calmly. In fact, Laura more and more seemed determined to strip Chauncey's house of *all* its breakables before the meal was finished.

Otto Orfizzi having attempted unsuccessfully to form an alliance with the shiekh by telling an anti-Semitic joke at which no one had laughed—not because it was anti-Semitic, but because it had been told badly, and because two of the guests happened in fact to be Jewish, and because in any case it wasn't very funny—Mavis Orfizzi turned her imitation-pitying smile toward Chauncey, saying, "I do apologize for Otto. He can be such an incredible boor."

It was only the thought that these witches and toadies were about to be burgled through his own intervention that kept the smile on Chauncey's face. "Oh, well, Mavis," he said. "Don't trouble yourself on my account. I think we should all take life as it comes."

"Do you?" An imitation-*self*-pitying smile took its place on Mavis's lips. "It must be comforting to have that philosophy."

"It is," Chauncey assured her. "After all, we never know what misfortunes may be heading our way, do we?" And for the first time all evening, the smile he bestowed on his guests was absolutely genuine.

11

Stately, plump Joe Mulligan paused in the privacy of the hallway to pull his uniform trousers out of the crease of his backside, then turned to see Fenton watching him. "Mp," he said, then nodded at Fenton, saying, "Everything okay down here."

Fenton, the senior man on this detail, made a stern face and said, "Joe, you don't want any of them princes and princesses see you walking around with your fingers up your ass."

"Aw, now," Mulligan said, embarrassment combining with a trace of indignation. "They're all at table up there. Besides, every man has to give a tug to his trousers from time to time."

"Stately plump men more than others," said Fenton, himself a skinny little dried-up man with porcelain teeth in his head. A bit of a martinet and a stickler for regulations, he liked the boys to call him Chief, but none of them ever did.

"Have another look at that back door while you're down here," he added, gave a sort of casual one-finger-to-forehead salute, and turned back to the stairs.

Joe Mulligan was one of the team of seven private guards on duty in the Chauncey house tonight, dressed like the others in a dark blue police-like uniform with a triangular badge on the left shoulder reading *Continental Detective Agency*. In his flat-footed walk and meaty bigness, Mulligan himself was police-like, as well he might be, having spent twelve years on the New York City force before deciding to get out of the city and join-ing Continental's Long Island office in Hempstead.

It used to be that policeman who displayed ineptitude or stupidity were sent *from* the city *to* the boondocks—"Pounding a beat on Staten Island" was the popular version of the threat —but as the Swinging Sixties swung more and more in the manner of a wrecker's ball, that usual direction of transfer be-came reversed. The quiet safe Staten Islands of duty became more highly prized, while the terrifying city lost its former attraction. For instance, Mulligan and his team were working in Manhattan now as direct punishment for having lost a bank out on Long Island two years ago. None of them had quit, all seven were still together, and Fenton himself had summed it up for all of them: "We'll do the job the same as ever. We're good men and we know it, and sooner or later we'll get back to the top. Out of New York and back to Long Island where we belong."

So they treated every unimportant minor assignment, every wedding, dog show and book fair, as though it were the D-Day landing. Tonight, they operated in three two-man teams, with Fenton roving among them. Each team was responsible for one area of the house, including the upper floors, though this last part was against the stated wishes of the client, who'd said, "Concentrate on the entrances downstairs, and let the upstairs go." But, as Fenton had told the team, "The reason they hire *us* is because we know the job and they don't."

Also, the teams traded places every half hour, to keep from becoming stale, too used to a single environment. Mulligan was alone now because his partner, Garfield, had gone to the second floor to replace Morrison and Fox, who would transfer to the first floor, releasing Dresner and Block to come down here, so Mulligan could go upstairs and rejoin Garfield.

But first the rear door, which continued as locked and un-sullied as ever. Mulligan peeked through the tiny diamond-pane window at the dark back yard, saw nothing, and let it go at that.

Footsteps on the stairs; Mulligan turned and here came Dresner and Block. "Hello, boys," Mulligan said.

Block nodded. "What say?"

Dresner said, "All quiet?"

"I believe we could have phoned in our part," Mulligan said. "See you, boys." And, with a certain amount of puffing he made his way up two flights of stairs to where Garfield, whose law-enforcement career had begun when he was a Military Police-man in Arizona and Paris, and who sported a Western-marshall moustache of amazing ferocity, was practicing his quick draw before the full-length mirror in Chauncey's bathroom. "Well, now," Mulligan said, a bit out of sorts from the combination of Fenton's remarks and the long climb upstairs, "it's Wyatt Earp you're expecting, is it?"

"Has it ever occurred to you," Garfield said, holstering his pistol and fingering his moustache, "that I'd be a natural for the movies?"

"No," Mulligan said. "Let's make our rounds."

So they went up *another* flight of stairs. The top floor, oddly enough, was grander than any of the others, possibly because its being strictly for guests had meant the decorators hadn't needed to worry overmuch about comfort and function. Chauncey's own bedroom suite on the next floor down was also sumptuously furnished, of course, but it was clearly a work-ing bedroom, whereas the rooms on the top floor, with their delicate chairs and tables, canopy beds, Persian carpets, hand-ironed cotton curtains, complementary wallpapers and up-holstery and bedspreads, were like display models in a mu-seum; one expected a plush rope across each doorway, permit-ting the visitor to look without touching.

Two of the suites were in current occupancy—by utter pigs. Garments, cosmetic jars, open luggage, pieces of paper and other litter formed a kind of archaeological layer over the original impersonality. Mulligan and Garfield strolled through these rooms, commenting to one another on stray artifacts—"I didn't know women wore brassieres like that any more," Garfield said, and Mulligan replied, "They don't"—and also discussing their hopes for an early return to Long Island. "Two years is long enough," Mulligan said truculently. "It's time we got out of New York and back to the bigtime."

"You couldn't be more right." Garfield said, touching his moustache. "Fenton ought to go see the Old Man for us, argue our case."

"Absolutely," Mulligan agreed. The two of them were returning to the central corridor then, and it was at that point Mulligan suddenly felt the unmistakable pressure of a gun barrel thrust against the middle of his back, and heard the quiet voice behind him speak the words of doom. Long Island flew away on mighty wings, and the voice said:

"Stick em up."

12

It seemed to Dortmunder, looking at the faces of the two private guards through the eyeholes of the ski mask covering his own face, that he'd seen them somewhere before, but that was both unlikely and irrelevant, so he dismissed it from his mind. He and Bulcher hustled the two disarmed guards into a closet in the unused guest room, locked the door, removed their ski masks, and returned to the central corridor, where an evidently nervous Kelp said, in a jittery whisper, "I thought the guards were supposed to stay downstairs."

"So did I," Dortmunder said. That had been quite a shock, as a matter of fact, when they'd come in from the elevator shaft to hear the sounds of conversation from one of the nearby rooms. Expecting no trouble, and not wanting to make any extra trouble for themselves in case of problems outside, none of them was carrying a gun, but fortunately a pair of socket wrenches from Chefwick's black bag had done just as well, convincing the guards long enough for Dortmunder and Bulcher to relieve them of their own artillery and put them away.

"Let's get going," Bulcher said, the commandeered revolver toylike in his mammoth fist, "before anything else happens." And he tucked the pistol into his hip pocket.

"Right," Dortmunder agreed. "The stairs are this way. Chefwick and Kelp, you hit the bedrooms. Tiny and I'll get the painting."

The robbery itself was quickly accomplished. Dortmunder and Bulcher removed the painting from the wall, turned it around, slit the canvas just beyond the edge of the painting all the way around, rolled it carefully into a tube shape, and fixed it with three rubber bands. Meanwhile, upstairs, Kelp and Chefwick were filling their pockets with earrings, necklaces, bracelets, rings, brooches, watches, tiepins, a golden dollar-sign money clip clutching nearly eight hundred dollars, and whatever other sparkly items attracted their magpie eyes. Bulcher and Dortmunder, with Dortmunder carrying the rolled painting, did the same for Chauncey's bedroom, where the pickings were surprisingly slim. Back in the sitting room, Dortmunder found two full bottles of that bourbon that had so impressed him his first time here, tucked them inside his leather jacket, and then he and Bulcher rejoined the other two on the top floor. "Some nice stuff," Kelp whispered, grinning, his nervousness forgotten now.

Dortmunder saw no reason to whisper. "Good," he said. "Let's get out of here."

Chefwick used one of his handy tools to open the elevator door, and Kelp went in first, reversing the route they'd used before. The elevator shaft was concrete-lined and about six feet square, with an open gridwork of metal beams inside it to support the elevator equipment. Kelp made his way via a horizontal beam on the left wall to another horizontal beam at the rear, and from there to the metal rungs set in the rear wall just opposite the doorway. Up the rungs he went, sidling past the electric motor and the chains and pulleys at the top, and out through the opened panel in the housing. Lowering a length of clothesline back through the opening, he waited while Chefwick tied his bag and the painting to the end, and then drew both up to the roof. (Dortmunder watched this part gimlet-eyed, waiting for Kelp to drop the goddam painting to the bottom of the elevator shaft—or rather to the top of the elevator, two stories below—but astonishingly enough Kelp did everything right.)

Chefwick himself went next, over to the metal rungs and up to the roof, followed by Bulcher. Dortmunder went last, pausing on the first metal beam to release the door, allowing it to slide closed, and the faint snick of the electric lock was immediately followed by a sudden whirring sound, and the small clanking of chains.

Yes? Dortmunder looked all around, and saw the elevator cables in motion. In motion? He looked down, and the top of the elevator was coming this way. The *elevator* was coming this way, sliding and clicking upward through its shaft.

God *damn,* but it was coming fast.

13

"I wonder if you've heard this one, Sheikh," Prince Elector Otto Orfizzi of Tuscan-Bavaria called across the table, his round-red-apple face thrust out among the candles.

"I should think I probably had," Sheikh Rama el-Rama el-Rama El responded, and turned to Laura Bathing to say, "Have you been in London recently?"

"Not for a year or so. Oops."

The Sheikh blandly watched her sop up red wine with her most recent napkin, while the black hand and white-clad arm of their host's serving boy reached through between them to pick up the shards of wine glass. "I was there two weeks ago," the Sheikh said.

"Watch out, you clumsy fool!" Laura shrieked at the servant. "You'll get glass in my meat!"

"I was buying a house in Belgravia," the Sheikh went on, unperturbed. His softly oiled chuckle came and went. "The poor English," he said pleasantly. "They can't afford their own capital any more, you know. They're all living in Woking and Hendon."

The Prince Elector, meanwhile, was trying to tell his joke to Lotte deCharraiveuneuirauville, who was ignoring him while grimly watching her husband, MuMu, thrust himself upon cosmetics heiress and frump Martha Whoopley. "What I've always felt about St. Louis," MuMu was saying, "is that it's somehow more *real* than most of the places I know. Do you feel that?"

Martha Whoopley used her tongue to clear brussels sprouts into her cheek pouches, then said, "More real? How d'ya mean?"

"After all the flitter of New York, Deauville, Paris, Rome—" MuMu gestured gracefully, candlelight sparkling on his rings and bracelets, a fraction of his collection. "All of *this*," he summed up. "Isn't it somehow more, more, oh I don't know, more *real* to get back to St. Louis?"

"I don't think it's more real," Martha said. She shoved a lot of French bread into her mouth and went on talking. "I grew up there. I always thought it stunk."

"But you still live there."

"I keep a house out by the plant. You've got to keep your eye on those manager people."

Film star and environmental activist Lance Sheath, a rugged escarpment at Martha's right, leaned toward her with his virile confidentiality, saying in the deep voice that had thrilled billions, "You oughta spend some time in Los Angeles. Get to know the future."

"We have a packaging facility in Los Angeles," Martha told him. "Out in Encino. I don't like it much out there. All that white stucco hurts my eyes."

Prince Otto was finishing his joke to whoever would listen. It concerned a Jewish woman checking in at the Fountainebleau Hotel in Miami Beach, asking for bellboys to get the luggage from the car, and then requesting a wheelchair for her husband. " 'Of course,' said the desk clerk,' " concluded the Prince. " 'I'm terribly sorry, can't your husband walk?' 'He can,' said the woman, 'but thank God he doesn't have to.' "

While the Prince laughed heartily at his own joke, Chauncey's mind delivered him, intact, a variant beginning, "A sheikh's wife enters the Dorchester Hotel in London—" and ending, " 'He can,' said the woman, 'but thank Allah he doesn't have to.' " Should he wait ten minutes or so, and then straightfaced tell that variant? No; revenge enough was already under way.

Meanwhile, Mavis Orfizzi was clutching her own bony breast in assumed horror at her husband's gaucherie. "I can't stand it any more," she cried, for the benefit of the table at large, and surged to her feet, knocking over her chair, and so up-staging Laura Bathing that *that* one gave off screeching at Thomas Jefferson, the serving boy, and gaped in astonishment. "Otto," Mavis announced over the other guests' heads, "you are as clumsy and oafish at table as you are in bed."

"In bed?" demanded the Prince Elector, stung out of his raconteur's role, "I'm afraid to touch you in bed for fear of cutting myself," he declared.

"I can't *stand* it!" Mavis cried out, but then, apparently realizing she'd become reduced to repeating herself, she clutched her brow with both hands, screamed, *"No more!"* and fled the room.

Her intent didn't occur to Chauncey until, in the astounded hush at the table following her exit, all at once he heard from afar the busy whirr of machinery. Elevator machinery. "No!" he cried, half rising from his seat, arm stretching out toward the doorway through which the damned posturing woman had made her melodramatic exit. But it was too late. Too late. Arm dropping to his side, Chauncey sagged back into his chair, and from the distance the sound of whirring stopped.

14

"I've been shafted," Dortmunder said.

Well, he had. He'd moved as fast as he could to the metal ladder rungs at the rear of the elevator shaft, but there just hadn't been time to get up and out of the way. The elevator remorselessly rose, like an engine of destruction in an old Saturday-afternoon serial, and before he could climb a single rung the thing had overtaken him, pinning him to the wall.

It was those damn bourbon bottles that trapped him. The top of the elevator had a lip around the edge, an overhang which had brushed its way up the back of his legs, shoved his rump aside, grazed his shoulderblades, and bunked him gently on the back of the head before halting just above him. There was a bit more room below the lip, but when he tried to climb the rungs to freedom he discovered that the bottles under his jacket gave him just that much extra thickness, front to back, and he couldn't clear the goddam lip. Nor did he have enough room to use his hands to open the jacket and remove the bottles. He could sidle up the rungs, bit by bit, until his head and shoulders were above the top of the elevator, but at that point he was stuck.

From above, the harsh whisper of Kelp floated down: "Come on! Dortmunder, come on!"

He looked up, but couldn't get his head back far enough to see the top of the shaft. Speaking to the concrete wall, he half whispered back, "I can't."

And then, from somewhere not too far away, a woman screamed.

"Terrific," Dortmunder muttered. Louder, he called up to Kelp, "You people go on! Stash the painting!"

"But what about you?"

"Go *on!*" And, to end the argument, Dortmunder crab-crawled his way down the ladder rungs again, putting his head out of Kelp's sight.

By now the woman had stopped screaming, but all at once more voices sounded, male and female. Turning his head as far as possible, Dortmunder could just see an air vent, and through it the interior of the elevator, the open elevator door, and a bit of hallway. And as he looked, and listened to the raised male and female voices, one of those goddam private guards—the fat one—suddenly ran by the open elevator door.

There was only one thing to do, and Dortmunder did it. *Down* he went, sidling past the back wall of the elevator, down as rapidly as he could into almost impenetrable darkness, lower and lower into the elevator shaft. Because who knew when it would occur to somebody to use the goddam elevator again.

Whirrrrrrrrr.

Yike. Zip zip zip zip went Dortmunder, descending and descending, but nowhere near as fast as the elevator, whose cables shushed and binkled near his right elbow, and whose dirty black metal bottom dropped toward him like an anal retentive's worst nightmare. He could sense it above his head, dropping and dropping, inexorable, closing down and down.

Whirrrrr-*clump*.

It stopped. Dortmunder's head, withdrawn like a turtle's into his neck, remained a good clear quarter-inch below the bottom of the elevator as he listened to the doors chunk open and heard the resonance of feet pounding outward; one or more of the private guards, gone to report. Meaning this was not the ground floor, but the main floor above it. Good thing they hadn't gone all the way down.

"All right, all right," Dortmunder whispered to himself, "let's not panic," and immediately the question came into his mind, *Why not?*

Well. He struggled for an answer, and finally found one: "Don't want to fall."

Very good. Not panicking, Dortmunder made his way down the rest of the ladder to the bottom of the shaft, which was in such utter blackness that he knew he'd arrived only when he started to reach his left foot down for the next rung, and slammed his toes into something solid at least three inches before he'd expected anything. "Ow!" he said aloud, and the well-like walls gave the word back to him.

So here he was at the bottom of things. Releasing the rungs, he began to move around this Stygian space and a sudden pain in his knee told him it was occupied. Another *ow* went the circuit, and then he began to feel about, this way and that, and finally came to the conclusion that what was at the bottom of this elevator shaft was some sort of huge spring. Could that be right? He visualized it in his mind, like a pink cross-section drawing from *The Way Things Work:* elevator shaft, elevator, elevator slips its gears and plummets, hits giant spring and goes ba-*roooong*-a, spring absorbs major portion of impact. By God, it might even work.

Whirrrrr.

Oh, no. Here the son of a bitch came again, heading this way. Dortmunder dropped to the oily, cruddy floor, wrapping himself like an open parenthesis around the base of the big spring, while the elevator descended to ground-floor level, the doors opened, male voices engaged in a conference of some kind, the doors closed, and the elevator whirred its way back up to the first floor.

Dortmunder stood, beginning to get pissed off. That crowd of Scotsmen at the theater, that was one thing, the accidents of life, you learned to roll with punches like that. But what was happening in this house was utter bullshit. He'd been promised no guards on the top floor, and there'd been *two* of them. He'd been promised the elevator would stay down and out of his way, and now the damn thing was treating him like an apple in a cider press. Was he going to tolerate this?

Probably.

Unless he could get the hell out of here. And now that his eyes had grown more accustomed to the dark, he could see breaks in the black, lines of light just over there, indicating a closed door, the bottom of which would be not very far above his head. The ground-floor door. If he could get through that, then somehow he'd manage to clear out of this house. Anyway, it was worth a try. And anything, finally, was better than just sitting forever in the bottom of an elevator shaft.

Circling the giant spring, Dortmunder approached the lines of light, touched the door, and tried to slide it open. It wouldn't go. He pushed harder, and it still wouldn't go.

Of course not. An electric lock was holding it in place, so long as the elevator was elsewhere. He had to get at that lock, which was about five feet up on the door judging from the one he'd seen at the top level.

Dortmunder sat on the spring—human beings are quickly adaptable to any environment, which makes them a fine stock for those interested in animal husbandry—to consider his present resources. Aside from his ski mask, clothing and those damned bourbon bottles, what did he have on his person?

Money. Keys. He would have had cigarettes and matches, but somehow May's chain-smoking had discouraged him, and about four months ago, after nearly thirty years of smoking Camels, he'd simply stopped. There'd been none of the usual withdrawal symptoms, no nervousness or bad temper, in fact not even much desire to quit. He'd simply awakened one morning, looked at the Everest of matches and butts in the ashtray on May's side of the bed, and decided not to have a cigarette just yet. Habit had kept him carrying his crumpled Camels another two weeks, but finally he'd realized he simply wasn't smoking any more, and that was the end of it. So he didn't have cigarettes, but more importantly under the circumstances, he also didn't have matches.

Yes, but what *did* he have? He had his wallet, with driver's license, money, blood-type card (you never know), a couple of credit cards he didn't dare use and a library card May had got him for obscure reasons of her own. In other pockets he had several cufflinks and tiepins belonging to Arnold Chauncey. He had—

Credit cards. Credit cards are tough plastic, they can be slipped between door and jamb to force open a latch. Could a credit card be inserted between the electric lock box and the metal plate on the elevator door, unlocking it?

There was only one way to find out. Clutching a credit card between his teeth like a pirate's sword, Dortmunder scrambled up the ladder and around the horizontal beams to the door. Credit card in position. Credit card pushed forward. Credit card pushed *harder,* pushed, pushed, wriggled, edged, pushed, sidled, *pushed* into the goddam space between box and plate, shoved in there until all at once it went, and there was a tiny *click.*

Yes? Holding on to the credit card—he didn't want to lose that into the darkness below, covered with his fingerprints— Dortmunder leaned forward against the concrete wall and used his other hand to push on the door.

Which slid open.

15

Arnold Chauncey sipped bourbon, stared at the spot on the wall where *Folly Leads Man to Ruin* had so lately hung, and tried not to look as pleased as he felt. The house was full of policemen, guests were shrieking in every corner, and somehow or other the plot seemed to have gone simultaneously completely wrong *and* completely right.

The dismay Chauncey had felt when Mavis Orfizzi had taken off in that elevator had been nothing to the cold acid-bath of doom that had washed o'er him when he'd discovered that two private guards, in *direct* contradiction of his *express* orders, had taken up posts on the top floor. As for his own behavior, he had to give himself low marks and consider himself *extremely* lucky that in the clatter of events nobody seemed to have noticed any of the false notes in his performance. His crying out, "No!" for instance, when Mavis entered the elevator. Then there'd been his reaction on seeing the guards come *down* from upstairs: an angry cry of, "What were you doing up *there?*"

Fortunately, after that last clinker Chauncey had finally got hold of himself and settled down to more or less appropriate behavior: initial shock and outrage, commiseration and apology toward his guests, helpful determination toward the policemen when they arrived, and stoic fortitude when counting up his own "losses" from his bedroom (Dortmunder & Co. had been damned efficient in there, by God). Statements had been taken from the dinner guests first, after which they'd been allowed to leave: Laura Bathing so startled she forgot to tip over a vase on the way out, Major General (Ret.) and Mrs. Homer Biggott limping out to be stacked into their Lincoln by their chauffeur, Sheikh Rama el-Rama el-Rama El departing with a smiling comment about "petty crime increasing as civilizations decline," Martha Whoopley the only one in the household to eat her portion of baked Alaska before departure, Lance Sheath helping her into her fur and leaving with her, chuckling mannishly deep in his throat. Chauncey himself had given the authorities a brief statement—the truth, that he had been at dinner with his guests until the screaming started.

And now the police were dealing with the houseguests, one by one, while the staff awaited their turn in the kitchen and the shamefaced private guards cooled their heels in the first-floor lounge next to the dining room in which the interviews were being held.

There was nothing left for Chauncey to do but wait for the dust to settle, and in the morning to call his insurance agent. Nobody could claim *this* was a faked theft; the closeting of the private guards, in fact, dangerous though their presence had been, adding yet another touch of verisimilitude to the affair. The first bourbon on the rocks he'd given himself had been medicinal in nature, a prescription for his jangled nerves, but the second had been in acknowledgment of a sense of relief, and the third was a toast to a dangerous crossing successfully accomplished. Cheers!

Chauncey was just draining this congratulatory tot when Prince Elector Otto Orfizzi wandered in, fresh from his interview with the police, saying, "Ah, there you are."

"Here I am," Chauncey agreed. His mood was becoming agreeably mellow.

"Bad timing, that," Orfizzi said, gesturing upwards with his thumb.

Not sure what the man meant, Chauncey said, "Was it?"

"If the damned woman had gone up there ten minutes earlier," the Prince explained, "the blighters might have shot her." He shrugged, evidently irritated at his wife's perverse insistence on remaining alive, then rallied himself and changed the subject. "I could hardly believe my eyes when I saw those policemen."

Now what? "I'm not sure I follow," Chauncey admitted.

"The man in charge." Prince Otto leaned forward, dropping his voice confidentially. "Black as the ace of spades."

"Ah, yes," Chauncey said, and the combination of nerves and liquor made him add, "Well, at least he isn't Jewish."

The Prince considered that. "I don't know," he mused. "With a Jew, you'd be certain in any event the fellow wasn't in league with the thieves."

"That's true," Chauncey said, and got to his feet, feeling the strong need of another drink.

"Would that be bourbon?" asked the Prince.

"It would. May I offer?"

"You certainly may. Say what you will about jazz, the Hollywood movie, the Broadway musical or the short story, *I* say America's contribution to the arts is bourbon."

"I agree with you," Chauncey said, in some surprise, and reached for the bottle, only to discover it was empty. And when he looked in the lower cabinet among the extras there was no bourbon to be seen. "Sorry," he said. "I'll have to go downstairs for more."

"Oh, don't bother, I'll be perfectly happy with Scotch. As happy as one can be with that woman in the house, of course."

"It isn't any bother," Chauncey assured him. "I'd rather stick to bourbon myself." And it would be pleasant to be away from the Prince for a few minutes.

But that was not to be. "I'll stroll along with you," the Prince announced, and did.

The main liquor storage was in a closet on the ground floor, next to a similar closet converted to a wine cellar, the latter with its temperature and humidity maintained at a dry fifty degrees. Chauncey and Orfizzi rode down together in the elevator, and to fill the time Chauncey described the wine cellar, as it was a recent conversion. "I'd like to see it," the Prince said.

"I'll show it you."

On the ground floor, they walked together down the corridor, and about halfway to the rear exit Chauncey stopped at a pair of doors on the right-hand side. "Liquor storage is on the left," he explained, "and this is the wine cellar." And he opened the door to look at the bleak eyes and shivering body of Dortmunder. "Ump!" Chauncey said, and quickly shut the door again, before the Prince could get around it to look inside.

"I didn't see it," said the Prince.

"Um, yes," Chauncey said. "I, um, I've just had an awful thought."

"You have?"

"I may be out of bourbon. Let's see." And Chauncey opened the other door, which displayed a floor-to-ceiling rank of horizontal bottle-storage spaces made of criss-crossed wooden slats, about two-thirds filled with liquor and liquor bottles. "Oh, of course," he said. "I have plenty." And he grabbed two bottles and put them in the startled Prince's hands, then took a third from the stacks for himself, the while gesturing with his free hand, saying, "You see the style. The wine cellar is identical, except of course for the humidity and temperature controls. Not needed in here, naturally."

"Naturally," agreed the Prince. He was holding the two bottles by the neck, as though they were small dead animals and he wasn't quite sure what he was expected to do with them.

Closing the door, Chauncey took the Prince by the elbow and led him off toward the elevator. "Now to our drink, eh?"

"But—" The Prince looked back over his shoulder at the closed wine-cellar door. "Oh," he said doubtfully, as Chauncey continued to propel him away. "Identical. Yes, um, right."

Back to the elevator they went, boarded, and Chauncey pushed the button before the door closed. But then, as the door was sliding into place, he suddenly thrust the third bourbon bottle into the Prince's arms, said, "Join you in a minute. Something I have to take care of," and slipped out of the elevator.

"But—" The Prince's startled face disappeared behind the closing door, and the elevator whirred upward as Chauncey *tore* down the hall, *flung* open the door, and cried, "What are you doing in *there?*"

"Freezing to death," Dortmunder told him. "Can I come out?"

Chauncey looked both ways. "Yes."

"Good." He emerged, and as Chauncey closed the door he said, "Get me out of here."

"I don't under— Yes, of course." Chauncey frowned up and down the corridor, chewing the inside of his cheek.

"We had guards," Dortmunder said. "*Not* to mention elevators."

"Things happened," Chauncey said, distracted by his own thoughts. "Come with me." He took Dortmunder by the arm, and as he led him down the corridor toward the back there was a faint *clink* from inside his leather jacket. A vision of two full bourbon bottles in the sitting-room storage cabinet came clear to Chauncey's mind, and he offered Dortmunder a sidelong jaundiced glance, saying, "I see."

Dortmunder seemed too disgusted by events to reply, and the two of them progressed as far as the mudroom by the back door, where Chauncey took out his keyring, slipped one key off, and handed it over, saying, "This unlocks the door to the passage. Also the one at the other end. Get it back to me later."

Dortmunder gestured at the door beside them. "Won't we set off the alarm when we open this?"

"I'll say it was me, I thought I saw something in the garden. Hurry, man."

"All right." Dortmunder took the key.

Struck by sudden doubt, Chauncey said, "Are there any more of you still in here?"

"Only me," Dortmunder said, as though the fact spoke volumes about his life.

"What about the painting? It's gone, isn't it?"

"Oh, yeah," Dortmunder said, looking surly. "*That* part went okay." And he left.

16

When Dortmunder's head disappeared for the last time behind the elevator, Kelp withdrew his own head from the open panel in the housing and said to the others, "What do we do now?"

"What he told us," Bulcher answered. "We get the hell out of here."

"But what about Dortmunder?"

Chefwick said, "Andy, he'll either get away or he won't. But it won't do *him* any good if we stand around on the roof and get caught with him."

Kelp cast another worried glance into the elevator shaft, where there was nothing to be seen. "He's going to blame me for this," he said. "I know he will."

"Come *on*, Kelp," Bulcher said, and he picked up the rolled painting from the tarred roof and strode away.

So Kelp left, with many backward looks, and joined the other two on the return journey across the roofs and up the rope and back into the theater building and down the stairs to the balcony. Bulcher led all the way, and he was the one who opened the door at the foot of the stairs.

Unfortunately, it was intermission time within, and the rear of the balcony was once again full of Scotsmen. When Bulcher unexpectedly shoved open the door, he knocked one Scotsman's full cup of whiskey all over another Scotman's kilt. Ignoring the damage, he made to push between them and go on about his business, but the empty-cupped Scotsman put a restraining hand on his chest and said, "Here, now. What do you think *you're* at?"

"Get out of my way," said Bulcher, who was in no mood for distractions. Behind him, Chefwick emerged from the stairs.

"By the Lord Harry you're a rude fellow," declared the drenched Scot, and he hauled off and punched Bulcher a good one on the ear. So Bulcher hit him back, and for good measure he then hit the other one, who staggered back into three more, spilling *their* drinks.

By the time Kelp got through the doorway the fight was merrily blazing away. People who had no idea what the brawl was all about were determinedly slugging people who had even less connection with it. "Well, for God's sake," Kelp said, standing in the doorway, gaping at a scene of surging fury and flashing knees and wildly swinging fists. Battle cries whooped and wailed above the fray, and somebody's rock-hard hand glanced off Kelp's forehead, causing him to stagger backward and sit down heavily on the steps.

What a view. In his dark stairway, there was a kind of muffled quality to the noise, and the belligerents staggering and swirling by the open doorway were like something in a 3-D movie. Kelp sat there a minute or two, bemused by the scene, until he suddenly realized that the white sticklike object he was from time to time seeing lifted in the air and then smashed down on one or another head was in fact the rolled-up painting, wielded in absentminded irritation by Tiny Bulcher.

"Not the painting!" Kelp came boiling out of the stairwell once more, plowing and bashing his way across the battlefield toward Bulcher, ignoring every buffet and deflection along the way, finally lunging upward like one of the figures in the Iwo Jima flag photo (which was posed, by the way, a later reconstruction; it's so hard to tell fiction from fact these days), wrenching the tubed painting out of Bulcher's great fist, screaming in his ear, "Not the painting!" and then abruptly bending double as about eleven different Scotsmen all let him have it at once in the breadbasket.

What a different perspective you get on the floor amid a sea of swirling kilts. Knees are knobbly, huge, dangerous-looking things, but over there was a pair of black stovepipes; Chefwick, in trousers. Kelp forced himself upward, climbing up handy sporrans to find that Bulcher had been swept away but indeed Chefwick was over there to the left, pressed defensively against the wall, clutching his black bag to his chest with both arms. Even in the middle of the fray, people recognized the true noncombatant when they see him, and so Chefwick remained like a rock in the ocean; it all swirled around him, but it never quite *got* him.

"Chefwick!" Kelp cried. Around him, a lot of Scotsmen wanted to play. "Chefwick!"

Light flashed from Chefwick's glasses as he turned his head.

"The painting!" Kelp cried, and launched it like a javelin, and went under for the second time.

17

Stan Murch eased the Caddy around the corner and came to a stop in front of Hunter House. As far as he was concerned, this job was a piece of cake. Nothing to do but sit here like some hired chauffeur out front of a concert hall, then when the guys came out drive clamly away. Piece of cake.

The car itself was a piece of sponge cake, with MD plates. Kelp had picked it up for Murch this afternoon. A pale blue Cadillac, it was loaded with options. Kelp preferred doctors' cars whenever available, believing that doctors baby themselves by buying cars loaded with every power-assisting gadget and padded with every creature comfort known to the engineers of Detroit. "Driving a doctor's car," he sometimes said, "is like taking a nice nap in a hammock on a Sunday afternoon. In the summer." He could wax quite lyrical on the subject.

Movement attracted Murch's attention, and he glanced over toward the concert hall, on his right. Was something happening in there? It seemed to him, looking through the row of glass doors, that activity of some sort had begun in the lobby; a lot of running around or something. Murch squinted, trying to see more clearly, and one of those doors snapped open and a body sailed out like a glider without wings, hit the pavement, rolled, popped to its feet and ran back into the lobby.

Murch said, "What?"

By golly, there was a *fight* going on in there. The same body—or another one—hurtled out again, this time followed by three men struggling and reeling in one another's arms like a rugby scrum, and then all at once the entire dispute boiled out of the theater and spread all over the sidewalk.

"Holy Jesus!" said Murch, and watched a body bounce off the hood of the Caddy and back into the fray.

A face appeared at the windshield, and because of the face's contortion and his own astonishment it took Murch a minute to realize it was Kelp, struggling to get away from a whole lot of people who wanted him to stay. Murch honked the horn, which startled Kelp's friends, and Kelp scrambled off the hood and ducked into the Caddy.

Murch stared at him. Kelp's clothing was ripped, his cheek was smudged, and he looked as though he might be getting a black eye. Murch said, "What in hell is going *on?*"

"I don't know," Kelp said, gasping for breath. "I just don't know. Here comes Chefwick."

And so he did, tiptoeing across the sidewalk, clutching his black bag to his chest, moving like a ballet dancer in a mine-field, and when at last he slipped into the Caddy and shut the door behind himself all he said, wide-eyed, was, "Oh, my. Oh, my."

Kelp asked him, "Where's Bulcher?"

"Here he comes," Murch said.

Here came Bulcher. He could be awesome when he was annoyed, and at the moment he was *very* annoyed. He had two of his opponents by the neck, one in each great ham-fist, and he was using them as battering rams to clear a path for himself through the melee, poking the two bodies out ahead of himself as he walked, battering them against raiding parties at his flanks, and generally cutting a swath. The path he'd bull-dozed on his way *in*to the hall was as nothing to the scorched-earth March To The Curb he effected on the way out. Reaching the Cadillac, he flung his assistants back into the riot while Chefwick opened a rear door for him. Then he hopped into the Caddy, slammed the door, and said, "That's enough of *that.*"

"Okay, Stan," Kelp said. "Let's go."

"Go?" Murch looked around, at Kelp beside him on the

front seat and Chefwick and Bulcher in back, and said, "What about Dortmunder?"

"He's not with us. Come on, Stan, they'll take the car apart next. Drive somewhere and I'll tell you on the way."

The car *was* rocking more than somewhat, from the bodies bouncing off it, and a few of Bulcher's recent playmates were beginning to look hungrily at him through the windows, so Murch put the Caddy in gear, pressed on the horn, eased away from the curb, and drove them away from there.

It took Kelp two right turns and a red light to explain Dortmunder's situation, finishing, as they headed downtown, "We can only hope he'll figure something."

"He's stuck in an elevator shaft, with private guards running around?"

"He's been in tighter spots than that before," Kelp assured him.

"Yeah," Murch said. "And wound up in jail."

"Don't talk defeatist. Anyway, the guy who lives there is on our side. Maybe he can give Dortmunder a hand."

"Yeah, maybe," Murch said doubtfully. Then, deciding to look on the bright side, he said, "But anyway, you did get the painting, right?"

"*That* part was easy," Kelp said. "Except when Bulcher thought it was a baseball bat."

"I got carried away," Bulcher said.

"All's well that end's well," Kelp said. "Let's see it, Roger."

Chefwick said, "Beg pardon?"

Kelp turned a suddenly glassy smile on Chefwick. "The painting," he said. "Let's see it."

"I don't have it."

"Sure you do. I gave it to you."

"No, you didn't. Bulcher had it."

"Kelp took it away from me," Bulcher said.

"That's right. And I threw it to Roger."

"Well, I didn't get it." Chefwick was sounding prissier and prissier, as though defending himself against unjust accusations.

"Well, I *threw* it to you," Kelp insisted.

"Well, I didn't *get* it," Chefwick insisted.

Kelp glared at Chefwick, and Chefwick glared at Kelp, and then gradually they stopped glaring and started frowning. They looked each other over, they frowned at Bulcher, they looked around the interior of the car, and all the time Bulcher watched them with his head cocked to one side while Murch tried to concentrate simultaneously on the Friday-night traffic and the events inside the car.

It was Murch who finally said the awful truth aloud. "You *don't* have it."

"Something—" Kelp lifted up and looked beneath himself, but it wasn't there either. "Something happened," he said. "In that fight. I don't know, all of a sudden there was this huge fight going on."

"We don't have it," Bulcher said. He sounded stunned. "We lost it."

"Oh, my goodness," Chefwick said.

Kelp sighed. "We have to go back for it," he said. "I hate the whole idea, but we just have to. We have to go back."

Nobody argued. Murch took the next right, and headed uptown.

The scene in front of the theater was *not* to be believed. The police had arrived, ambulances had arrived, even a fire engine had arrived. Platoons of Scotsmen were being herded into clumps by wary policemen, while other policemen in white helmets trotted into the hall, where the controversy was apparently continuing.

Slowly Murch drove past Hunter House along the one lane still open to traffic, and was waved on by a cop with a red-beamed long flashlight. Sadly Kelp and Chefwick and Bulcher gazed at the concert hall. Kelp sighed. "Dortmunder is going to be very upset," he said.

18

Dortmunder took the subway to Union Square, then walked the rest of the way home. He was in the last block when a fellow came out of a doorway and said, "Pardon me. You got a match?"

"No," said Dortmunder. "I don't smoke."

"That's all right," the man said. "Neither do I." And he fell into pace with Dortmunder, walking along at his right hand. He had a very decided limp, but seemed to have no trouble keeping up.

Dortmunder stopped and looked at him. "All right," he said.

The man stopped, with a quizzical smile. He was an inch or two taller than Dortmunder, slender, with a long thin nose and a bony sunken-cheeked face, and he was wearing a topcoat with the collar turned up and a hat with the brim pulled down, and he was keeping his right hand in his topcoat pocket. Some sort of black orthopedic shoe was on his right foot. He said, "All right? All right what?"

"Do whatever you're here to do," Dortmunder told him, "so I can knock you down and go home."

The man laughed as though he were amused, but he also stepped back a pace, twisting on the lame foot. "I'm no holdup man, Dortmunder," he said.

"You know my name," Dortmunder mentioned.

"Well," said the man, "we have the same employer."

"I don't get it."

"Arnold Chauncey."

Then Dortmunder did get it. "You're the other guy the lawyer found for him. The killer."

The killer made a strangely modest gesture with his left hand, while the right remained in his pocket. "Not quite," he said. "Killing is sometimes part of what I do, but it isn't my real job. The way I like to think of it, my job is enforcing other people's wishes."

"Is that right."

"For instance," the killer said, "in your case, I'm being paid twenty thousand dollars, but not to kill you. I get paid whether you live or die. If you give back the picture, that's fine, you live and I collect. If you *don't*, if you make trouble, that's not fine, and you die and I collect." He shrugged. "It makes no difference."

Dortmunder said, "I don't want you hanging around me the next six months."

"Oh, don't worry," the killer said. "You'll never see me again. If it's thumbs down, I'll drop you from a distance." Grinning, he took his right hand out of his pocket, empty, made a pistol shape with the fingers, pointed it straight-arm at Dortmunder's face, closed one eye, grinned, sighted along his arm, and said, "Bang. I'm very good at that."

Somehow, Dortmunder believed him. He already knew that he himself was precisely the kind of reliable crook Chauncey had asked for, and he now believed that this fellow was precisely the kind of reliable killer Chauncey had asked for. "I'm happy to say," he said, "that I don't intend to do anything with that painting except hold on to it till I get paid, then give it back to Chauncey. Fancy is not my method."

"Good," said the killer, with a friendly smile. "I like getting paid for doing nothing. So long." And he started away, then immediately turned back, saying, "You shouldn't mention this to Chauncey."

"I shouldn't?"

"He doesn't want us to meet, but I thought we should have one chat." His grin flickered. "I like to see my people," he said. His eyes glittered at Dortmunder, and then once again he turned away.

Dortmunder watched him go, tall and narrow and dark, body twisting as he strode on his game leg, both hands now in his topcoat pockets, and he felt a faint chill up the middle of his back. Now he understood why Chauncey had said Dortmunder wasn't dangerous; it was because he'd had that fellow as a comparison. "Good thing I'm an honest man," he muttered to himself, and he walked on home, where he found

Kelp and Murch and Chefwick and Bulcher and May all waiting for him in the living room.

"Dortmunder!"

"John!"

"You made it! I knew you would!"

They gave him cheers and pats on the back, and he gave
them Chauncey's bourbon, and then they all sat down with
glasses of the stuff—terrific bourbon, almost worth the trouble
it caused—and Kelp said, "How'd you do it? How'd you get
away?"

"Well, I went down to the bottom of the elevator shaft,"
Dortmunder started, "and then . . ." And he stopped, struck
by something vaguely wrong. Looking around at the attentive
faces, he saw they were more glazed than attentive. Bulcher's
and Kelp's clothes were all messed up, and Kelp maybe had
the beginnings of a black eye. There was a kind of sub-
terranean tension in the room. "What's the matter?" he said.

May said, "John, tell us how you got out of the elevator
shaft."

He frowned at May, he frowned at the others, he listened
to the silence, and he *knew*. Looking at Kelp, he said, "Where
is it?"

"Now, Dortmunder," Kelp said.

"Where *is* it?"

"Oh, dear," said Chefwick.

Murch said, "There was a fight in the theater."

"It wasn't anybody's *fault*," said Kelp.

Even Tiny Bulcher was looking abashed. "It was just one
of those things," he said.

"WHERE IS IT?"

An electric silence. Dortmunder watched them stare at the
floor, and finally it was Kelp who answered, in a tiny voice:
"We lost it."

"You lost it," Dortmunder said.

Then all of them were talking at once, explaining, justifying,
telling the story from a thousand different directions, and
Dortmunder just sat there, unmoving, stolid, letting it wash
over him until at last they all ran down. In that next silence,

Dortmunder sighed, but didn't speak, and May said, "John, can I freshen your drink?"

Dortmunder shook his head. There was no heat in him. "No, thanks, May," he said.

Kelp said, "Is there anything we can do?"

"If you don't mind," Dortmunder told him, "I'd like to be alone for a while."

"It wasn't anybody's fault," Kelp said. "It really wasn't."

"I'm not blaming you," Dortmunder said, and oddly enough it was the truth. He *didn't* blame anybody. Fatalism had captured another victim. "I just want to be alone for a while," he said, "and think about how I've got six months to live."

THE SECOND CHORUS

1

Amid the merry flocks of Christmas shoppers, Dortmunder looked like some sort of rebuttal; the wet blanket's answer to Santa Claus. As he stood in the perfume department at Macy's, the word *HUMBUG* seemed to float in a balloon in the air over his head, and the eye he cast on the salesgirl would have to be called jaundiced. "What's that one?" he said.

The girl was holding a tiny glass phial shaped like a 1920's floorlamp without the shade; a spread-out pancake at the bottom, where the eighth of an ounce of perfume was, and then a long skinny neck with nothing in it at all, except the tube of the atomizer. "Ma Folie," said the girl. "It's French."

"Oh, yeah?"

"It means, 'My Folly.' "

"Yours, huh? Let me smell it again."

The girl had already sprayed a mite on her wrist, which she obediently re-extended in Dortmunder's direction. It felt weird to lean over and rest his nose on some unknown female's wrist—bony, gray-white skin, thin blue vein tracings—and all Dortmunder knew after he'd sniffed was the same as he'd learned last time; the stuff smelt sweet. He wouldn't have known Ma Folie from peach brandy. "How much is it?"

"Twenty-seven fifty."

"Twenty-seven *dollars?*"

"Foreign currency can be exchanged on the sixth floor," she told him.

Dortmunder frowned at her. "I don't have any foreign currency."

"Oh. I'm sorry, I thought . . . well, anyway. It costs twenty-seven dollars and fifty cents."

"I oughta knock *this* place over," Dortmunder muttered, and turned to look around at the store, the customers, the exits, the escalators—kinda casing the joint. But it wasn't any good, of course. They had private cops, closed-circuit TV, electric eyes, all kinds of sophisticated defenses. And the real cash would be kept in the offices, way upstairs; you'd never get out of the building, even if you managed the score.

"Sir?"

But Dortmunder didn't answer. He remained frozen in position, having just that second noticed a face he knew on the Down escalator, descending steadily from the ceiling; a bright cheerful Christmassy face, gazing birdlike this way and that as he glided down that long diagonal. Dortmunder was so taken aback that it didn't occur to him to avert his own face until too late; Kelp had seen him, Kelp had flashed a huge smile, Kelp was up on tiptoe on the escalator waving one hand high over his head.

"*Sir?*"

"Christ," Dortmunder muttered. He gave the girl a bilious look and she backed away, uncertain whether to be frightened or offended. "All right," Dortmunder said. "The hell with it, all right."

"Sir?"

"I'll take the goddam thing."

Kelp was struggling his way through the multitudes, the bewildered husbands, the snotty-nosed children, the self-absorbed secretaries, the massed family groups, the smirking pairs of teenage girls, the short stout women carrying nine shopping bags, the tall slender women wearing fun furs over their shoulders and yellow-lensed sunglasses on top of their heads, all the flux and flow of gift-time in the metropolis, and Dortmunder, now that it was too late, lifted one shoulder to shield his face while he slipped the girl three crumpled sawbucks.

"Dortmunder!"

"Yeah," Dortmunder said.

"What a coincidence!" Kelp was carrying a full Korvette's shopping bag; working some dodge, no doubt. "I just called your place about an hour ago, May said she didn't know where you were."

"Christmas shopping," Dortmunder said, as another man might say, "Cleaning the cesspool."

Kelp glanced at the girl, currently putting a fresh perfume bottle in a complicated little cardboard box, and he leaned closer to Dortmunder to say, quietly, "Whadaya wanna *buy* that stuff for? We hit one of them shopping centers out on the Island, we make a profit on it."

"For a Christmas present?" Dortmunder shook his head. "A Christmas present is different," he said. "A Christmas present is something you buy."

"Yeah?" Kelp received that as though it were a brand-new idea, but one possibly worth further thought.

"Besides," Dortmunder said, "I still got some of that Chauncey money." The five of them had split nearly seven thousand dollars after fencing all the jewelry and other goods from the fiasco.

Kelp was surprised. "You do? That was over a month ago!"

"Well, I'm not a big spender."

The girl came back with Dortmunder's purchase in a bag, and his change. "That's twenty-nine seventy," she said, and dropped a quarter and a nickel into Dortmunder's palm.

"You told me twenty-seven fifty."

"Plus tax."

"Well, shit," Dortmunder said, put his change in his pocket, picked up his parcel, and turned away.

"And Merry Christmas to *you*," the girl told his back.

"Listen," Kelp said, as they moved away from the counter, "I got to talk to you, that's why I was looking for you. It's too crowded in here, you want a lift home?"

Dortmunder gave him a wary look. "No new capers," he said.

"Nothing *new*," Kelp said, with funny emphasis. "I promise."

"Okay, then."

They went out to Herald Square. It was nearly six, quite dark, not quite freezing, and slowly, slightly, sloppily snowing. Jammed traffic and roly-poly bundled people were everywhere. "Colder'n hell," Dortmunder said.

"It isn't the cold, it's the humidity," Kelp told him. "The air's so damp, it gets right into your bones. If it'd get down below freezing, dry the air out, we wouldn't feel so cold."

Dortmunder looked at him. "Everything's gotta be the opposite with you," he said.

"I'm just saying."

"Don't. Where's your car?"

"I don't know yet," Kelp said. "Wait right here, I'll be back." And he sloshed away, carrying his Korvette's shopping bag into the swirling crowds and the gathering snow.

It was after Kelp was out of sight that what he'd said ricocheted in Dortmunder's mind. Aloud, he muttered, "He doesn't *know* yet?" Escape suggested itself, but when he thought about his alternatives—the subway in the Christmas rush, trying to find a cab in Herald Square at six o'clock on a shopping day in December, walking twenty-five blocks home in the snow and the cold—he realized he might just as well stay where he was. So he leaned his back against the wall of Macy's, near the entrance doors, put his hands in his overcoat pockets—his right hand closing around the box of perfume—and settled down to wait. Snow gathered on his shoulders and his black knit cap, snow melted on his forehead and caused little icy rivulets to run down his nose and cataract onto his coat buttons, and icy slush transmitted previews of the grave through his wet shoes to his feet.

He'd been standing there about five minutes when a distinguished gent in an astrakhan hat and white moustache and fur-collared coat paused in front of him, stuffed something into the breast pocket of Dortmunder's overcoat, and said, "Cheer up, old chap. And a merry Christmas to you." And walked on. Dortmunder stared after him, nonplussed, then fingered his pocket and drew out a neatly folded dollar bill. "Well, Jesus H. Jumping Christ," he said.

A car was honking. Dortmunder looked past the dollar and saw a tan Mercedes-Benz at the curb, and somebody inside it waving. Kelp?

Kelp. And, yes, the Mercedes had MD plates; from Connecticut, as it happened. Dortmunder trotted around to the passenger side, slid into the car, and felt dry warmth bask over him as Kelp shot the Mercedes forward. "Ahhhh," said Dortmunder.

"Im-*possible* traffic," Kelp said. "Even Stan Murch wouldn't get anywhere in this stuff. I picked up this beast a block away, can you believe it? Took me that long just to come back." He glanced over. "What's with the dollar bill?"

Dortmunder was still holding it in his hand, and now he shoved it away in his side pocket. "I found it," he said.

"No kidding. Maybe this is your lucky day."

What an idea. "Yeah," said Dortmunder.

"In fact," Kelp said, "this *is* your lucky day."

Dortmunder closed his eyes. He could enjoy the comfort of the car, and just not listen to anything Kelp had to say.

"For instance," Kelp said, "there's that question of the painting, and what happens six months from now."

"Four and a half," Dortmunder said. His eyes were still closed.

"Okay, four and a half."

"And I figure maybe I can leave the country," Dortmunder said. "Go to South America, maybe. Me and May, we could open up a bar or something. Is the guy gonna follow us all over the world for twenty grand?"

"Yes," said Kelp. "So long as they're looking for the painting, they'll look for you, and you know it."

Inside his closed eyes, Dortmunder sighed. "You could let me at least have my little dreams," he said.

"I got something better," Kelp told him. "I got an out."

"You don't."

"I do."

"You don't. Not unless you got the painting, and you don't. When Chauncey comes around and wants it back, there aren't gonna be any outs."

"One," Kelp said, and suddenly flew into a frenzy at the wheel, honking his horn in a mad bebop rhythm of toots, the while yelling, *"Move your goddam ass whatsa matter don't you wanna go home!!!"*

Dortmunder opened his eyes. "Take it easy," he said.

"They give anybody a license," Kelp grumbled, subsiding. Then he said, "Listen, I can't talk in this traffic. You got any of that good bourbon left?"

"You're kidding."

"I tell you what," Kelp said. "I'll buy a bottle of bourbon on the way downtown—not Chauncey's brand, but something nice. Something bottled in Kentucky."

"Yeah?"

"Invite me up to your place," Kelp said. "We'll have a drink, I'll give you my idea."

"You know what I think of your ideas," Dortmunder told him.

"Can it be worse than a visit from Chauncey's friend?"

Dortmunder sighed.

"I'll buy two bottles," Kelp said.

2

"You remember my nephew Victor," Kelp said.

"The FBI man," Dortmunder said.

"The *ex*-FBI man," Kelp corrected him. "It makes a difference."

"They threw him out," Dortmunder said, "because he kept putting a suggestion in the FBI suggestion box that they oughta have a secret handshake, so they'd be able to recognize each other at parties."

"That's not necessarily so," Kelp said. "That's just a theory."

"It's good enough for me," Dortmunder told him. "It helps me remember the guy. What about him?"

"I was talking to him at Thanksgiving," Kelp said, "at my grandmother's. She makes the most fantastic turkey, you wouldn't believe it."

What was there to say to a remark like that? Nothing; so that's what Dortmunder said. He settled himself more comfortably in his personal easy chair in his warm dry living room— May was out at the Safeway, where she was a cashier—and he sipped a little more bourbon. It was bottled in Kentucky (as opposed to being distilled in Kentucky, shipped north in railroad cars and bottled in Hoboken) and it was pretty good; a firm stride upward from the stuff at the O. J. Bar and Grill, which was probably also *distilled* in Hoboken, from a combination of Hudson and Raritan waters.

Kelp was going on with his story. "The point is," he said, "Victor was telling me about a guy that lives in his neighborhood now, that he'd worked on his case back in the FBI. The guy was a counterfeiter."

"Yeah?"

"Only he didn't *print* the money," Kelp said. "He *drew* it." He made vague drawing gestures in the air. "One bill at a time. All twenties."

Dortmunder frowned past his glass at Kelp. "This guy drew individual twenty-dollar bills?"

"Apparently he was terrific at it. He'd take a sheet of paper, he'd paint five or six bills on it, cut them out, paint the other side, pass em all over town."

"Strange fella," Dortmunder decided.

"But terrific," Kelp said. "According to Victor, you couldn't tell his bills from the real thing. Every one of them, a work of art."

"Then how'd they get him?"

"Well, a couple ways. First off, he always worked in water-color. With oils, you get too much build-up on the paper, the texture's wrong. So his bills, they were fine when he first passed them, but pretty soon they'd begin to run."

"This sounds *exactly* like the kind of guy you'd know," Dortmunder said.

"I don't know him," Kelp said. "My nephew Victor knows him."

"And you know Victor."

"Well, he's my nephew."

"I rest my case," Dortmunder said. "What was the other way they caught this guy?"

"Well, he usually stayed right there in his own neighbor-hood," Kelp said. "He's a very unworldly sort of guy, he's really an artist, he just did these twenties to keep himself in potatoes and blue jeans while he did his own art. So like, when all these twenties kept getting traced back to the same Shop-Rite, the same drugstore, the same liquor store, the Feds staked out the neighborhood, and that's how Victor met this guy Porculey."

"Porculey?"

"Griswold Porculey. That's his name."

"It is, huh?"

"Absolutely. Anyway, the Feds nailed Porculey, but all he got was a suspended sentence when he promised not to do it any more."

"They believed him?"

"Well, yeah," Kelp said. "Because it made sense. Once they got him, and they figured out how he was doing those things, they talked to him, and it turned out he was spending five hours just to do one side of one bill. You know, those twenties, they're all full of tricky little stuff."

"Yeah, I've seen some," Dortmunder said.

"Well, anyway, that means ten hours per bill, and not even counting the cost of materials and overhead, paper, paint, de-preciation on the brushes, all the rest of it, the most he's making is two bucks an hour. He could do better than that *delivering* for the Shop-Rite, part time."

Dortmunder nodded. "Crime doesn't pay," he said. "I'm gradually coming to that conclusion."

"Well, the point is," Kelp went on, "this guy used to live up in Washington Heights, he had his studio up there and all, but the rent kept going up, they priced him out of the neighborhood and he moved out to Long Island. Victor ran into him in the shopping center."

"Passing twenties?"

"No," Kelp said, "but he's thinking about it. He told Victor he was looking for some way to do a bunch of bills all at once. Victor figures he's about halfway to inventing the printing press, and he's worried the guy'll get in trouble. And that's where we come in."

"I was wondering where we came in," Dortmunder said.

"We can put a little honest cash his way," Kelp said, "help him avoid temptation."

"How do we do that?"

"You don't get it?" Kelp was so pleased with himself he was about to run around in front and kiss himself on both cheeks. Leaning forward, gesturing with his half-full bourbon glass, he said. "We fake the painting!"

Dortmunder frowned at him past his own half-empty glass. "We what?"

"This is a famous painting, right, the one we copped from Chauncey? So there'll be pictures of it, copies of it, all that stuff. Porculey's a real artist, and he can imitate *anything*. So he runs up a copy of the painting and that's the one we give back!"

Dortmunder studied Kelp's words one by one. "There's something wrong with that," he said.

"What?"

"I don't know yet. I just hope I find it before it's too late."

"Dortmunder, it's better than getting shot in the head."

Dortmunder winced. "Don't talk like that," he said. Already in anticipation, the last few weeks, he was getting headaches every time he passed a window.

"You gotta *do* something," Kelp told him. "And this is the only something in town."

Was that true? Dortmunder considered again his dream of escaping to some South American seacoast town with May, opening a little restaurant-saloon—May's famous tuna casserole would make them an instant success—he himself would run the bar; he wasn't sure whether to call it May's Place or The Hideaway. But as he visualized the dream once more, himself behind a gleaming black bar with bamboo fittings—somehow South America was very South Pacific in his imagination— in walks a tall narrow fellow with a bad limp. He ups to the bar and he says, "Hello, Dortmunder," and his hand comes out of his topcoat pocket.

"*Un*," said Dortmunder.

Kelp looked at him, concerned. "Something wrong? Bourbon no good?"

"Bourbon's fine," Dortmunder said.

Kelp said, "Listen, why don't I call Victor, have him set up the meet? Dortmunder? I'll do that, right? Why don't I?"

May's Place faded, with its unwelcome customer. "Okay," Dortmunder said.

3

"I don't see why we had to meet him at a shopping center," Dortmunder grumbled, watching the windshield wipers push snow back and forth on the glass. Today's doctor's car was a silver gray Cadillac Seville, with a tape deck and a selection of tapes by Tom Jones, Engelbert Humperdinck and Gary Puckett & The Union Gap. (The Seville was Cadillac's response to the oil crisis and the need for smaller cars; *dan de* was removed from the middle of the Cadillac Sedan de Ville, resulting obviously in a shorter lighter car: the Seville.)

"What difference does it make?" Kelp said, slithering through the erratic traffic on the Southern State. "We meet Victor at the shopping center, he takes us on to Porculey's place."

"It's Christmastime," Dortmunder pointed out. "That's what difference it makes. We're going out to Long Island in a snow-storm to a shopping center a week before Christmas, that's what difference it makes."

"Well, it's too late to change it now," Kelp said. "It won't be that bad."

As a matter of fact, it was that bad. When they left the parkway, they immediately found themselves in endless clogged traffic, windshield wipers slap-slapping in the headlight-lit darkness all around them, auto windows all steamed up, smeary child-faces peering out every side and back window, people honking furiously and pointlessly at one another, and the same people revving like mad and spinning their wheels when they found themselves on a bit of ice, instead of gently accelerating. And the huge sprawling parking lot of the Merrick Mall, when they reached it, was if possible even worse; in addition to at least as much stalled traffic, there were also millions of pedes-trians slipping and sliding around, some of them pushing shop-ping carts full of Christmas packages and some of them pushing baby carriages full of Christmas packages and babies. "This is teriffic," Dortmunder said. "Your nephew Victor is still the same giant brain he always was."

"The Dunkin' Donuts," Kelp said, peering through the wind-shield and pretending he hadn't heard Dortmunder's comment. "We're supposed to meet him at the Dunkin' Donuts."

The Merrick Mall, in the manner of most shopping centers, was designed like a barbell, with a branch of a major depart-ment store at one end, a branch of a major supermarket at the other end, and several zillion smaller stores in between. As Kelp inched along amid the shoppers, the familiar electric logos gleamed out at them from the darkness: Woolworth's, Kentucky Fried Chicken, Thom McAn, Rexall, Gino's, Waldenbooks, Baskin-Robbins, Western Auto, Capitalists & Immigrants Trust. Then the record stores, the shoe stores, the ladies' clothing stores, the Chinese restaurants. However, inflation and unem-ployment have affected the shopping centers at least as much as the rest of the economy, so that here and there among the brave enticements stood a storefront dark, silent, its windows black, its forehead nameless, its prospects bleak. The survivors seemed to beam the more brightly in their efforts to distract attention from their fallen comrades, but Dortmunder could see them. Dortmunder and a failed enterprise could always recognize one another.

"There it is," Kelp said, and there it was: Dunkin' Donuts, with its steamy window full of do(ugh)nuts. Kelp pootled around a while longer, found a parking place at the far end of a nearby row, and he and Dortmunder squelched through the slush and the hopeless vehicles to find Victor seated at a tiny formica table in the Dunkin' Donuts, actually dunking a do(ugh)nut into a cup of coffee.

Kelp's nephew Victor, a small neat dark-haired man who dressed as though he were applying for a job as a bank teller, was more than thirty years of age but looked barely out of his teens. His slenderness and boyishly unlined face helped to give that impression, confirmed by the eager anticipatory quality of his every expression. What he most looked like was a puppy seen through a pet-store window, except he didn't have a tail to wag.

"Mr. Dortmunder!" he said, hopping to his feet and sticking out the hand with the dunked do(ugh)nut in it. "Nice to see you again." Then he realized he was still holding the do(ugh)-nut, chuckled sheepishly, stuck the whole thing out of sight in his mouth, wiped his hand on his trousers, stuck it out again, and said, "Murf nur murf."

"That goes for me, too," Dortmunder told him, and shook his sticky hand.

Victor gestured for them to sit at his table, while he hurriedly and noisily swallowed, then said, "Coffee? Donuts? Uncle?"

"Not for me," Dortmunder said. Neither he nor Kelp had taken the invitation to sit.

"Victor," Kelp said, "I think we'd just rather go see this fellow Porculey, okay?" Kelp tended to get a little nervous when in the presence simultaneously of Dortmunder and Victor.

"Oh, sure," Victor said. Standing beside the table, he gulped his coffee down, patted his mouth with a paper napkin, and said, "All set."

"Fine," Kelp said.

Victor led the way outside, and turned right, to walk along the semi-protected sidewalk. The few other pedestrians slogging past weren't even trying to look imbued with Christmas cheer. A roof extended over the walk, but a gusty cold breeze shot little clumps of wet snow in under it from time to time. Kelp, his uneasiness expressing itself in a fitful desire to keep some sort of conversation going, said, "Well, Victor. Still got your old Packard?"

"Oh, yes," Victor said, with his modest little chuckle. "It's a fine car. Ask the man who owns one."

"Do you want us to follow you, or should we all ride in the Packard?"

They were just passing one of the empty stores; black windows, a bit of trash in the doorway. "We're here," Victor said, and stopped.

This was so unexpected that Kelp and Dortmunder kept going, until they realized they'd left Victor behind. When they looked back, Victor was knocking on the glass door of the empty store.

Now what? The door was opening and light was spilling out into the snowy dark. A voice was speaking, Victor was grinning and replying, Victor was crossing the threshold, smiling and gesturing for Dortmunder and Kelp to follow. They did, and entered another world.

The stocky man who shut the door behind them remarked, genially, "Terrible out there tonight," but Dortmunder paid no attention, absorbing the interior of the store. In its most recent commercial manifestation it had apparently been a women's clothing boutique, the long narrow space separated into sections by platforms of various heights, all edged with elbow-high black wrought-iron railings, each platform covered in carpeting of another color, all shades of blue or gray. With the walls covered in burlap painted dark blue and the plate-glass windows painted black, the final effect was somewhere between a garden and a garret, flooded in moonlight.

Probably when the platforms had borne racks of skirts and
sweaters and jumpsuits the garden effect had been predominant,
but now the feeling was much more of a garret, helped by the
bits of clothing and old rags draped carelessly over most of the
railings. The nearest couple of platforms featured ratty pieces
of living-room furniture, while a platform toward the middle
bore several plain wooden kitchen chairs and an old trencher
table. Toward the rear were two easels, a high stool, and a
library table covered with the impedimenta of painting: tubes
of color, water glasses full of slender brushes, rags, palette
knives. Unframed canvases were stacked in corners and hung
on the walls. Above the easels, the standard shop ceiling gave
way to a recess containing a domed skylight.

The store was warm after the snowy night outside, and
despite its narrow length and endlessly shifting levels, it was
somehow cosy. People lived here, you could see that, and had
made a place of their own in what had once been a desert of
impersonality.

People. Two of them, one a girl of about twenty curled up
on the sofa, with an old plaid throw rug draped across her
legs. She was slender, but with roundnesses and softnesses, like
the world's tastiest peach, and her smile made her cheeks plump
and delectable. Dortmunder could have gone on looking at her
for thirty or forty years, but he forced himself to give some
attention to the other person as well.

This was the man who had let them in. He was a roly-poly
sloppy man of about fifty, wearing bedroom slippers, paint-
stained dark corduroy trousers, a mostly-green plaid shirt and
a dark green ratty cardigan sweater with leather elbow patches.
He hadn't shaved today, and it was possible he hadn't shaved
yesterday.

Victor was making the introductions, announcing each name
as though that person were a particular discovery of Victor's
own: "Griswold Porculey, I'd like you to meet my uncle, Andy
Kelp, and his friend, Mister John Dortmunder."

"W'r'ya," Dortmunder said, shaking Porculey's extended
hand.

"How do you do. How do you do. Victor's uncle, eh?"

"His mother is my older sister," Kelp explained.

Porculey gestured at the girl on the sofa, saying, "And this is my friend, Cleo Marlahy, an ever-present comfort."

Throwing off the throw, Cleo Marlahy uncurled her legs and sprang to her feet, saying, "Coffee? Tea? Wine?" Then doubtfully, to Porculey, "Do we have any liquor?"

"We might have vermouth."

"I'd love some coffee," Kelp said.

Dortmunder said, "Me, too."

Victor said, "May I have wine? I'm older than I look."

Porculey said, "Red or white?"

"Red, please."

"Done," said Porculey. "We don't have any white."

The girl was wearing black velvet pants and a white blouse. She was barefoot, and her toenails were painted an extremely dark red; the color of drying blood. She bounded away on these feet like the little mermaid, while Porculey directed his guests into chairs and himself dropped with a grunt into the sofa.

Kelp said, "This is quite a place. Very clever idea."

"Only rent I could afford," Porculey said, "to get this much space *and* north light." He gestured toward the skylight. "They gave me a good rent," he went on, "because they had so many empty stores, and because I agreed to make one or two turns around the place after the shops all close. Sort of a night watchman. Cheaper for them, cheaper for me. I'm a night bird anyway, and I walk anyway, so it's no hardship. We took down the partitions in the changing rooms, put our bedroom back there. Only problem's the lack of a kitchen, but we don't need much. Couple of hot plates, little refrigerator, use the sink in the lav. Perfect, really. They give more heat than any landlord in *my* experience, there's no nosy neighbors to poke and pry, and any shop I want is right outside that door."

Cleo returned, with a mismatched pair of white mugs for Dortmunder and Kelp, and an empty jelly glass for Victor. Distributing the mugs, she then picked up a gallon jug of Gallo Hearty Burgundy from the floor beside the sofa, half filled the jelly glass, gave it to Victor, and said, "Porky? More wine?"

"Don't mind if I do. Don't mind if I do."

Porculey drank from a tapered pilsner glass meant for beer, in which the dark red wine looked like something in a laboratory experiment. Cleo's glass, which she rescued from way under the sofa, was a small glass stein which had originally held mustard. She filled it to the top with hearty burgundy, plopped onto the sofa next to Porculey, raised her stein, and said, "Absent friends."

"May they rot," said Porculey, lifting his pilsner glass in the toast, and took a healthy swig. Then he said, looking at Dortmunder, "I understand you folks have a problem."

"We do," Dortmunder agreed. "We helped a fellow fake an art theft, to get the insurance. He wants the painting back, but we don't have it any more. It got lost. Kelp seems to think you could run up an imitation and we could give that back to the guy instead of the original."

Kelp said, "We'd make it worth your while, of course."

Porculey grunted in amusement. "Yes, I should think you would," he said. The hand not holding the pilsner glass had strayed over to Cleo's near thigh and was massaging it gently. The girl sipped wine and smiled comfortably to herself. Porculey said, "What painting is this?"

"It's called *Folly Leads Man to Ruin,* by somebody called Veenbes."

"Veenbes." Porculey put his head back, gazing up toward the corner of the ceiling. His hand stroked and stroked. "Veenbes. *Folly Leads Man to Ruin.* Mm, mm, possibly. Book," he decided, all at once, and released Cleo's leg in order to heave himself out of the sofa and onto his feet.

Book? There were any number of books in sight, though no bookcases. Paperbacks were heaped up in corners and under tables, while large hardcover volumes were stuck between uprights of the railings along platform edges. It was to these that Porculey went, carrying his wine, muttering under his breath as he ran his free hand along their spines. Then he stopped, pulled out one book, set the pilsner glass on the floor, thumbed through the volume, shook his head in annoyance and shoved the book back again.

This might take some time. While waiting, Dortmunder looked around, absorbing this weird dwelling place and noticing here and there on the dark walls unframed paintings, presumably Porculey's. They were all different, and yet they were all the same. In the middle foreground of each was a girl, either naked or wearing something minimal like a white scarf, and in the background was a landscape. The girls were mostly seen full length, and they were always very absorbed in what they were doing. One of them, for instance, sitting on the grass with some ruined castles behind her, plus in the distance a couple of trees and a small pond at which two deer drank, was studying a chess set laid out on the grass in front of her. Another showed a girl on a beach, leaning over the gunwale to look inside a large stranded rowboat, with a huge storm way out at sea in the background. (This was the girl with the scarf.)

The girls were not quite identical. Glancing around, Dortmunder saw maybe four different girls among the paintings, and it was with a sudden shock that he realized one of them was Cleo Marlahy. *So that's what she looks like with her clothes off,* he thought, blinking at a picture in which, against a background of an apple orchard white with spring flowers, an unsmiling girl was rather leggily climbing over a rail fence.

"Ah *hah!*"

Porculey had found something. Back he came, lugging a large book, and showed the page to Dortmunder. "That it?"

"Yes," said Dortmunder, looking at the small color illustration taking up half the page. The jester pranced, the people followed, the darkness yawned. Below the illustration were the title, the painter's name and dates, and the words *Private Collection.*

"Here," Porculey said, dumped the book in Dortmunder's lap, and padded off again.

Kelp, leaning over from his chair, said, "That's it, all right."

Dortmunder looked at him. "You never even saw the thing."

"Well, you described it."

Porculey came back with two more books, both also containing reproductions of the painting. He added these to Dortmunder's lap and returned to the sofa. Cleo, meanwhile, had gone off to rescue the pilsner glass, and now brought it back and handed it to Porculey. "Thank you, my dear," he said, and she patted his cheek and sat down again beside him.

Dortmunder's lap was full of books, all open to illustrations of folly leading man to ruin. He said, "So anyway you know what it looks like."

"There are also larger reproductions available," Porculey said. "Prints. Photographs of the original."

Kelp said, eagerly, "So you can do it?"

"Not a chance," Porculey said.

Even Dortmunder was surprised at that. Not that he'd ever believed, really believed, there was anything in Kelp's idea, but the suddenness with which it had been shot down left Dortmunder for just a second without a reaction.

But not Kelp. Sounding almost outraged, he said, "Not a chance? Why not? You've got the copies, the reproductions, you're the guy can do endless perfect twenty dollar bills!"

"Not from photographs," Porculey said. "Look at those three illustrations. There isn't one color reproduced the same in all three. Which is the original color, or is the original something entirely different? And even if we could be absolutely sure we had every one of Veenbes' dozens of colors right, what about the brush-strokes? How is the paint laid on the surface, how does it reflect light, where is it thick, where thin? The man who owns that painting must have looked at it from time to time, he must *know* what his painting looks like. I might be able to do something that would fool a buyer, maybe even a gallery operator or a museum curator, but the *owner* of the painting? I'm afraid not."

Cleo, her smile sympathetic, said, "Porky really does know about art. If he says it can't be done, it can't be done."

"So that's that," Dortmunder said.

Kelp was frowning so hard he looked like a crumpled piece of paper. "But that *can't* be that," he insisted. "There *has* to be a way."

"Sorry," Porculey said.

Dortmunder slugged down the rest of his coffee. "Maybe I will have some wine after all, he said."

4

'Twas the night before Christmas, and all through the house floated the aroma of May's tuna casserole. The apartment was filling up with guests, and Dortmunder, a cup of bourbon-spiked eggnog in his hand, sat in his personal chair in the living room —partly because he felt like sitting there, but mostly because if he stood up somebody else would be sure to cop his seat— and contemplated the Christmas tree. He wasn't sure about that tree. He'd been dubious about it from the beginning, and he was still dubious about it.

He'd been dubious, in fact, from before he'd actually seen the thing. Two days ago, when May had walked in with a cardboard carton the right size and shape to hold maybe four rolled-up window shades, and had said, "I bought us a Christmas tree at the hardware store," Dortmunder had been dubious at *once*. "At the hardware store?" he'd said. "And it's in that box?"

"Yes and yes. Help me set it up."

So then she'd opened the box and taken out a lot of fuzzy silver sticks. "That's no tree," Dortmunder'd said. "That's a lot of imitation corncobs."

"We have to put it together," she'd told him, but when they did all they wound up with was a tapering fuzzy silver thing that didn't look at *all* like a Christmas tree. "There, now," May said. "What does *that* look like?"

"A man from Mars."

"Wait till we put the ornaments on."

Well, now it had the ornaments on, and a lot of gift-wrapped presents underneath, but it still didn't look like a Christmas tree. In the first place—and this is just the first place, mind, this isn't the whole objection—in the first place, Christmas trees are *green*.

Still, whatever the thing was it did give off a kind of cheerful glitter, and it made May happy, so what the hell. Dortmunder kept his doubts to himself and his feet up on his old
battered hassock, and he grinned and nodded at his guests.
A funny thing to have, guests. Not people in to talk about
setting up a score, or splitting the take afterward, or anything
else in the way of business. Just people to come over and eat
your food and drink your liquor and then go home again.
Strange sort of idea, when you thought about it. It had been
May's idea, like the Christmas tree, intended to cheer Dortmunder up.

One thing about throwing a party; you offer people free food
and free drink, they're very likely to show. Astonishing number
of familiar faces here, some of them people Dortmunder hadn't
seen in years. Like Alan Greenwood over there, a fellow he'd
worked with a bunch of times until all of a sudden it turned
out Greenwood had been leading a double life; all the time
Dortmunder had thought of him simply as a good utility-
infielder-type heistman, Greenwood had had this secret life as
an actor. *Boom,* he got discovered, he got his own television
series, he didn't need to run around on fire escapes any more.
And here he was, in his blue denim leisure suit and his string
tie and his lace-frilled shirt, with this incredible gaunt blond
beauty named Doreen on his arm. "Nice to see ya, Greenwood."

"What's happening, baby," Greenwood said, and shook
hands with his left.

Then there was Wally Whistler, one of the best lockmen in
the business, just out of prison, having got sent up for absentmindedly unlocking a lock while he was at the zoo with his
kids; it had taken hours to get the lion back in his cage. And
Fred Lartz, a onetime driver who had given up driving after
an experience he had one time when he got drunk at a cousin's
wedding out on Long Island, took a wrong turn off the Van
Wyck Expressway, wound up on Taxiway Seventeen out at
Kennedy Airport, and got run down by Eastern Airlines flight
two-oh-eight, just in from Miami. Fred's wife Thelma—the

lady out in the kitchen with May, with the funny hat—did all the driving for the family these days.

Also present, and scoffing down the eggnog pretty good, was Herman X, a black man whose other life as a radical political activist in no way interfered with his primary career as a lockman. The lady he'd brought with him, and introduced as Foxy, was another stunner, tall and skinny and stylish and gleaming black. Foxy and Alan Greenwood's Doreen tended to stalk in slow circles around one another, remote and wary.

The crew from the painting fiasco were present, in force. Roger Chefwick had showed up with his round, pleasant, motherly wife, Maude. Tiny Bulcher was there with a small, sweet-faced, rather plain girl named Eileen, who looked terrified; Dortmunder kept expecting her to slip somebody a note reading, "Rescue me from this man." Stan Murch was there with his Mom, who had come direct from work and so was still in her taxi-driving duds: checked slacks, leather jacket, soft cap. And Andy Kelp was there, of course, with his nephew Victor.

Oh, it was quite a party. Besides the eggnog, there was straight bourbon, or beer in the refrigerator, and a big jug of Gallo Hearty Burgundy exactly like the stuff Dortmunder had drunk at the shopping center the other night. Christmas music played on the phonograph, Herman X and Foxy and Greenwood and Doreen danced from time to time, and Stan Murch and Fred Lartz and Wally Whistler sang along with some of the more well-known songs, such as "Jingle Bells" and "God Rest Ye, Merry Gentlemen," and "Rudolph, the Red-Nosed Reindeer." May and Thelma Lartz and Maude Chefwick were putting together a nice buffet supper in the kitchen, and generally people were having a real nice time. Also, most of the guests had showed up with a gift, and from the size and shape of those gifts, now under the poor excuse for a tree, Dortmunder suspected most of them were bottles of bourbon, so the party couldn't be considered a dead loss. All in all, Dortmunder would have to describe the occasion, and even himself, as damn near cheerful.

Over came Murch and Fred Lartz and Wally Whistler, grouping themselves around Dortmunder in his chair, Murch explaining, "We need a fourth, and you're it. All together now. Good King Wen-ces-las—"

Dortmunder knew about half the words, but it hardly mattered. He mumbled along in his throat, his usual singing style, and the other three belted the tune back and forth among them like a medicine ball, occasionally fumbling it enough to make nearby conversations falter. Joy and good cheer flowed like floodwaters through the apartment, and Dortmunder grinned around his eggnog cup and let the flood float him away.

The next album was orchestral music, so the glee club wandered off to refresh its drinks. Kelp came by with a new cup of eggnog for Dortmunder, then hunkered down next to his chair and said, "Nice party."

"Not bad," Dortmunder agreed.

"Listen, do you mind a little discussion for a minute?"

Dortmunder looked at him, uncomprehending. "A little discussion? About what?"

"Chauncey," Kelp said.

Dortmunder closed his eyes. "And just when I was sort of feeling good," he said.

Kelp patted his arm. "Yeah, I know. I'm sorry, I wouldn't break in on the party spirit and all that, but I got an idea, and it means Porculey doing a copy after all, and if you think it's as good an idea as I do then he ought to start right away."

Dortmunder's eyes opened, the better for frowning. "A copy? Porculey said it wouldn't work."

"It'll work with my idea," Kelp told him. "Can I give it to you?"

"You might as well," Dortmunder said, "but my guess is it stinks."

"Just wait," Kelp said, and leaned close to murmur in Dortmunder's ear. Dortmunder listened, his head cocked a bit, his eyes watching his guests moving and talking and dancing and singing all over his apartment, his left hand holding his eggnog cup and his feet up on the old hassock in front of his chair.

At first he seemed pessimistic, but then he looked a bit surprised, and then almost amused, and finally he seemed to be considering the situation, thinking it over. Kelp finished, rocked back on his heels, grinned at Dortmunder's profile, and said, "Well? Whadaya think?"

"Jesus," Dortmunder said. "It's almost dumb enough to work."

"Do I tell Porculey go ahead?"

"Jesus."

"*Think* about it, Dortmunder." Kelp's excitement was so intense his fingers were jittering.

"I am thinking about it."

"Do I tell him go ahead?"

Slowly Dortmunder nodded, then slowly nodded again. "Yes," he decided. "Let's give it a shot."

"Way to talk!" Kelp told him, and jumped to his feet. "I got a feeling about this one," he said. "Something tells me this is gonna be our finest hour."

Second thoughts could be seen gathering on Dortmunder's face, but at that point May called from the dining-room doorway, "Feedbag's on!" Pointing across the room at Dortmunder, she said, "You stay right there, John, I'll bring you a plate."

"And another eggnog," Kelp said, his hand out for the cup. "Swig that down."

So Dortmunder swigged it down, and he was brought a plate heaped high with steaming food, plus a fresh cup of eggnog, and the living room filled up with people holding plates of food in one hand and drinks in the other, trying to figure out how to pick up their fork.

"To the founder of the feast!" Kelp suddenly cried out. "John Dortmunder!"

"Aw, come on," Dortmunder said, but a full-bodied cheer drowned him out. And then goddam Stan Murch had to start singing "For He's a Jolly Good Fellow," despite "Oh, Little Town of Bethlehem" currently emanating from the phonograph, and everybody else had to join in, and Dortmunder had to sit there like a fool, the hot dish burning his lap, and get sung at.

After which everybody put their plates and glasses and cups and beer cans down and applauded their own singing or something, and turned bright cheery eyes on Dortmunder, who realized he was expected to say something. He looked around and his eye fell on Kelp's sparkling face.

He lifted his fresh eggnog. "God help us," Dortmunder said, "every one."

5

Andy Kelp had friends everywhere, even in the Police Department. Shortly after the New Year, he called a police friend named Bernard Klematsky. "Hi Bernard," he said. "It's me, Andy Kelp."

"Well, hello, Andy. Calling to confess?"

Kelp chuckled. "Always the kidder," he said. "Lemme buy you a drink when you come off."

"Why?"

"I wanna pick your brains."

"In that case," Bernard said, "you can buy me spaghettini with clam sauce. At Unfredo's. Ten-thirty."

"I'll be there," Kelp promised, and he was, but Bernard was fifteen minutes late. "Over here," Kelp called, when Bernard at last arrived, and waved at him across the half-empty restaurant from his table in the corner.

It took a while for Bernard to disencumber himself of his fur hat, his silk scarf, his leather gloves and his wool overcoat, storing them all on the hanger-jangly metal rack by the front door, and then he stood revealed as an average-appearing fellow of thirty-something, with bushy black hair, a rather long and fleshy nose, a rumpled dark blue suit with a rumpled dark blue necktie, and the indefinable air about him of a teacher of mathematics. A lay teacher, in a parochial school. He came over to the table, rubbing his hands together for warmth, saying, "Cold out tonight."

"You mean you want a drink *and* spaghettini."

"A Rob Roy straight up would be a very nice thing."

Kelp caught the eye of Sal the waiter, ordered the Rob Roy, and said, "And another bourbon and soda."

"You wanna order?"

"We might as well," said Bernard. "I'll have the escalope limone and spaghettini on the side, with clam sauce."

"Aw, Bernard," Kelp said, giving him a reproachful look.

Bernard didn't care. He was very happy to be indoors in the warm. Smiling at Kelp, he said, "What about the wine? A nice Verdicchio?"

"Bernard, you're holding me up."

"Whoever heard of a cop holding up a robber?"

"Everybody," Kelp said, and told Sal the waiter, "I'll have the chicken parmigiana, spaghetti on the side with the red sauce, and we'll take the Verdicchio."

Sal the waiter went away, and Bernard shook his head, saying, "All that tomato."

"I like tomato. Can we talk now?"

"Wait'll I been bribed," Bernard said. "What've you been up to lately, Andy?"

"Oh, this and that," Kelp said.

"One thing and the other, huh?"

"More or less," Kelp agreed.

"Same old thing, in other words."

"In a manner of speaking," Kelp said.

"Well, you're looking good," Bernard told him. "Whatever you're up to, it agrees with you."

"You look good, too," Kelp said, and the drinks arrived.

"Ah, the bribe," Bernard said. He swigged down half his Rob Roy, beamed, patted his belly, and said, "There. *Now* we can talk."

"Good." Kelp leaned closer over the white tablecloth. "I need a guy's name and address."

"Wait a minute," said Bernard. "You want to pick my brains, or you want to pick Police Department records?"

"Both."

"Andy, fun's fun, but maybe you're about to overstep, you know what I mean?"

Kelp was uncertain on that score himself, and the uncertainty made him nervous. He put away a bit more of his second bourbon and soda, and said, "If you say no, it's no. I wouldn't argue with you, Bernard." He tried a friendly grin. "And I wouldn't ask for the spaghettini back either."

"Or the Rob Roy," Bernard said, and finished it. Then he said, "Okay, Andy, try it on me, and if I say no there won't be any hard feelings on either side."

"That's what I like to hear." Kelp cleared his throat, and blinked several times.

Bernard pointed at Kelp's face. "Whenever you blink a lot like that," he said, "you're about to tell a lie."

"No, I'm not," Kelp said, blinking furiously.

"So let's hear it," Bernard said.

Kelp willed his eyelids to remain up. His eyes began to burn. Looking with great sincerity through his burning eyes at Bernard, he said, "What I'm about to tell you is the absolute truth."

"Relax, Andy," Bernard told him. "Nobody says I have to believe you. If it's a good story, I'll do what I can."

"Fair enough," Kelp said, and permitted himself to blink. "I have this cousin," he said, blinking, "and he's got himself in hot water with some people."

"Would I know these people?"

"For your sake," Kelp said, "I hope not."

"You worry about me. That's nice."

"Anyway," Kelp went on, "you know me, you know my family, we've never been violence-prone."

"That's true," Bernard said. "That's one of the nice things about you, Andy."

"My cousin's the same way. Anyway, he has the idea these people put a hitman on him."

Bernard looked interested. "Really? Does he want police protection?"

"Excuse me, Bernard," Kelp said, "but from what I can see, all police protection ever does for anybody is they get to fall out the window of a better class hotel."

"We won't argue the point," Bernard said, which was what he said any time he lacked arguments on his own side. "Tell me more about your cousin."

"He wants to do his own protecting," Kelp said. "And in order to do it, he has to identify this guy for sure. Now, he knows some things about him, but he doesn't have the guy's name and address. That's where we need help."

Bernard looked somber. He said, "Andy, maybe now you *should* tell me the truth. Is this cousin of yours figuring to hit the hitman? Because if so, I can't—"

"No no no!" Kelp said, and his eyes didn't blink at all. "I told you, Bernard, non-violence, it's an old family tradition. There's more than one way to skin a cat."

"They all leave the cat dead."

"I swear to God, Bernard," Kelp said, and actually raised his hand in the Boy Scout pledge. "My cousin strictly wants to know for sure who the guy is, and his dealing with the problem will absolutely one hundred per cent *not* include physical violence."

"He wants to outbid the other side?"

"I have no idea what's in my cousin's mind," Kelp said, blinking like mad.

"All right," Bernard said. "Tell me what you know about the guy."

"He's white," Kelp said. "He's tall, skinny, black haired, he's got a game leg. The right foot's in a big orthopedic shoe, and he limps. Also, he got picked up for something late in October, I don't know for what, and a very famous lawyer called J. Radcliffe Stonewiler got him off."

Bernard frowned deeply. "You know a lot of funny details about this guy," he said.

"Please, Bernard," Kelp said. "Don't ask me where I get

my information, or I'll have to make up some cockamamie lie, and I'm no good at that."

"Oh, Andy," Bernard said, "you underestimate yourself." And the food and wine arrived. "Nice," Bernard said. "Let's eat a while, and I'll think about this."

"Great idea," said Kelp.

So they ate, and they drank wine, and at the end of the meal Bernard said, "Andy, can you promise me, if I get you anything on this bird, nothing illegal will happen?"

Kelp stared at him. "*Nothing* illegal? Bernard, you can't be serious. Do you have any idea just how many laws there *are?*"

"All right," Bernard said, patting the air. "All right."

But Kelp had momentum, and couldn't stop all at once. "You can't walk down the *street* without breaking the *law,* Bernard," he said. "Every day they pass new laws, and they never get rid of any of the old laws, and you can't live a normal *life* without doing things illegal."

"Okay, Andy, okay. I said okay, didn't I?"

"Bernard, just off the top of your head, how many laws would you say you broke so far today?"

Bernard pointed a stern finger across the table. "Lay off, Andy," he said. "Now I mean it."

Kelp stopped, took a deep breath, got hold of himself, and said, "I'm sorry. It's a subject that's close to my heart, that's all."

Bernard said, "Let me rephrase it, Andy, okay? No major crimes. No, wait, you'll be talking about industrial pollution in a minute. No *violent* crimes. Is that a fair request?"

"Bernard," Kelp said, with solemnity, "it is not my intention, or my cousin's intention, to harm one hair of this fellow's head. He won't get killed, he won't get wounded. All right?"

"Thank you," Bernard said. "Let me make a phone call, see what I can do." He pushed his chair back and said, "While I'm gone, order me an espresso and a Sambuca, okay?" And he got to his feet and headed toward the phone booth in the back.

"Bernard," Kelp muttered after his departing back, "you're

a highway robber." But he ordered the espresso and Sambuca from Sal the waiter, and the same for himself, and was chewing on one of the coffee beans from the Sambuca when Bernard came back. Kelp gave him an alert look, but first Bernard had to taste his Sambuca, then he had to put a sugar cube in his espresso. Finally, stirring the espresso, he looked seriously at Kelp and said, "Your cousin's tangled with a wrong guy."

"I thought so," said Kelp.

"His name's Leo Zane," Bernard said, "and he has the worst kind of no record."

"I don't think I follow."

"Picked up lots of times, always on very serious stuff— murder, attempted murder, aggravated assault, twice for arson —but never convicted."

"Slippery," Kelp suggested.

"Like a snake. And twice as dangerous. If your cousin wants to deal with this guy, he better wear gloves."

"I'll tell him. Did you happen to get an address while you were on the phone?"

Bernard shook his head. "Zane isn't a homebody," he said. "He lives in furnished rooms, residence hotels, he's a loner and moves around a lot."

"Drat."

"There's one thing that might help," Bernard said. "There's a clinic up in Westchester he goes to sometimes. On account of his foot. Apparently, that's the only place he ever goes for treatment, that one clinic."

"What's it called?"

"Westchester Orthopedic."

"Thanks, Bernard," Kelp said. "I'll tell my cousin."

Bernard pointed a serious finger at Kelp. "If anything happens to Zane," he said, "anything at all, I'll connect it back to you, Andy, I swear I will."

Kelp spread his hands in utter innocence. Not a blink marred his eyes. "Don't you think I know that, Bernard? I know you're a straight guy. I wouldn't have called you if I figured to pull something like that."

"All right," said Bernard. Relaxing, he looked down at his Sambuca, smiled, and said, "You ever try this?"

"Try what?"

Bernard took out a pack of matches, lit one, held it over the Sambuca, and a small blue flame formed on top of the liqueur, where the coffee beans floated. Bernard shook out the match, and sat smiling at the blue flame.

Kelp didn't get it. "What's that for?" he asked.

"The idea is," Bernard said, "it like roasts the coffee beans."

"But what's that burning?"

"The alcohol, of course."

"Then why do it?"

Bernard looked startled. "By God, you're right," he said, and blew out the flame.

"I hope you made a wish," Kelp said.

6

The scrawny black cat jumped from the floor up to the windowsill, where Leo Zane was pouring milk into the saucer. Setting the milk carton on the table nearby, Zane stood at the window a minute longer, scratching the cat behind the ear as it lapped up milk. A dreary March rain dribbled down the glass, and Zane's foot continued to ache. It was the weather, of course, the dampness of the end of winter, and the trip to the clinic, his first in almost six months, had done no good at all.

He ought to go away for a while, somewhere warm and dry. Maybe Los Angeles, sit in the sun, absorb some warmth into the bones of his foot. Absorb warmth into his body, his entire body was cold and achy now; the damp pain, like death, crept up through his frame from his foot, filling him with chills and cramps. No matter how much clothing he wore, no matter how warm the room or how much hot coffee he drank, the cold torment was still there, deep in his bones.

What was keeping him in New York? Very little, beyond his own lethargy. Every year around this time he made the same vague plans to leave, but he never went, he always found some excuse, he seemed wedded to the climate that made him sick. And this year?

Well, in fact, this year there were one or two jobs still open. The psychiatrist's wife, for instance; she was turning out to be surprisingly difficult to dispatch. Of course, the jobs that had to look like accident or natural causes were always the most difficult. And then there was the Chauncey job, that was still on tap.

Not that Zane expected actually to *do* anything on the Chauncey job. His one conversation with that fellow Dortmunder, plus the occasional interval of observing the man, had convinced him Dortmunder would try no tricks. Once Chauncey collected from the insurance company—possibly next month, more likely in May—Dortmunder would assuredly turn over the painting, Chauncey would pay Zane the remaining fifteen thousand due on the contract, and that would be that.

The psychiatrist's wife. If only she drove a car. You'd think, in this day and age—

Movement beyond the window attracted Zane's attention. Down below, a man hunched against the rain as he entered his automobile, a dark blue Jaguar sedan, parked by the fire hydrant. It had MD plates, from over in New Jersey, and Zane reflected again on what a dodge that was. Put MD plates on a car, you could park anywhere you wanted, just as though doctors still made housecalls. Up at the clinic they were parked all over the—

Hadn't there been a Jaguar sedan parked outside the clinic? Dark blue, like this one?

Down below, the Jaguar's windshield wipers clicked into

motion, swiping back and forth. As Zane watched, the Jaguar moved away, rolling sedately down the block, its yellow right directional blinking, an intermittent bright spot in the rain. He wasn't positive it was the same sort of car as he'd seen near the clinic. Same color, perhaps, but a different make?

"Grrowww!" said the cat, and scratched at Zane's wrist.

Startled, Zane released his grip—lost in thought, he'd been strangling the thing—and the cat ran away to hide under the daybed. Zane picked up the milk carton, for something to do, and limped with it to the refrigerator. The cat's eyes peered out at him from under the bed, but he ignored it. His mind was moving again, away from the unanswerable questions about the car, on to other concerns. He sat at the formica table, brooding, his eyes vague, his hands relaxed with curved fingers on the tabletop, the aching in his foot forgotten for the moment, everything forgotten for the moment.

The psychiatrist's wife. An accident, a fall. Hmmmmmm ...

7

Kelp was so happy he was crowing. "Don't say I never did anything for you, Dortmunder," he said. "Not after this."

"All right," Dortmunder said. Owing a debt of gratitude to another person always made him nervous, and that other person being Kelp didn't improve the situation.

"Over *two months* I staked out that clinic," Kelp pointed out. "I musta gone through a thousand paperback books. Day after day, three, four days a week, and boy, I finally hit it."

"For sure," Dortmunder said. "This time it's positively for sure." In the last two months Kelp had three times followed limping men home from the Westchester Orthopedic Clinic, a site that by the very nature of things would be bound to provide a certain steady quota of limping men, and all three times Kelp had insisted Dortmunder accompany him on expeditions to remote neighborhoods to look at these guys, and none of them had been even *remotely* like the killer Dortmunder had met back in November.

But this time Kelp was sure. "Absolutely," he said. "And you know why? Because I waited after he went in his building, and then I followed him and looked at the mailboxes, and there it was: Zane, room thirteen."

"All right," Dortmunder said.

"So we got him."

"We'll have to check every once in a while," Dortmunder said. "Be sure he doesn't move."

"Oh, sure." Kelp then looked slightly pained and said, "Maybe the other guys could do some of that, huh? I spent more time in cars the last two months than A. J. Foyt."

"Oh, naturally," Dortmunder said. "We'll all take our turns."

"Good," said Kelp, and then there was a little silence.

Dortmunder sniffed. He rubbed a knuckle against his nose. He hitched his pants. "Kum, kak," he said, and coughed, and cleared his throat.

Kelp said, "What?" He was leaning forward, looking alert and helpful.

"Um," said Dortmunder. He stuck his finger in his ear and jiggled it, looking for wax. He took a deep breath. He put his hands behind his back and clasped them together tight. "Thanks, uh, Andy," he said.

"Oh, sure," Kelp said. "Don't mention it."

8

"That's pretty good," Dortmunder said.

Griswold Porculey gave him a look. "Pretty good? Dortmunder, I'll tell you what this is. It's a work of genius."

"I said it was pretty good," Dortmunder said.

They were both right. The nearly finished painting on Porculey's easel was an incredible piece of work, a forgery so brilliant, so detailed, that it suggested true genius perhaps *did* reside within the unlikely corpus of Griswold Porculey after all, just as genius has so often in the past chosen other unlikely vessels for its abode. The paint-smeared hand holding the paint-smeared brush, the bleary washed-out eye observing the work, these had turned a lumpish array of pigment into a painting Jan Veenbes himself might have been proud to claim.

Tacked and taped on the wall to Porculey's left were nearly two dozen representations of *Folly Leads Man to Ruin,* ranging from full-size photographic reproductions to reduced-size copies torn from art books. The differences in color and detail among these many imitations were enough to discourage the most determined copyist, but somehow Porculey had maneuvered this minefield and had made so many right choices that Dortmunder, looking at the almost-completed work, thought he was seeing an exact duplicate of the painting in Arnold Chauncey's sitting room. He wasn't, of course, but the differences, though pervasive, were minute.

Porculey was contemplating now that darkness in the lower right, where the road curved away and down a dim slope. This was the most difficult part because it was the vaguest, with the least specific detail and yet it was far from being a featureless wash of umbra. It was a *peopled* gloom, its obscurity filled with faintly seen writhings, hints of grotesquerie, suggestions of shape and form and movement. Porculey's brush moved cautiously over these deeps, touching lightly, pausing, returning, moving on.

It was early April, three weeks since Kelp had finally found the killer, and Dortmunder was back in this garret-boutique for the first time since that night in December when Porculey had thrown such cold water on Kelp's original idea. Dortmunder had wanted to return, several times, to see for himself what Porculey was up to, but his exploratory phone calls to the painter had received unrelenting negatives. "I don't want a lot of amateurs breathing down my neck," Porculey had said, and when Dortmunder had tried to point out it was his *own* neck that was being breathed down, and by a professional killer at that, Porculey had merely said, "I'll call you when there's something to see," and had hung up on him.

So it came as a surprise this morning, and a very happy one, when Porculey himself had gotten in touch, calling Dortmunder at home and saying, "If you still want to see what I'm doing, come along."

"I will, right away."

"You can bring your partners, if you want."

But Dortmunder hadn't wanted; this painting was too important to him, and he preferred to see it without a lot of conversation going on all over the place. "I'll come by myself," he said.

"Up to you. Bring a bottle of wine, you know the stuff."

So Dortmunder had brought a gallon of Hearty Burgundy, some of which Cleo Marlahy had at once poured into the usual disparity of drinking vessels, and now he stood holding his white mug of wine and watching Porculey's brush make small tentative decisions on the surface of the painting. In the last four months, it seemed, laboring away in his shopping-center sanctuary, Porculey had been bringing forth a miracle.

Which he was willing to talk about. Stepping back from the easel, frowning at that troublesome darkness in the lower right, he said, "Do you know how I did it?"

"No."

Porculey nodded. "I began," he explained, continuing to brood at the painting as he spoke, "with research. The Frick has one Veenbes, and three more hang in the Metropolitan. I studied those four, and I looked at every copy of them I could find."

Dortmunder said, "Copies? Why?"

"Every artist has his own range of colors. His palette. I wanted to see how Veenbes' other pictures reproduced, to help me get back to the original colors in this one."

"I get the idea," Dortmunder said. "That's pretty good."

Cleo, sipping her wine and musing at Porculey and the painting as though she herself had invented both and was pleased with the result of her labors, said, "Porky's had a wonderful time with this. He got to rage and carry on and throw things and make disgusting statements about art, and then preen himself at being better than anybody."

"Better than most, at any rate," Porculey said comfortably. His brush tip, having grazed briefly at his palette, darted out at the gloom again, altered it infinitesimally. "Because I did more than just dry research," he went on. "I looked at the paintings, but more than that I tried to look *through* them, past them. I tried to see Veenbes in his studio, approaching the canvas. I wanted to see how he held his brush, how he stroked the paint into place, how he made his decisions, his changes. Did you know his brush strokes move diagonally upward to the left? That's very rare, you might think he was left-handed, but there are two portraits done by his contemporaries that show him at his easel with the brush in his right hand."

Dortmunder said, "What difference does it make?"

"It changes the way the picture takes the light," Porculey told him. "Where it reflects, and how the eye is led through the story."

All of which was over Dortmunder's head. "Well, whatever you did," he said, "it looks terrific."

Porculey was pleased. Smiling briefly over his shoulder, he said, "I wanted to wait till I had something worth showing. You see that, don't you?"

"Sure. And it's just about done, huh?"

"Oh, yes. Another two or three weeks, probably no more."
Dortmunder stared at the back of Porculey's head, then at
the painting. "Two or three *weeks?* That's a whole painting
there already, you could fool a lot of people the way it is
right now."

"But not Arnold Chauncey," Porculey said. "Not even for
a second. I did some research on your customer while I was
about it, and you chose a difficult man to fool. He isn't just
another culture merchant, buying and selling works of art as
though they were coin collections. He's a connoisseur, he
knows art, and he *certainly* knows his own paintings."

"You're making me unhappy," Dortmunder said.

Cleo, friendly and sympathetic, was immediately at his elbow,
holding up the glass jug of wine. "Have some more," she suggested. "Everything'll work out. Porky's doing you proud."

"It isn't Pork, uh, Porculey I'm worried about," Dortmunder
told her. "I got talked into another Andy Kelp Special, *that's*
what I'm worried about."

"Seems like a nice fellow, Kelp," Porculey said.

"Doesn't he," said Dortmunder.

Porculey stepped back to give his work the critical double-O.
"You know," he said, "I really am quite good at this sort of
thing. Better even than those twenties. I wonder if there's a
future in it."

"There's ten thousand from us," Dortmunder reminded him,
"if the scheme works and we get Chauncey's money. That's the
only future *I* know about."

"Ah," Porculey said, "but what if I took my knowledge of
Veenbes, his subject matter, his palette, his style, and what if
I did a Veenbes of my *own?* Not a copy, but a brand-new
painting. Unknown old masters crop up all the time, why not
one by me?"

"I wouldn't know," Dortmunder said.

Porculey nodded, thinking it over. "A *lot* better than drawing
twenties," he said. "Very dull, that was. No palette at all. A
few greens, a black, and that's it. But a Veenbes, now." His

eyes were half-closed, no longer seeing the semi-Veenbes in front of him. "A medieval convent," he said. "Stone walls and floor. Candles. The nuns have just removed their habits. . . ."

9

Eight days later, Dortmunder entered the main borough office of the Unemployment Insurance Division and waited his turn to be inspected by the guard just inside the door. The guard was examining the purse of a woman client in search of guns or bombs or other expressions of political discontent, and he was in no hurry to finish. Dortmunder was dressed today in dark green work pants, a flannel jacket and a heavy workman's belt festooned with tools, and he was carrying a clipboard.

The woman client, whose brown skin and surly manner had made her a prima facie subject for official suspicion, had proved too clever for Authority this time, having left all her guns and bombs at home. The guard reluctantly let her through, then turned to Dortmunder, who plunked his clipboard onto the rostrum and said, "Typewriter repair."

"Which department?" Since Dortmunder was tall and male and white and and not a client and not carrying any packages that might conceal guns or bombs, the guard had no reason to suspect him of anything.

"Beats me," Dortmunder said. Running a finger down the top sheet on his clipboard, he said, "They just give me this address, that's all. The typing pool, it says."

"We got four typing pools in this building," the guard said.

"I'm just the guy they send around," Dortmunder told him.

"Well, how do I know what department?"

"Beats me," Dortmunder said.

There's a difference between a client and a workman, and

the difference holds true everywhere, not merely in the Unemployment Insurance Division of the Department of Labor of the State of New York. The difference is, the client is there because he wants something, but the workman doesn't give a damn what happens. The workman won't extend himself, won't try to help, won't provide explanations, won't in fact do anything but just stand there. The client wants to be liked, but the workman is just as willing to go back to his boss, shrug, and say, "They wouldn't let me in."

Everybody knows this, of course, including the guard on the door, who looked unhappily into Dortmunder's unhelpful eyes for a moment, then sighed, and said, "All right. I'll call around." And he picked up his phone from the rostrum, simultaneously scanning his list of interior phone numbers.

The guard struck gold the first try, which didn't surprise Dortmunder at all. "I'll send him right up," he told the phone, cradled it, and said to Dortmunder, "Osro."

"What?"

"Out-of-State Resident Office, upstairs. Go to the end of that hall there, take the elevator to the third floor."

"Right."

Dortmunder, following instructions, eventually found himself in Osro, a large room full of desks and clerks and typewriters, semi-separated from one another by clusters of filing cabinets. He went to the nearest desk, bearing the sign IN-FORMATION, and told the girl there, "Typewriter repair. They just called up from downstairs."

"Oh, yes." She pointed. "The typing pool. Down past the second bunch of filing cabinets and turn right."

"Fine," Dortmunder said, and went to the typing pool, where the woman in charge, a tall gray-haired person with a face and body the texture of concrete, frowned at him, and said, "Do you know it's been nearly *three weeks* since we put in our Form Two-Eighty-B?"

"I just do my job, lady," Dortmunder said. "Where is it?"

"Over here," she said, grumping, and led the way.

Of course, every large bureaucracy has many typing pools,

and every typing pool's typewriters break down from time to time, and no request for repairs ever takes less than four months to filter through that particular bureaucracy, so the woman in charge should have been grateful to Dortmunder for being so prompt, instead of complaining; but there's too little gratitude in this world.

The woman left Dortmunder alone at the typewriter, a large Royal electric. He plugged it in and turned it on and the thing buzzed at him. He hit a few keys in his normal terrible typing style, and found that the machine's problem was a refusal to automatically return when the automatic return button was pushed. He spent another two or three minutes fiddling with it, then unplugged it, picked it up—the thing weighed a ton—carried it over to the ungrateful woman's desk, and said, "I'll have to take it to the shop."

"We *never* get machines back that go to the shop," the woman said, which was probably true. It was certainly true of the last machine Dortmunder had taken from this building, about two years ago.

Dortmunder said, "I'll leave it if you want, but it needs work in the shop."

"Oh, very well," she said.

"Do I need a pass or something with the guard on the door?"

"I'll phone down."

"Okay."

Dortmunder carried the typewriter downstairs, where the guard nodded hello and waved him through. Outside, he put the machine on the passenger seat of the Plymouth he'd stolen for this trip, then drove back to Manhattan and to a friend of his who ran a pawn shop off Third Avenue. This man had never been known to ask anybody any question other than, "How much?" Dortmunder handed him the machine, accepted forty dollars, and went out to the street.

It was a pleasant day late in the month of April, one of the few days all month without rain, so Dortmunder decided to leave the Plymouth where he'd parked it and walk home. He'd gone about half a block when he suddenly realized he was looking at Stan Murch through the windshield of a car parked next to a fire hydrant. He started to grin and wave a big hello, but Stan made a tiny negative gesture with his head and the hand on the steering wheel, so Dortmunder converted his own movement into a cough, and walked on.

May wasn't at home, since she had the afternoon shift down at the Safeway, but a note was Scotch-taped to the front of the TV set:

Call Chauncey

"Oog," said Dortmunder, and went out to the kitchen to pop open a can of beer. He stayed in the kitchen, not wanting to be reminded of that message on the TV, and was working on his second beer when the doorbell rang.

It was Stan Murch. "Yeah, I'd love one," he said, looking at the beer in Dortmunder's hand.

"Sure. Sit down."

Dortmunder brought a beer from the kitchen to the living room, where Murch was now seated, looking at the TV. "You call yet?"

"He wasn't home," Dortmunder lied. "How come you give me the office out there?"

"I was following Zane," Murch said, and swigged some beer.

"Oh." Since they believed that so far Zane hadn't positively identified any of Dortmunder's partners in the robbery, the group had been taking turns occasionally trailing Leo Zane around, trying to find the right handle to use on him later.

Then Dortmunder frowned. "What was he doing down around there?"

"Following you," Murch said. "Someday you'll have to tell me how you do that typewriter bit."

"Following *me?*"

"Yeah." Murch drank beer and said, "I'm following him and he's following you. Pretty funny, in a way."

"Hysterical," Dortmunder said, and went to the phone to call Chauncey.

10

Chauncey had called Zane first, upon arrival in New York: "Chauncey here."

"You got it, did you?" Zane's rather weedy voice, empty of strength or emphasis, suggested a kind of wasting menace that Chauncey found thrilling; like a Brueghel allegory.

"Yes, I did." This time, apparently, the robbery had been so unreproachably real that the insurance investigation had been barely a formality, bringing settlement much sooner than anticipated. "And your pet?" Chauncey asked. "How has he been keeping?"

"In his cage. He doesn't even *want* to fly away."

"Good. I'll see him soon. You'll keep an eye out?"

"I'll follow him," Zane said, until you're finished. You won't see me, but I'll be there."

"Exactly right."

"When do you do it?"

"As soon as possible," Chauncey said. "I'll call you back." And he phoned Dortmunder, leaving a message with the rather dry-voiced woman who answered the phone.

It was nearly three hours before the man called back, and then his voice had such a grudging surly quality that Chauncey became at once suspicious, despite Zane's assurances. "The painting's all right?"

"Sure it is," Dortmunder said. "Why wouldn't it be?"

"Then you'll bring it here. I have the money."

"In cash?"

Chauncey grimaced. Nobody uses cash any more, unless buying a newspaper, so Chauncey hadn't thought at all about the actual physical transfer of funds from himself to Dortmunder. But of course he couldn't very well offer the man a check, could he? And even if he could, Dortmunder certainly couldn't accept it. Nor was Dortmunder likely to be on Diners Club or Master Charge.

"Chauncey?"

"I'm thinking," Chauncey told him. "Wait there, Dortmunder, I'll have to call you back." But when he tried, half an hour later, the line was busy, and this was why:

———

"I'm telling you, Dortmunder, it isn't *finished*."

"And *I'm* telling *you*, Porculey, the goddam man is in New York and he wants his goddam picture back."

"You can't give it to him unfinished."

"I have to turn it over, period."

"You told me I had till May."

"He's here *now*, and he wants his painting."

"It isn't ready."

(And so on, for several minutes, more and more of the same, while Chauncey kept dialing Dortmunder's number and getting the same infuriating busy signal, until Dortmunder finally asked the following question:)

"How long?"

"What?"

"How long to get it done?"

"To do it right. Two weeks. Two weeks minimum."

"*Not* to do it right. Come on, Porculey, help me on this."

There was a brief pause. The faint slobby sound in Dortmunder's ear was Porculey sucking on his lower lip, as an aid to thought. Finally Porculey sighed, another distasteful sound, and said, "Friday. It won't be perfect, but—"

"This is Tuesday."

"I know what day it is, Dortmunder."

"Three days?"

"I have to bake it, antique it, it has to dry. Do you want it to smell of fresh paint?"

"Three days," Dortmunder insisted. "You can't make it shorter."

"*Shorter?* Dortmunder, d-d-d-d-do you ree-ree-ree—"

"Okay, okay. I'll take your word for it."

"I mean, after all."

"I believe you," Dortmunder said. "Friday."

"Friday night."

"Aw, come on."

"Friday *night.*"

"Eight o'clock."

"Ten o'clock."

"Eight-thirty."

"Avoid the rush-hour traffic, Dortmunder. Ten o'clock."

"The rush hour doesn't go that late. Nine o'clock."

"Make it nine-thirty."

"*Nine,*" Dortmunder said, and slammed the phone down, and it rang at him.

———

It was of course Chauncey, dialing yet again, ready to bite the receiver in half if he got a busy signal one more time, and being so astonished when he got the ring sound instead that at first he didn't say anything at all when Dortmunder said, "Hello?" Then, when Dortmunder said it again—"Hello?"— even though Chauncey recognized the voice and knew it was the person he was trying to call, his surprise made him say, "Dortmunder?"

"Chauncey."

"You've been on the phone."

"It's a friend's birthday," Dortmunder said.

Chauncey was again surprised, this time pleasantly. Sentimental comradeship in the criminal classes; how charming. "That's nice," he said.

"About the money," Dortmunder said. Apparently sentiment didn't leave much of an afterglow with the man.

"Yes." Chauncey cleared his throat and said, "It turns out cash is a difficult thing to acquire, at least without creating questions."

Dortmunder, sounding exasperated, said, "Chauncey, after all this, are you saying you don't have the money?"

Chauncey was too concerned with his own problems to wonder what *after all this* referred to. "Not at all," he said. "I have the *money,* but I don't yet have the *cash.*"

"Money and cash are the same thing," said Dortmunder, who apparently lived in a much simpler world.

"Well, not exactly," Chauncey told him. "The thing is, it'll take me a while to get the cash together. I'm sorry, I hadn't really thought about the problem before."

"Meaning you'll have it when?"

"This isn't a stall, Dortmunder, I do have the money."

"When do *I* get it?"

"Not till Friday, I'm afraid."

"This is Tuesday."

"I realize that. I apologize, and I've started on it, but the fact is I can't take that much cash from any one source. I'll need several business days to do it. I've made a beginning, and by Friday I'll have it all."

"Make it Friday night."

"Fine. You remember the passage from my back yard to the next street?"

"Sure."

"You come there Friday at midnight, and I'll let you in."

"Good." Then Dortmunder said, "I won't be alone."

"You won't? Why not?"

"We're talking about a lot of cash," Dortmunder reminded him. "The rest of my string'll be with me."

Chauncey wasn't sure he liked that idea, his house filling up with crooks. "How many?"

"The driver stays outside. Me and three others come in."

"Four of you? Dortmunder, don't misunderstand me, I trust *you* but how can I be sure of these other people?"

"I vouch for them," Dortmunder told him. "You can trust them completely."

11

Friday night. Leo Zane, in his own car, his only permanent possession, a black Mercury Cougar with a special stirrup-like accelerator so he could drive without too much pain in his right foot, was following Dortmunder and an unidentified man in a bright red Volkswagen Rabbit through the rain-splashed streets of Manhattan. The windshield wipers splashed back and forth, the cold damp spread through the metal frame of the car, and Zane peered steadily at the Rabbit taillights out ahead.

Presumably, Dortmunder was on his way to the meeting with Chauncey at midnight, half an hour from now, but in that case why was the Rabbit aiming itself so completely downtown? Appropriately enough, the Rabbit was heading for that warren of streets south of 14th and over by the Hudson River known as the West Village. The westernmost part of Greenwich Village, this area is almost nothing but trucking companies and warehouses, because of the proximity of the docks and the Holland Tunnel.

The Rabbit traveled south on Washington Street, ever deeper into this maze, the streets lined with parked trucks, no pedestrians out in the rain except the occasionally lonely gay hoping to meet a new friend; in the gay world this neighborhood was known as The Trucks, and with no local residents to complain, a certain virbrant streetlife often took place here after dark. But not on a chilly wet night like this; the few solitary strollers slogging along with their hands in their jacket pockets looked more like homeless cats than liberated swingers.

At last the Rabbit turned off Washington Street, but in the rainy dark Zane couldn't make out exactly what street he was following it onto. Was it somewhere near Charles Lane, or

Weehawken Street? Or farther south around Morton or Leroy Streets? For all he knew, in this poor visibility, with his eyes so exclusively on the taillights of the Rabbit ahead of him, they were south of Canal Street by now, down around Desbrosses or Vestry Streets.

And not every trucker or shipper or warehouse, apparently, was completely closed for the weekend; ahead of Zane, a large tractor-trailer was backing and filling, taking up most of the width of the street, facing from left to right, trying to back into position somewhere on the left. A great bulky monster of a man, in a rain-slick poncho and knit cap, was standing in the middle of the street, directing the tractor-trailer in its movements, and he'd flagged down the Rabbit, stopping it so the big truck could keep juggling itself left and right across the cobblestones.

Drat. Not wanting to be too close to the Rabbit, Zane slowed the Cougar, stopped several car lengths back, and waited for the jam-up to end. But the burly man in the street came trotting through the puddles, waving at Zane to move forward. With mighty gestures he informed Zane to get farther over to the left, where a large delivery van was parked half up on the sidewalk. Following directions, Zane tucked in beside the parked van, his door handle almost touching the van's olive-green side.

Next, the big man motioned for the Rabbit to back up, urging it also to move in close against the side of the van. Zane ducked his head, shielding his face with one hand as the Rabbit approached, its white reversing lights gleaming. When those lights clicked off, the Rabbit was still perhaps a car length ahead, but too close for Zane's comfort.

And now what were these people up to? While headlights in his rear-view mirror told him some other car was becoming involved in this mini traffic jam, the huge tractor-trailer that was causing all the trouble pulled completely out into the street, turning in his direction, apparently intending to start all over again in its effort to pull into the alley or loading dock or whatever it was up there. Sweeping out and around, it angled in from Zane's right until it was as close to the Cougar on that side as the delivery van was on his left, except that the tractor-trailer was headed the other way.

When *would* they get this over with? The tractor-trailer just stood there, apparently unable to figure out its next move, and Zane didn't realize anything was wrong until the lighting suddenly began to change.

First, the Rabbit's taillights went out. It was hard to tell from here, but its headlights seemed to have been switched off as well.

. Second, the Rabbit's interior light went on, because somebody had opened its door. Both doors, in fact; Dortmunder and the driver were both getting out of their car, only the back half of which was jammed between the delivery van and the tractor-trailer.

Third, as Dortmunder and the driver shut their doors behind themselves, so that the Rabbit's interior light snapped off again, the headlights in Zane's rear-view mirror *also* went out.

Where were Dortmunder and the other one going? Was *this* their destination? What in hell was going on?

Some other vehicle was out front, something much larger than the Rabbit. Slowly, that vehicle was pushing the Rabbit toward Zane's Cougar. Zane instinctively switched into reverse, but with that other car behind him there was nowhere to go. Then he shifted into drive, but if he tried to push back against that larger vehicle he would simply smash his own car against the Rabbit.

The Rabbit stopped. The other vehicle—a truck of some sort— remained where it was.

Nothing at all happened.

"This is ridiculous," Zane said. He honked his horn: *yap yap yaaaaap.* The sound disappeared in the rain. The Rabbit made no response, nor did the tractor-trailer on his right, nor did the car behind him, nor did the delivery van on his left.

"Well," he said, and opened the door. It opened about half an inch, and then it stopped.

At last Zane got the picture. Quickly switching off the Cougar's engine, releasing his foot from the stirrup-accelerator, he

slid across to the passenger door, pushed it open, and heard
the thunk when it hit the side of the tractor-trailer.

Wider on this side; almost a full inch.

With the engine off, the windshield wipers had stopped, and
it was through tears of rain on the glass that Zane looked out
at the Rabbit, with the truck parked beyond it. No way to
push through. Twisting around, he tried to look through the
water-smeared rear window, but though he could make out
little about the vehicle blocking him from behind, he was certain in his heart about one thing: it would have too much
weight for his Cougar to move it.

Trapped. Dortmunder *was* up to something, that son of a
bitch. He'd trapped Zane here, he was pulling something, he
was *doing something right now.* "When I get out of here,"
Zane muttered, and thumped the dashboard with a closed fist.

When he got out of here? Good God. Zane knew when he'd
get out of here. When the real operators of these trucks came
back to work, that's when, and not a second before.

On Monday.

12

At exactly midnight, Arnold Chauncey put the key into the
inside lock of the passage door, turned it, opened the door, and
nobody came in.

What? Holding the door ajar, blinking in the misty rain,
Chauncey peered out at the street and saw no one and nothing.
Where was Dortmunder? Much more important, where was
the painting?

All right; no reason to panic. Anyone can be a bit late.
Keeping the door partway open, turning up the skimpy collar
of his suede jacket against the rain and the chill, Chauncey
settled himself to wait. Dortmunder would be here. And if

something went wrong with Dortmunder, then Zane would take over. Not to worry.

The passage behind Chauncey's house was unheated, and in fact unroofed, the top only lightly covered with a trellis overgrown by vines. This offered less than no protection; the vine leaves, rather than stopping the rain, merely collected the tiny droplets into large gushes, which were dumped all at once down the back of Chauncey's neck. Meantime, his suede jacket and silk ascot and calf-height calf-leather boots, all of which had been designed primarily for indoor stylishness, were proving themselves effete and inadequate in the harsh reality of the outside world; rather like the French aristocrats of 1789.

Fortunately, Chauncey didn't have very long to wait, shivering in the darkness just inside the passage, peeking through the slightly open door, ducking back at the appearance of every non-Dortmunder pedestrian. After barely five minutes of this, a large dark car arrived, double-parked itself outside there, and Dortmunder's unmistakable figure—fairly tall, very narrow, stoop-shouldered, with lowered head—hopped out and hurried tippy-toe in his direction, trying to avoid puddles *and* dogshit at the same time. Three others emerged scrambling from the car in Dortmunder's wake, and followed his progression through the minefield, but Chauncey's eye was primarily taken by the long cardboard tube in Dortmunder's hand. Folly, home from the wars.

Dortmunder bounded through the doorway Chauncey held open for him, turned his collar down, and immediately turned it back up again, saying, "It's raining in *here*."

"There's no roof," Chauncey told him, and reached for the cardboard tube. "Shall I hold that?"

But Dortmunder held the tube out of reach, saying, "We'll *switch* inside."

"Of course," said Chauncey, disappointed, and led the way to the house. At the back door, Dortmunder paused, saying, "Doesn't this trigger the alarm?"

"I told Watson I'd use this door tonight."

"Okay."

The house was wonderfully warm and dry. They climbed

the two flights of stairs to the sitting room where Chauncey, sounding rather more regretful than hostlike, said, "I suppose you'd all like drinks."

"You bet," everybody said. They were standing around rubbing their hands together, working their shoulders up and down, grimacing and twitching the way people do when they leave the cold and wet for the warm and dry.

Chauncey took drink orders—they all wanted bourbon, thank you—and while he poured he said to Dortmunder, "You were late."

"We had a little chore to take care of first."

Chauncey handed around glasses, then raised his own in a toast: "Success to all our schemes."

"Hear, hear. Okay. I'll drink to that."

They did, and Chauncey had his first real opportunity to study Dortmunder's "string." And what a motley collection they were, all in all, dominated by a man monster with a face like a homicidal tomato, plus a skinny sharp-nosed bright-eyed fellow who looked like a cockney pickpocket, and a mild-mannered gent who looked like a cross between a museum curator and a bookkeeper out of Dickens. So these four—with the driver outside—were the team of burglars, were they? Except for the monster, they looked perfectly ordinary. Chauncey, who had been rather nervous at the prospect of having these people all together in his house, was almost disappointed.

But mostly his thoughts were on Folly. He sipped at his drink, waiting impatiently for the others to finish their first tastes—with many aaahhhs and lip-smackings—and then he said, "Well. Shall we get to it?"

"Sure," Dortmunder said. "You got the money?"

"Of course."

From another cabinet near the liquor supply he brought out a small black attaché case. Opening this on a side table, Chauncey revealed stacks of bills, all fifties and hundreds, neatly filling the interior of the case. "I suppose you'll want to count this," he said.

Dortmunder shrugged, as though it didn't matter, saying, "It couldn't hurt." He nodded to the cockney pickpocket and the museum curator, who stepped over to the money, little smiles on their faces, and started flipping through the stacks. Meanwhile, Dortmunder was removing the rolled painting from its cardboard tube. "Hold this, Tiny," he said.

Tiny? As Chauncey stared in disbelief at the monster, who apparently did answer to that name, Dortmunder handed the fellow one corner of the painting and then backed away, unrolling it. Tiny (!) held two edges, Dortmunder held the other two, and there was Folly, revealed in all his splendor.

Not exactly, of course. There were still creases and curves in the surface, from the rolling-up, and the light struck it differently from this angle, making everything seem slightly different, slightly strange. But it was his Folly, all right, and Chauncey smiled in welcome as he stepped toward it, leaning forward to get a better look at the details. Odd how different that market basket looked in this—

"Hold it right there!"

The voice, cold and loud and aggressive, came from the doorway behind Chauncey, and when he spun around he was absolutely astounded to see the room filling up with terrorists.

At least, they *looked* like terrorists. Three of them, all wearing ski masks and brown leather jackets and all carrying machine pistols with those skimpy-looking tubular metal stocks. They moved very professionally, one hurrying to the left, one to the right, the leader remaining in the doorway, the barrel of his pistol moving lazily from side to side, prepared to stitch a line of bullets across the entire room. From his hands he was a black man, while the other two were white.

"Good *God!*" Chauncey cried, and these people looked so exactly like terrorists in the weekly newsmagazines that at first he thought it was a coincidence, that he was about to be kidnapped as a capitalist oppressor and held until Outer Mongolia, say, or Lichtenstein, had released a selected list of fifty-seven political prisoners.

But then he heard a *thwap* behind him, and knew that either Dortmunder or Tiny had released his end of the painting, allowing it to snap back into a roll, and all at once he understood. "Oh, no," he said, almost under his breath. "No."

Yes. "We'll take that," the leader was saying, gesturing with the machine pistol past Chauncey, at Dortmunder behind him. Then the machine pistol angled toward Dortmunder's two partners over by the attaché case, their hands full of stacks of bills, their faces showing the most complete—under other circumstances comical—surprise. "That, too," the leader said, and the satisfaction in his voice was like molasses.

"You son of a bitch," Dortmunder said, his voice almost a growl.

"Dortmunder," Chauncey said, warning him. Life is better than death, said the tone of his voice. This is merely one battle, not the whole war. All of those sentiments, however expressed over the centuries, were summed up in the tone of Chauncey's voice when he spoke Dortmunder's name. And Dortmunder, who had been teetering forward on his toes, hands clenched, shoulders bunched, now slowly relaxed, settling onto his heels once more.

From here, everything moved with professional speed and assurance. It was Tiny who held the rerolled painting, and at the leader's orders he put it into its cardboard tube and turned it over to the man on the left. The attaché case was refilled, closed, and given to the man on the right. Those two backed from the room, leaving the leader in the doorway. "We'll watch this door for ten minutes," he said. "Check your watches. Anybody through too soon gets shot." And he was gone.

The stairs were carpeted, so the people in the room wouldn't hear the trio leave, or know when they left, or how many stayed behind. Chauncey just stood there, gaping at the empty doorway, and the true fact of his loss—the painting *and* the money—didn't come home till Dortmunder was suddenly in front of him, glaring.

"Who'd you tell?"

"What? What?"

"Who did you tell?"

Tell? Tell someone about the insurance fraud, about the exchange of painting and money here tonight? But he *hadn't* told anyone. "Dortmunder, I swear to God— Why *would* I, man, think about it."

Dortmunder shook his head: "We're pros, Chauncey, we know our job. Not *one* of us would say a word to anybody. You're the amateur."

"Dortmunder, who is there for me to tell?"

"There they go!" cried the cockney pickpocket. He and the other two were over by the front windows, looking out into the rain. "Dortmunder!"

Dortmunder hurried to the windows, Chauncey following him. Tiny was saying, "One, two, three. They didn't leave anybody."

"Four!" cried the cockney pickpocket. "Who's that?"

Chauncey stared out the window. He couldn't believe what he was looking at. Over there, diagonally across the way, near the streetlight, three men in brown leather jackets had crowded around a fourth. Their faces were bare, now, but too far away to see. One carried the cardboard tube, another the attaché case. But it was the fourth man who held Chauncey's attention, held him frozen. Tall, narrow, dressed in black . . .

"He can't move fast with that limp," Tiny was saying. "Come on, Dortmunder, we'll trail them, we'll get our goods back."

"Z-z-z-z-z," said Chauncey, but stopped himself before making that mistake. The limping man and the other three hurried away toward the corner, out of the light.

Dortmunder's men were running from the room. Dortmunder had paused, was staring now into Chauncey's eyes as though to read his mind. "You're sure," Dortmunder said. "You told nobody. You don't know how this happened."

How could he admit it? What would happen to him? "Nobody," he answered, and looked Dortmunder straight in the eye.

"I'll get back to you," Dortmunder said, and ran from the room.

Chauncey sat down and drank half a bottle of bourbon.

13

It was Christmas all over again, in May's new apartment. The same crowd as at Christmastime, the same tasty aroma of tuna casserole wafting through the air, the same spirit of joy and good fellowship.

The gifts this time, though, weren't booze and perfume, they were solid cash and a sense of solid accomplishment, and maybe even the renewed gift of life itself. The lost painting was dealt with, Chauncey was cooled out and would be sending around no more hired killers, and on that table where once had stood the miserable fake tree the attaché case now yawned wide, gleaming with crisp new greenery.

Dortmunder sat in his personal chair with his feet up on his old hassock and a glass of bourbon-on-the-rocks in his left hand, and he damn near smiled. Everything had worked out *exactly*, even the moving of all the furniture and goods from May's old apartment to this new one six blocks away. And now everybody was relaxing here, less than half an hour since they'd left Chauncey's house, and all Dortmunder could say was, it was the best worked-out goddam plan *he'd* ever seen in his life.

Andy Kelp came by—good old Andy—with an open bourbon bottle in one hand, an aluminum pot full of ice cubes in the other. "Top up your drink," he said. "It's a party."

"Don't mind if I do." Dortmunder topped up his drink, then found himself actually grinning at good old Andy Kelp. "Whadaya think?" he said.

Kelp stopped, paused, grinned, cocked his head to one side, and said, "I'll tell you what I think. I think you're a goddam genius. I think you been operating under a cloud too long, and it was about time your true genius shone through, and it did. *That's* what I think."

Dortmunder nodded. "Me, too," he said simply.

Kelp went away, to top up other drinks around the room, and Dortmunder settled down to sip and smile and consider the harvest, at long last, of his own genius. The original notion had been Andy's, but the *plan* had been all Dortmunder.

And how *well* it had worked! Dortmunder always planned well, nobody could argue that, but things never worked out the way they were supposed to. This time, though, the pieces had clicked into place one after the other like a stunt drill team.

It was at the Christmas party that Kelp had suggested to the other guests they could do an old buddy a favor and at the same time pick up some pocket money for themselves, and once they'd understood the situation they'd all agreed. Wally Whistler, the lockman whose absentmindedness in releasing a zoo lion from its cage had resulted in an only-recently-completed involuntary vacation upstate, had followed Roger Chefwick's route in bypassing Chauncey's alarm system and coming down through the elevator shaft while Dortmunder, purposely late, had kept Chauncey out of his house. Fred Lartz, the former driver who had quit driving after he'd got run down by Eastern Airlines flight two-oh-eight, and Herman X, the radical black lockman, had completed the terrorist trio, and their timing, manner and efficiency just couldn't have been bettered. (Dortmunder raised his glass thrice: to Herman X, dancing once more with his sleek girl friend Foxy to an Isaac Hayes record; to Fred Lartz, comparing routes in a corner with Stan Murch; and to Wally Whistler, absentmindedly fumbling with the catch on the spring-leaf table. Whistler and Lartz raised their glasses in return. Herman X winked and raised his right fist.)

A strange string, that; two lockmen and a non-driving driver. The driving for that bunch, in fact, had been done by Fred Lartz's wife, Thelma, the lady in the crazy hat out in the kitchen helping May. Thelma did all Fred's driving for him now that he'd quit, but this was her first time driving *professionally,* and she'd been cool and reliable all the way. (Dortmunder raised his glass to Thelma, who couldn't see him because she was in the kitchen. Three or four other people saw him, though, and grinned and raised their glasses back, so that was all right.)

But the coup de grace had been the little play put on for Chauncey's benefit on the street outside. And for that, who better than an actor? Alan Greenwood, the former heistman and now television star, had been delighted at the idea of playing the limping killer, Leo Zane. "It's the kind of role an actor can get his teeth into," he'd said, and he'd made a special trip back from the Coast just to appear in Dortmunder's private production. And what a job he'd done! For just a second, seeing him out there under that streetlight, Dortmunder had actually believed he *was* Zane, somehow free of the trap and ready to blow the gaffe on all of them. Wonderful performance! (Dortmunder raised his glass to Greenwood, also dancing. At first, he'd thought Greenwood was here with Doreen again, the girl from Christmas, but this time Greenwood had introduced her as Susan, so maybe she was somebody different. Anyway, they were dancing, and over Susan's shoulder Greenwood gave the English thumbs-up salute and smiled with several hundred teeth.)

So now they had it all. Porculey's copy of *Folly Leads Man to Ruin* looked terrific thumbtacked over the sofa, and the attaché case full of money looked just as terrific on the table across the room. One hundred thousand dollars, every last dollar of it present and accounted for. The money had to be spread a bit thinner than if the original robbery had worked out, but so what? The point was, they'd done the job at last and *they had the money.* Ten thousand would go to Porculey for the fake, and the man had earned every penny of it. One thousand each would go to Wally Whistler and Fred Lartz and Herman X as a token payment of appreciation, and one thousand to Alan Greenwood to cover his expenses in coming to town just for this gig. It had been agreed by everybody concerned that May should get a thousand, both to help fix up the new apartment and also as a kind of testimonial to her world-renowned tuna casserole. And that left eighty-five thousand dollars. Split five ways (Kelp would give his nephew Victor a little something as a finder's fee out of his own piece), it left

Dortmunder and Kelp and Murch and Chefwick and Bulcher a solid reasonable seventeen thousand dollars each. What was wrong with that? Nothing. (Dortmunder raised his glass to the attaché case. It didn't offer any visible response, but it didn't have to. Its presence was enough.)

Of course, there *was* something a little strange about the fact that, when success finally did arrive, it came in the form of a fake robbery of a fake Old Master, but just so long as the money was real—and it was, they'd looked it over very carefully—what the hell. Right?

And here was Kelp—good old Andy Kelp—back with more bourbon and more ice cubes. Dortmunder was astounded to realize his glass was practically empty; nothing in it but one naked ice cube. He added a second, Kelp filled the glass to the top, and the party went on.

Dortmunder was never exactly sure afterward when the party did come to an end. After a while May and Thelma brought out the food, and then a while later the money was divvied up—May took her share and Dortmunder's share away to the bedroom, where she'd already worked out this apartment's hiding place—and then a while later Wally Whistler's absentminded fiddling with the catch on the spring-leaf table resulted in a lot of dishes and glasses and peanuts clattering to the floor with a *hell* of a racket when the table collapsed to Wally's utter embarrassment, and a while after that people started going home, all of them stopping to thank Dortmunder for a nice party and to say a word or two about tonight's success. Dortmunder just smiled at them all, and nodded happily whenever his glass was refilled, and somewhere in through there he must have fallen asleep, because you can't wake up unless you've been asleep, and just like THAT Dortmunder woke up. He stared around an empty room gray with daylight, and he said out loud, "What's going wrong?"

Then he heard the echo of his own voice, and sat back in his chair. He had the fuzzy mouth and the muzzy headache that come from sleeping sitting up in a chair with your clothes on after you've had just a bit too much to drink. Moving his tongue around inside his head as though it were a sock he was trying to put away somewhere, he silently answered his own question: *Nothing's* going wrong. Chauncey was cooled out. Zane was certainly not cooled out, but his credibility was destroyed in Chauncey's eyes because *Chauncey didn't know Dortmunder knew what Zane looked like,* and in any event Dortmunder was going to make himself very hard to find for the next few months. Besides moving their apartment, he and May intended to take some of that money and have a real vacation, a real spree for themselves, and by the time they came back this whole business would have blown over. Why would a professional like Zane spend the rest of his life, with no employer, on a manhunt that had no profit in it? Zane would eventually stop being upset, he'd get back to his own life, and that would be the end of that.

So what could go wrong? Nothing. This job was done, and it had been a complete success.

Dortmunder closed his eyes. Ten seconds later, the left eye opened halfway, and watched the empty room.

THE BRIDGE

1

Andy Kelp met them at the airport, grinning from ear to ear. "What a great tan," he said.

"Yeah," Dortmunder said. "Hello."

May said, "I made him go out on the beach. All he wanted was sit in the hotel and look at television."

"I went to the casino," Dortmunder said, defending himself.

Kelp said, "Yeah? You win?"

Dortmunder looked around, frowning. "Where do we pick up our stuff?"

Pointing at signs, Kelp said, "Baggage, that way."

The three of them set out, along with several million other travelers, following the lit BAGGAGE signs and arrows suspended from the ceiling. This was a Sunday evening in early June, and the terminal was full of people who had not at all terminated; they were insistent, every one of them, on pushing toward some farther destination. Sunday is when most people finish their vacations, and when the disorganized finally get started. Pale faces and vinyl luggage going out, peeling faces and wicker baskets coming back. Walking along through this mob, May told Kelp, "We had beautiful weather. The whole thing was just perfect."

Kelp was delighted. "You had a good time, huh?"

Dortmunder nodded, slowly and thoughtfully, as though it had taken much soul-searching to come to this conclusion. "Yeah," he said. "It was okay."

The trip had been strictly May's doing, from beginning to end. She'd gone to the travel agency, she'd brought back the brochures full of white sand beaches and blue swimming pools, she'd talked it over with Dortmunder, and then she herself had chosen the package tour to Puerto Rico: fourteen days and thirteen nights in a first-class hotel in beautiful San Juan, air fare included, complimentary cocktail with dinner the first night in the hotel. May had done the packing, completed the arrangements with the travel agency, and made a lightning swoop on Korvette's to stock up on dark glasses, suntan oil, floppy hats and clogs.

Dortmunder had helped by expressing doubts. "If the Puerto Ricans all come *here*," he'd said, for instance, "how come it's such a hot idea for us to go *there*?" Another time, he'd expressed the opinion that airplanes were too heavy to fly, and a little later he'd pointed out he didn't have a passport. "You don't need a passport," May told him. "Puerto Rico's part of the US." He stared at her. "The hell it is." But it turned out she was right about that; Puerto Rico wasn't exactly a state, but it was *something* in the United States of America—maybe it was "of." Anyway, May's accuracy about that one detail had encouraged Dortmunder to trust her with the rest.

And, as he had gracefully admitted, it had worked out okay. Nice beach, nice casino—they closed it too early, though—nice driving around in a rain forest, nice boat trips to a lot of like little islands; all in all, nice. Except for an ashtray from the El Conquistador restaurant and a couple towels from the hotel, Dortmunder hadn't boosted a thing the whole trip. A real first-class vacation.

Dortmunder said, "How are things around town?"

"About the same," Kelp said. "No nice scores, not even a hotel hit. We're still the champs."

Dortmunder grinned. Over a month after the event, the Chauncey caper could still bring a warm glow to his heart, a sense of a good job well done. "Yeah, that's okay," he said.

"Chefwick retired," Kelp said.

Dortmunder showed his surprise. "Retired? How come?"

"Some guy in California bought a Chinese railroad, and Chefwick's gonna run it. He took his piece from the job, and him and Maude went on out there."

Dortmunder gave Kelp a wary look. "Is this one of your stories?"

"It's *true.*"

"They're always true. A Chinese railroad?"

"Yeah," Kelp said. "It used to go from someplace to someplace else in China, but now they use planes and buses and—"

Dortmunder said, "A *real* railroad? Not a model?"

"That's right. Apparently, this was a very famous early railroad. It was built with Irish labor, and they—"

"All right," Dortmunder said.

"I'm just telling you what Roger told me. This guy in California bought it, that's all. A couple locomotives, some railroad cars, some of the old switches, even one little railroad station like a pagoda. Same as that guy in Arizona bought the London Bridge and set it up in Arizona. Exactly the same."

"Fine," Dortmunder said.

"They're putting down some track," Kelp said, "and building an amusement park around it, like a Disneyland, and Chefwick's gonna run the railroad. Him and Maude, they'll live in the railroad station."

Smiling, May said, That's nice."

Dortmunder also smiled, and nodded his head. "Yeah, that's okay," he said. "Chefwick's got himself a real railroad. That's okay."

"Of course, he'll still set up his model," Kelp said.

"Don't tell me," Dortmunder said. "In the railroad station."

"Where else?"

"Sure," Dortmunder said.

Kelp nodded, and said, "Oh, and Tiny Bulcher's back in jail."

"What for?"

"He beat up a gorilla."

Dortmunder said, "Stop."

May said, "Did you say he beat—"

"Don't ask him, May," Dortmunder told her. "He'll only answer."

"It was in the *Daily News* and everything," Kelp said, as though that were an adequate defense. "It seems he was—"

"I said stop," Dortmunder told him.

"You don't even want to hear about it?"

"No."

"*I* do," May said.

"Tell her later," Dortmunder ordered, and they reached the place where they were supposed to pick up their baggage.

It was a madhouse. Several circular constructions skirted by moving conveyor belts offered an array of luggage from several different airplanes to travelers packed three and four deep in all directions. Dortmunder and May and Kelp at last found the right conveyor belt, struggled their way to the front rank, and spent the next ten minutes watching other people's luggage go by.

"Boy," Kelp said after a while, "there's sure a lot of goods in the world." Impossible, his expression seemed to say, for *anybody* to steal it all. Impossible even to scratch the surface.

After several million alien impedimenta had appeared on the conveyor belt—some of them circling over and over again, apparently having arrived at a destination other than that of their owners—May suddenly said, "That's ours," and Dortmunder obediently plucked the old brown suitcase off the conveyor belt.

Kelp said, "One more, right?"

"We bought some stuff," Dortmunder muttered, looking the other way.

"Oh, yeah?"

It took another ten minutes for May to feel they'd wrenched the last of their own possessions from the passing parade, and by then she and Dortmunder and Kelp were standing in the middle of a redoubt formed of seven pieces of luggage. In addition to the two lumpy ordinary suitcases they'd had with them on departure, they now claimed: two flimsy-looking wicker baskets, each about the size of a typewriter case, both tied with stout cord; a tennis racket(!); a smallish bright-colored carton announcing in red and yellow letters for all the world to know that the contents were duty-free liquor and duty-free cigarettes; and a scruffy cardboard carton wrapped in length after length of thin string. "Jeepers," Kelp said. "I guess you *did* buy some stuff."

"They had some really wonderful bargains," May said, but like most returned travelers her expression suggested that doubt was beginning to set in.

"Let's get outa here," Dortmunder said.

"Well," Kelp said, cheerily picking up both wicker baskets and the tennis racket, "wait'll you see what the medical profession has for us this time."

They pushed their way through the crowd, found the outside world, and then walked endlessly through parking lot No. 4. It was a cool, damp, overcast spring night with a hint of rain in the air, and they just kept walking around in it. "The car's here someplace," Kelp kept saying, looking left and right over the acres of cars glittering in the infrequent floodlights. "It's right around here."

"What is it?" Dortmunder asked him. "What does it look like?"

"I want it to be a surprise. I know it's around here someplace." So they walked, and they walked. Dortmunder carried both suitcases, with the string-wrapped carton under one arm. May carried the box of duty-free liquor and cigarettes. And they kept walking.

Until Dortmunder stopped, put everything down on the blacktop, and said, "That's enough."

"But it's very close," Kelp said. "I know it's right around here."

"Unless it's *here*," Dortmunder told him, "you can forget it."

May said, "Here's a car with MD plates." She was gesturing at a dusty Mustang II with crumpled fenders and a metal coathanger for an antenna.

Kelp gave the Mustang a look of scorn. "That belongs to some intern."

"We'll take it," Dortmunder decided. "Get out your keys."

Kelp was shocked, hurt, distraught. "But I picked one *special*," he said. "A silver Rolls-Royce, with a TV *and* a bar! A wonderful car, it must belong to some doctor has his own hospital, I'll bring you home in style."

"We'll take this one," Dortmunder said, pointing at the Mustang.

"But—"

May said, softly but meaningfully, "Andy."

Kelp stopped, looked at May, looked at Dortmunder, looked with hatred at the Mustang, looked desperately around the endless parking lot, and then sighed, and reached for his bunch of keys.

One of the keys opened the Mustang's doors and started the engine, but none of them would open the trunk, so they went to Manhattan with May in the front seat next to Kelp, while Dortmunder rode in back with the two suitcases, the cardboard carton, the two wicker baskets, the duty-free carton and the tennis racket.

They left the Mustang a block from home, carried everything to the building and up the stairs, and May unlocked the front door to let them in. They walked inside, May first and then Dortmunder and then Kelp, and in the living room Leo Zane limped forward with a cold smile while Arnold Chauncey turned from the fake painting thumbtacked to the wall and said, "Dortmunder." He gestured at the painting. "Before Leo shoots you people," he said, "would you mind telling me what in *hell* that's all about?"

2

"It's a fake," Dortmunder said.

"I *know* it's a fake," Chauncey answered. "What's it *for?*" Before Dortmunder could work out an answer—a memento? I've been practicing?—Kelp stuck an oar in, crying, "Say! Isn't that the guy highjacked us? You remember, Dortmunder? The guy outside with the limp."

It was a nice try, but Dortmunder knew from the cold smile on Zane's face and the cold frown on Chauncey's that it wasn't going to work. Nevertheless, having nothing better to do, he went along with the gag: "Could be him, I don't know. I only got a quick look."

Chauncey shook his head in irritation, saying, "Don't waste everybody's time, Dortmunder. I know everything. I know Leo disobeyed my orders and made contact with you last November. I know you tied him up in a cocoon of trucks downtown while you had some stooge imitate him in front of my apartment. I know you staged that robbery, and I know you turned the painting over to another buyer, and I know—" with an angry gesture at the luggage all over the floor "—you've just been away on a nice vacation on *my* money. The only thing I don't know," Chauncey finished, flinging his arm out toward the painting on the wall, "is what *that* goddam thing is for."

"Listen," Dortmunder said.

"Don't tell me lies," Chauncey warned him.

"Why would I lie to you?" Dortmunder asked, but hurried along without waiting for an answer. "Just because this guy sold you a bill of goods, you blame me. I think he *was* in on that highjack. It sure looked like him outside the window. What makes you believe him instead of me?"

Chauncey seemed to give that question more consideration than it actually deserved. Everybody watched him think it over (except May, who was frowning uncertainly at Dortmunder), and finally Chauncey nodded and said, "All right, I'll make you a trade. A story for a story. I'll tell you why I *know* Leo's telling the truth, and then you'll tell me what in hell you're doing with a grade-A imitation of the painting you stole."

"It's a deal," Dortmunder said.

Leo Zane said, "Mr. Chauncey, you're the employer, so it's up to you, but aren't we wasting time? Why don't I just pop these three, and we go home?"

"Because I'm curious," Chauncey told him. "I'm fascinated. I want to know what's going on." To Dortmunder he said, "My story first. No more than a minute or two after you people left my house that night of the so-called robbery, the phone rang. It was Leo, calling from a phone booth down in Greenwich Village."

Dortmunder shrugged. "So he said."

"And so he proved. He told me how you people had blocked him in, and how he'd smashed the rear window of his car so he could crawl out and get away. He gave me the phone number at the booth where he was, and I called back, and he was there. I drove downtown to meet him, and that phone booth did have that number, and his car was boxed in as he'd described."

"Hmmm," Dortmunder said.

"Leo went looking for you," Chauncey went on, "but of course you'd moved, and it took a while to find the trail."

Kelp suddenly broke in, saying, "Wait a minute. Listen; how about this? What if Zane himself set up a fake Zane, so then when he proved he was someplace else you'd naturally think somebody *else* was trying to frame him? How about that?"

While Dortmunder and May both looked embarrassed, Chauncey gave Kelp a look of scorn, then said to Zane, "If that one says anything else, shoot him right away."

"Absolutely," said Zane.

Kelp looked hurt and unappreciated, but kept his mouth shut.

Chauncey returned his attention to Dortmunder. "All of which is annoying enough," he said, "but now it's even worse. There's been another development."

Dortmunder's expression was wary. "Oh, yeah?"

"The painting has turned up. In Scotland, with an apparently authentic pedigree. They claim it's been in the same family more than a hundred fifty years."

"Then it's not yours," Dortmunder said.

"Three experts in London," Chauncey told him, "have affirmed it *is* the original. It's listed for auction at Parkeby-South in September, and expected to sell at better than two hundred thousand pounds." A faint trembling in Chauncey's voice suggested his calm was only skin deep. "On the assumption the experts are right," he said, "and the painting has been in

Scotland the last one hundred fifty years, my insurance company now believes only a copy was stolen from me, and they're suing. They want their money back."

"Oh," Dortmunder said.

Did that twitching in Chauncey's cheek indicate anger? "Perhaps the Scottish painting is mine," he said, "and the pedigree is faked; you'll know that better than I. On the other hand, perhaps Veenbes did that subject twice, and both are originals. It's been known to happen before, and it's certainly the defense I'll try in court. But in either case *our* situation is the same. You have taken my money, you have taken my painting, and you have laid me open to a lawsuit from my insurance company." Chauncey took a deep breath, got himself under control, and went on. "That's my story," he said. "Now tell me what this copy is for, so Leo can shoot you and I can go home."

Dortmunder frowned, and in the lengthening silence he seemed to hear the faint skirl of bagpipes. "Scotland," he said, thoughtfully, while fighting men in kilts reeled before his eyes.

"Never mind Scotland." Chauncey jabbed a finger once more at Porculey's fake. "*That's* what I want to know about."

Dortmunder sighed. "Sit down, Chauncey," he said. "As much as it goes against my principles, I think I'm gonna have to tell you the truth."

3

"And that's the truth," Dortmunder finished.

"By God, it sounds it." Chauncey sat back on the sofa, shaking his head. He was the only one seated; Zane stood over near the door, silent as the grave, while Dortmunder and Kelp and May stood in a row facing Chauncey.

Dortmunder had told the whole story himself, but now Kelp chimed in, with a nervous glance toward Zane, saying, "The thing is, Mr. Chauncey, it wasn't Dortmunder's fault. He was stuck in that elevator shaft when it got lost. If he'd been along, it never would have happened. You wanna know whose fault it is, it's whoever took that elevator ride."

Chauncey said to Dortmunder, "Why didn't you tell me all this before?"

Dortmunder looked at him, saying nothing.

Chauncey nodded. "You're right." Twisting around, looking at the copy on the wall once more, he said, "It is good, I have to admit it. Your friend is very very good."

"Maybe you'd like to see some of his other stuff," Dortmunder said. "I could introduce you to the guy. His name's Porculey."

Chauncey gave Dortmunder a sharp look, and shook his head. Getting to his feet, he said, "I'm sorry, Dortmunder. I know you're trying for the human touch, and it may be you're just the victim of circumstance, but the fact is, I've been very badly dealt with. I'd never be able to look myself in the mirror again if I did nothing about it." He looked uncomfortable but determined. "You've been effective to this extent," he went on. "I no longer want to be present when it happens." Turning to Zane, he said, "Wait a minute or two after I leave." And he started for the door, stepping over the array of suitcases and wicker baskets.

"Uh," Dortmunder said. "Uh, wait a minute."

Chauncey paused, but only just; looking back over his shoulder, his attention clearly already out of the room. Even his voice seemed to come from far away: "Yes?"

"I might, uh—" Dortmunder spread his hands, shrugging. "I might have an idea," he said.

THE FINAL CHORUS

1

Ian Macdough (pronounced Macduff: no relation to Macbeth's friend) was a happy man. He had been unknown, and he would be famous. He had been poor, and he would be rich. He had been an unwilling country squire confined by circumstance to the family manse near Inverness, and he would be a London toff. A bluff, big-boned, red-haired, hearty, freckled gent of forty-odd, Ian Macdough was a happy man, and he wanted the world to know it. "Bring us another bottle of Teacher's," he told his floor valet at the Savoy, though it was barely lunch time, "and a lit-tle glass for yourself."

"Thank you, Mr. Macdoo," said the floor valet, who was a Portugee or Eyetie or some other sort of swarthy unfortunate, "but I shouldn't drink on the job. I'll bring the bottle straight away."

"Macduff," said Macdough, a bit shortly. He didn't like people who refused to drink with him, nor did he like them to get his name wrong. Most of the people he'd met so far in London would drink with him right enough, but few and far between were those who'd get his name right first crack out of the box. Macdoo indeed. Up north in the Grampians *everybody* knew his name.

"Mick-duff," agreed the Mediterranean, and bowed himself out of the suite.

Well, what could you expect from a foreigner? Nothing could spoil Macdough's mood for long these days, so while he waited for the bottle to arrive he stood smiling out of his sitting-room windows at the Thames, gleaming and glistening beneath midsummer sunshine.

London. All roads elsewhere might lead to Rome, but all roads in the British Isles lead to London. (Which is one of the reasons the traffic is so snarled.) A Scotsman or a Welshman or an Ulsterman might sit at home and think his dour dark thoughts about *England,* that often bullying big kid of the United Kingdom, but when his thoughts turned to a *city,* a real city, it wasn't of Edinburgh or Cardiff or Belfast he thought, but of London. Happy is he who can stand at the window of a suite in a major hotel in one of the world's queen cities, and smile out at the summer sun.

Bring bring, went the phone. *Bring bring. London calling.* The smile still lighting his ruddy face, Macdough turned from the view and replied: "Are you there?"

An extremely English male voice, one of those voices in which the vocal cords seem determined to strangle each word before it can struggle out to freedom, said, "Mister Macdow?"

"Macduff," said Macdough. The combination of the mispronounced name *and* a public-school accent was enough to curdle his smile completely.

"I'm so sorry," garbled the voice. "Leamery here, from Parkeby-South."

Which put Macdough's smile right back on his face, redoubled. "Ah, yes," he said. "They did tell me you'd call."

"Praps you could drop over this afternoon? Would four be convenient?"

"Certainly."

"Fine, then. Just ask for me at the cashier's desk."

"At the cashier's desk? Certainly. At four o'clock."

"Till then."

As Macdough cradled the receiver, his mind turned idly to the amazing series of events that had led him to this happy moment. The brawl in New York last winter, during the Queen's Own Caledonian Orchestra's performance (which he had attended through the generosity of old fellow-officers from the Brigade), his own lucky escape from the swarming police, and his utter astonishment when, in his hotel room next morning, he had awakened (a bit hung over) to find himself in possession of an extremely valuable painting stolen—according to the newspaper brought by room service with his breakfast—just the evening before. The terror he'd felt while smuggling the thing home (concealed inside a great mawkish framed landscape purchased for twenty-five dollars specifically for that purpose, the valuable Old Master undetected behind the dreadful New Monstrosity) was only a dim memory now, as was the utter bewilderment he had felt when faced with the question of how to turn his stroke of luck into actual cash. If Aunt Fiona hadn't chosen that moment to pass away (not prematurely; she was eighty-seven, as mad as an African general and as incontinent as Atlantis), Macdough would still be at a loss. Blessed Aunt Fiona, nothing became her life like the leaving of it.

The Macdough clan, which included Ian and his Aunt Fiona among its scores and multitudes, was one of the oldest and least successful families in all of Scottish history. Over the centuries, whenever the Scots fought the English they seemed to do so on Macdough land, and the Macdoughs got the worst of it. If Scot fought Scot, the Macdoughs invariably lined up on the wrong side. The Campbells and MacGregors might ebb and flow, but the Macdoughs immemorially ebbed.

So it was with low expectations that Macdough, as Aunt Fiona's sole heir, had first learned of her demise. The old lady had never owned anything in her life except rubbish bequeathed her by prior indigent Macdoughs. Several sheets of the inventory attached to the will were actually in scrabbly spidery eighteenth-century handwriting, describing pikestaffs and saddles and pewter plates which, while theoretically passing from hand to hand down the generations, had actually remained untouched and unwanted in various barns and basements and in the still-enclosed portion of the uninhabitable Castle Macdough high in the grim Monadhliath Mountains. However, the rituals had to be observed, and so Macdough had sat in a cluttered musty solicitor's office in Edinburgh and listened to the reading of the will, which included an endless droning recital of the inventory—what *rubbish* was here being gallantly preserved!—and was very nearly asleep when he suddenly sat bolt upright and stared at the solicitor, who, startled, stared right back. "What?" said Macdough.

The solicitor blinked. "I beg your pardon?"

"What was that? What you just read there."

The solicitor found his place in the list: "Mead barrels, oak, six, with bungs."

"No, before that."

"Wounded stag with two rabbits, bronze, height sixteen inches, broken antler, one."

"Good God, man, before *that*."

"Frame, wood, gilt, ornate, with painting, oil, comic figures."

"Frame, wood," Macdough muttered. "Painting, oil. Comic figures?"

"So it says."

"Where is this, er, frame?"

"Mmm, nmmm." The solicitor had to leaf back through two pages of inventory to the nearest heading. "Castle Macdough."

"Ah," Macdough said. "I might find a use for a good wood frame." And he napped through the rest of the inventory, then drove his venerable Mini at high speed (well, its highest speed) north from Edinburgh, through Perth and Pitlochry on the A 9, turning off beyond Kingussie on the old road not even on the maps. More trail than road, and more gully than either, it climbed into the inhospitable mountains and arrived at last at Castle Macdough, a ravaged ruin covered with mildew. Some of the ground floor remained, windows broken and floors buckled, while below were fairly weathertight storerooms strewn with rubbish, all of it carefully recorded in that everlasting inventory which now nestled against Ian Macdough's own will. (Macdough being a confirmed bachelor of a bluff, hearty, masculine yet asexual, peculiarly northern type, the next recipient of all this muck was slated to be a nephew of his, one Bruce Macdough, currently nine years of age.)

Stumbling over a baton used in relay races, Macdough struggled his way by flashlight from room to room until one bit of debris glittered back at him. Gilt? Yes. Frame, wood? Indubitably. Ornate? Good heavens, yes. Macdough pulled the object from its recess and found it to be almost exclusively frame; nearly four feet square, it was runnel and channel and riband and curlicue of gilded wood vastly surrounding a murky little picture possibly sixteen inches by eighteen. Dragging the thing into the light of day, Macdough found the tiny illustration thus so sumptuously engarbed was in fact an awkward amateurish comic drawing in oil of three drunken kilted men staggering on a road, trying to hold one another up. The moon in the sky was lopsided, though not by apparent intent.

Hadn't the inventory mentioned a double-bladed battle-axe? Descending into the depths, Macdough found the thing, carried it with some difficulty—it was damned heavy—up the slimy stone stairs, and proceeded to reduce the frame, wood, gilt, ornate, *with* its painting, oil, comic figures, to several zillion slivers. These were packed into the Mini and distributed into the air a few at a time over the next fifty miles.

It took another trip to Edinburgh to find an appropriately old frame which would match both the inventory's description and the stolen masterpiece's dimensions. This frame, happily, already contained an old painting—of a grandmotherly lady asleep in a rocker by the fire, a kitten and a ball of wool in her lap—so Macdough could use the same tacks to put the valuable Veenbes in its place. Another solitary trip to Castle Macdough was necessary, to seed the Veenbes there, and then Macdough awaited the right moment to introduce the subject of his inheritance into a conversation with a pair of old drinking pals, Cuffy and Tooth (both of whom had, as a matter of fact, been along on the night of the New York concert). Was it Cuffy who finally said, "Damn it, man, there could be something of value there. Why not have a looksee?" It might have been Tooth. In any event, it wasn't Macdough; he'd steered the conversation, but he'd let the others make the decisions, and when he asked them to join him for the projected looksee they fell in with the idea at once.

Neither of them, however, turned out to have the brains or the taste of a donkey, and after they'd *both* stumbled past the Veenbes without a second look Macdough had finally to discover the thing himself. "Now, look at *this* picture. Might be worth something, don't you think?"

"Not a bit of it," Cuffy said. "It's a mere daub, anyone can see that."

"The frame might be worth something," Tooth suggested.

"I'll take it along for the frame, then," Macdough decided, and so he did, and was subsequently astounded and delighted when word came from the Edinburgh art dealer that what he had was, in point of fact, a masterpiece of incredible value.

Borrowing on his prospects—the Parkeby-South valuation was security enough for Macdough's Inverness bankers—he had come here to London in July, two months before the auction that would make him rich, and was staying at the Savoy while looking about for a more permanent London abode; some flat, maisonette, pied-à-terre, some little somewhere to stay from now on, whenever he was "in town." Oh, by *glory,* but life was turning good!

A knock at the door. Macdough turned from his views—the outer view of London and the inner view of well-deserved success—and called, "Come in."

It was the floor valet, with a bottle of Scotch on a silver salver. And, Macdough noted at once, two glasses. "Ah hah," he said, with an amiable smile. "You will join me after all."

The man's own smile was both sheepish and conspiratorial. "You're very kind, sir. If you'll permit me to change my mind?"

"Certainly, certainly." Macdough came forward to pour with his own hands. "Take your opportunities, that's my advice," he told the fellow. "In this life, never let your opportunities slip you by."

2

To Dortmunder's surprise, he *could* get a passport, He'd paid his debts to society—at least the ones society knew about—and the privileges of citizenship were his for the asking. With the other necessary preparations, it was already July before everything was ready, but by God here he was, on a 747, leaving the United States of America, bound for London. In England.

And beside him was Kelp, who was grumpy. "I don't see why *we* can't ride in first class," he said, for about the fifteenth time.

"Chauncey's paying," Dortmunder answered, for maybe the seventh time. "So we do it his way."

Chauncey's way, as it happened, was that he and Leo Zane would travel beyond the maroon curtain in first class, with the free liquor and wine and champagne, and the prettier stewardesses, and the wider seats with more legroom, and the spiral staircase to a bar and lounge on an upper level, while Dortmunder and Kelp would travel in economy: the cattle car, here in back. Dortmunder had an aisle seat, so at least he could stretch his feet out when nobody was walking by, but Kelp had the middle seat, and a stout elderly Indian lady in a sari, with a red dot on her forehead, had the window seat. Kelp was sort of squeezed in there and—particularly since Dortmunder had won the struggle over whose elbow would have the armrest —Kelp was apparently pretty uncomfortable.

Well, it would only last seven hours, and when the plane landed they would be in London, and it would then be up to Dortmunder to make good on his latest brainchild. He'd be hampered in more ways than one—by not knowing the city at all, for instance, and by having to limit himself to a string consisting of one Kelp and two amateurs (Chauncey and Zane)

—but there really hadn't been much choice. It was either find some way to help Chauncey or become fresh notches on Zane's gun. If that cold son of a bitch ever did anything as human as notching a gun.

The plan, as with others of Dortmunder's, combined the simple with the unusual. In this one he proposed to *switch* the copy and the original before the sale took place in September. Chauncey could then, in defending himself against the insurance-company lawsuit, insist the version at the auctioneers be reappraised. It would be denounced as a fake, the lawsuit would stop, and Chauncey would retire with his painting and money intact.

All Dortmunder had to do was figure out the *details* of that one simple act, in a foreign city, with a half-amateur crew, while a gun was held at his head.

As far as he was concerned, this plane could stay up here in the sky forever.

3

Chauncey loved London, but not like this. In the first place, this was *July*. Nobody ever came to London in July, that's when the place was crammed with Americans and foreigners. In the second place, Chauncey's companions on this trip left much—in fact, everything—to be desired. In the cab from Heathrow, he and Zane occupied the rear seat, with Dortmunder and Kelp facing them on the jump seats, and while Chauncey noticed that Kelp very carefully made sure his knees were not annoying Zane in any way, Dortmunder wasn't controlling his own knees at all. Chauncey's legs were crammed over against the door, his view was of nothing but Dortmunder's lugubrious pan, and the damp English air blowing in through the open side windows was absolutely *hot*.

Still, it was all in a good cause. Beyond Dortmunder's beetled brow, and beyond the meter ticking away just past Dortmunder's right ear, Chauncey could see the mound of their luggage piled up in the space beside the driver, and prominent among his own Hermès and Zane's American Touristers and Kelp's six canvas ditty bags and Dortmunder's anonymous brown elephant-skin two-suiter with the straps loomed the golf bag behind the lining of which lurked the Griswold Porculey imitation of *Folly Leads Man to Ruin*. Sometime soon—very soon, please God—the imitation would go away and the *original* would slip into its place in the golf bag, and Chauncey would leave this city of teeming millions and fly away to Antibes, where everybody sensible was spending the summer.

In the meantime, the only thing to do was make the best of a bad situation. Oppressed by the continuing silence in the cab, these four large bodies sweating lightly in the hot July London air, Chauncey made a desperate stab at smalltalk: "This your first trip to London, Dortmunder?"

"Yeah." Dortmunder turned his head slightly to look out the window. The cab, having come in the M 4 from Heathrow, was now inching through the normal traffic jam on Cromwell Road. "Looks like Queens," Dortmunder said.

Chauncey came automatically to the city's defense. "Well, this is hardly the center of town."

"Neither is Queens."

Cromwell Road became Brompton Road before Chauncey tried again: "Have you traveled much outside the United States?"

"I went to Mexico once," Dortmunder told him. "It didn't work out."

"No?"

"No."

Kelp unexpectedly said, "You were in Canada a couple times."

"Just hiding out."

"Still."

"Just farmhouses and snow," Dortmunder insisted. "Could of been anywhere."

The cab finally reached Hans Place, a long oval around a tree-filled park, fringed by tallish orange-brick nineteenth-century houses done in the gabled ornate style termed by Sir Osbert Lancaster "Pont Street Dutch." When the cab stopped, Chauncey gratefully ejected himself onto the sidewalk and paid the fare while the others unloaded the luggage. Then Edith and Bert appeared from the house to welcome Chauncey back and to carry *his* baggage while the others could do as they wished with theirs.

This house had been divided long ago into four separate residences, complexly arranged. In Chauncey's maisonette, staff quarters and kitchen were on the ground floor rear, a front-windowed sitting room and rear-windowed dining room were on the first floor, and a spiral staircase from the dining room led up to two bedrooms plus bath at the rear of the second floor. Edith and Bert, a tiny shriveled couple who spoke an absolutely incomprehensible form of cockney in which *R* was the only identifiable consonant, were the maisonette's only full-time residents, with their own small room and bath downstairs behind the kitchen. They grew brussels sprouts in their bit of a garden in back, they did their shopping two blocks away at Harrods on Chauncey's charge account, they pretended to be valet and cook during those occasional intervals of Chauncey's presence in town, and all in all they lived the life of Reilly and knew it. "Hee hee," they said to one another, tucked into their teeny bed together at night. A maisonette in Knightsbridge! Not bad, eh, Mum? Not bad, Dad.

With much piping and chortling and recourse to the letter *R*, this happy couple welcomed Chauncey home. He perceived the sense, if not the substance, and told them, "Show these gentlemen to the guest room."

"Aye. Aye. R, r, r, r."

In the house they all went, and up the half flight to the sitting room, and thence up the spiral stairs, Edith and Bert struggling like trolls with Chauncey's luggage, cheerfully barking all the way. Zane went next, limping so garishly up the spiral staircase he seemed a living parody of a Hammer film, followed by Kelp, whose half dozen ditty bags gave him no end of trouble, constantly tangling and snagging with the staircase's banister rails and his own legs and—for one terrifying instant—with Zane's bad foot. The look Zane shot down at him was so cold, so lethal, that Kelp staggered backwards into Dortmunder, who'd been plodding steadily and unemotionally around the spiral like the mule circling an Arab well. Dortmunder stopped when much of Kelp landed on his head, and said, with tired patience, "Don't do that, Andy."

"I'm— I'm just—" Kelp righted himself, dropped two of his bags, stuck his rump in Dortmunder's face as he gathered them up, and climbed on.

Chauncey brought up the rear at rather a safe distance, and when he reached the top, Edith and Bert were already unpacking his bags in his room, while a dispute was starting in the guest room. Dortmunder expressed the core of the problem in a question to Chauncey: "All three of us in here?"

"This is it," Chauncey told him. "On the other hand, the sooner the job is done, the sooner you'll be able to leave and go home."

Dortmunder and Kelp and Zane looked around at the room, which had been designed with married—or at least friendly— couples in mind. One double bed, one dresser, one vanity, one chair, one writing desk, two bedside tables with lamps, one closet, one window overlooking the garden. Kelp, looking apprehensive but determined, said, "I don't care. He can shoot me if he wants, but I'm telling you right now I won't sleep with Zane."

"I believe there's a fold-up cot in the closet," Chauncey said. "I'm sure you'll sort something out."

"I can't sleep on a cot," Zane said. "Not with this foot."

"And I can't sleep with *you*," Kelp told him. "Not with that foot."

"Take it easy, you," Zane said, pointing a bony finger at

Kelp's nose.

"Let's all take it easy," Dortmunder suggested. "We'll draw straws or something."

Zane and Kelp were both objecting to that plan when Chauncey left the room, closing the door behind him, and entered his own civilized quarters, where Bert and Edith had not only finished his unpacking but had laid out a change of clothing on the bed and were starting a hot tub. "Lovely," Chauncey said, and then told them, "Now, those men with me, they're very eccentric Americans, just pay them no mind at all. They'll be here for a few days, on business, and then they'll be gone. Just ignore them while they're here, and if they behave at all strangely, pretend you don't notice."

"Oh, r," said Edith.

"Aye," promised Bert.

4

Leaning against a Chippendale chifferobe, Dortmunder watched two Japanese gentlemen bid against one another for a small porcelain bowl with a bluebird painted inside it. That is, he assumed it was the two Japanese gentlemen who were doing the bidding, since their slight head-nods were the only activity in the crowded room apart from the steady chanting of the impeccably dark-suited young auctioneer: "Seven twenty-five. Seven-fifty. Seven-fifty on my right. Seven seventy-five. Eight hundred. Eight twenty-five. Eight twenty-five on my left. Eight twenty-five? Eight-fifty. Eight seventy-five."

They'd started at two hundred, and Dortmunder had by now become bored, but he was determined to stay here in this spot long enough to find out just how much a rich Japanese would spend on a peanut bowl with a bird in it.

Here was one of the auction rooms at Parkeby-South, a large

auctioneer-appraisal firm in Sackville Street, not far north of
Piccadilly. Occupying a bewildering cluster of rooms and staircases in two adjacent buildings, the firm was one of the oldest
and most famous in its line of work, with connections to similar
companies in New York, Paris and Zurich. Under this roof—
or these roofs—were miles of rare books, acres of valuable
carpet, a veritable Louvre of paintings and statuary, a bull's
dream of china and glass, and enough armoires, commodes,
tallboys, chiffoniers, secretaries, wardrobes, rolltop desks and
cellarets to fill every harem in the world. The place looked like
San Simeon, with Hearst just back from Europe.

There were three kinds of rooms at Parkeby-South. There
were half a dozen auction rooms filled with people seated on
rows of wooden folding chairs as they bid incredible amounts
for marble thises and crystal thats; there were display rooms
crammed with everything from a life-size bronze statue of
General Pershing's horse to a life-size blown-glass bumblebee;
and finally there were rooms behind closed doors featuring the
discreet notice: PRIVATE. Modest unarmed gray-haired guards
in dark blue uniforms made no ostentatious display of themselves, but to Dortmunder's practiced eye they were everywhere,
and when Dortmunder experimentally pushed open a PRIVATE
door to see what would happen, one of these guards immediately materialized from the molding and said, with a helpful
smile, "Yes, sir?"

"Looking for the men's room."

"That's up on the first floor, sir. You can't miss it."

They were already *on* the first floor. Dortmunder thanked
him, collected Kelp from his mesmerized pose in front of a
glass cabinet full of gold rings, and went on upstairs, where
he was now watching a pair of Orientals struggle with one another for a jelly-bean bowl.

He was also brooding. There must be over a million dollars
worth of goods in this building. Guards were all over the joint
like flu in January, and so far as Dortmunder could see there
were no burglar alarms on the windows. Which could only
mean live guards in the place all night long.

"Eleven hundred," said the auctioneer. They were going by fifties now. "Eleven-fifty. That's eleven-fifty on my left. Eleven-fifty? No? Eleven-fifty on my left." *Clack* went the hockey puck in his left hand onto the top of his wooden rostrum. "*Sold* for eleven-fifty. Item number one fifty-seven, a pair of vases."

While a pair of gray-smocked employees held up the pair of vases—also porcelain, they featured one-footed flamingoes on their sides—Kelp whispered in disbelief, "They paid eleven hundred fifty dollars for that little bowl?"

"Pounds," Dortmunder whispered back. "English money."

"Eleven hundred fifty pounds? How much is that in cash?"

"More," said Dortmunder, who didn't know.

"Two grand?"

"Something like that. Let's get out of here."

"Two grand for a little bowl," Kelp said, following Dortmunder out to the hall. Behind them, the auctioneer had started the bidding on the vases at six hundred. Pounds, not dollars.

Out on the street, Dortmunder turned toward Piccadilly, but Kelp lagged behind, looking wistfully back. "Come on," Dortmunder said, but Kelp still dawdled, looking over his shoulder. Dortmunder frowned at him: "What's the matter?"

"I'd like to live there," Kelp said. He turned to grin wistfully at Dortmunder, but his expression changed almost immediately into a puzzled stare. He seemed to be looking now at something across the street.

Dortmunder, facing the same way, saw nothing. "What *now?*" he said. "You wanna live in that silver store?"

"I thought— No, it couldn't have been."

"You thought what?"

"Just for a second—" Kelp shrugged and shook his head. "There was a guy looked like Porculey," he said. "Fat like him. He went in one of those doors over there. You know the way people look like other people. Especially out of town."

"People look like other people out of town?"

"Couldn't have been him, though," Kelp said, and at last he moved briskly forward, leaving Dortmunder staring after him. Looking back, Kelp said, "Well? You coming?"

5

"I'm discouraged," Dortmunder said.

Chauncey looked up fom his brussels sprouts. "I'm sorry to hear you say that."

The four of them were at dinner in Chauncey's apartment, the meal prepared by Edith and served with many whispered *r*'s by Bert. This was their first repast together since their arrival yesterday, the jet lag caused by the five-hour time difference having thrown them all off for a while. Chauncey had kept himself awake yesterday with Dexedrine and asleep last night with seconal and by this morning had become completely adjusted to British time. The others seemed to have fared less well, with Zane the most obvious sufferer. The man's bleached face was even more pallid and gaunt than usual, and his limp had progressed to a level of grotesquerie not seen in these parts since the days of the Black Death.

As for Dortmunder and Kelp, jet lag and a strange environment seemed merely to confirm both in their pre-existing personalities. Dortmunder was more dour, Kelp giddier, though Kelp this morning had briefly been in an extremely foul mood, apparently brought on by the ultimate arrangement of sleeping accommodations in the guest room. Zane, through a combination of medical necessity and native harshness, had occupied the double bed, alone, with Dortmunder taking the cot; leaving Kelp to sleep on an assemblage of pillows and comforters on the floor. The opened-out cot, however, having already taken up most of the available extra space, Kelp had been forced to recline with his head under the dresser and his feet under the bed, which had resulted in his doing himself some sort of injury when he'd awakened, startled, from a bad dream in the middle of the night.

Kelp's essential good humor had soon returned, however,

and he'd seemed basically cheerful when he and Dortmunder left early this afternoon to look over the situation at Parkeby-South. Chauncey himself had gone out not long after, having tea with friends in Albert Hall Mansions, and had seen none of his guests until dinnertime, when his question to Dortmunder about the result of his visit to Parkeby-South had produced the word *discouraged.*

A word on which Dortmunder was willing to expand: "The place is full of rich stuff," he said. "And full of guards. And it looks to me like there's guards in there at night, when they're closed. I didn't see any alarm systems, but there could be."

"You mean you can't get in?"

"I can get *in,*" Dortmunder said. "I can get in and out anywhere. That's not the problem."

"Then what is the problem?"

"The idea," Dortmunder reminded him, "is to switch these paintings without anybody knowing it. Now, you turn off a burglar alarm and you're home free, you can come and go and nobody the wiser. But you can't walk in and out of a place full of live guards without somebody *seeing* you."

"Ah," said Chauncey.

Zane, pausing with a forkload of lamb chop and mint jelly halfway to his mouth, said, "Create a distraction."

"Very good!" Chauncey said, and beamed hopefully at Dortmunder. "What about that?"

Dortmunder looked dubious. "What distraction?"

Zane answered again: "Rob the place. Go in with guns, steal a few things, and while you're there switch the paintings."

"Lovely," Chauncey said.

Dortmunder didn't seem to think so. He said, "*Another* fake robbery? If we're stealing stuff, why don't we steal the painting? The cops'll want to know about that."

"Mm," said Chauncey.

But Zane wouldn't give up that easily. He said, "Did you actually *see* the picture while you were there? Is it on display?"

"No. I guess they keep the most valuable stuff locked up somewhere until it's sold."

Shrugging, Zane said, "So you didn't see it, that's why you didn't steal it."

Chauncey, tired of shifting between hope and despair, merely raised an eyebrow at Dortmunder this time, waiting for his negative response.

Which didn't come. Frowning, Dortmunder poked brussels sprouts here and there on his plate, saying at last, "I don't know. It sounds complicated. Just the two of us, we don't know how many guards they got in there, we've got to fake a robbery in one part of the place and at the same time find the painting locked up in some other part *and* get through that lock without anybody knowing, *and* switch the paintings without anybody seeing, *and* get away before the cops show up. It doesn't sound good."

Chauncey said, "What sounds better?"

Dortmunder slowly shook his head, having nothing to say. He was brooding, thinking, quite apparently getting nowhere.

It was Zane who broke the silence again, saying casually to Chauncey. "I was looking at that back yard of yours. High walls, nobody can see in, nice soft dirt. Plenty of room back there for a couple graves."

Dortmunder went on brooding as though he hadn't heard, but Kelp babbled, "Don't you worry about a thing, Mr. Chauncey! Dortmunder'll figure it out. He's figured out tougher problems than this one. Haven't you, Dortmunder?"

Dortmunder didn't answer. He continued to brood, pushing and poking at the brussels sprouts on his plate. His fork hit one too hard, and it dropped off the edge and rolled forward to bunk against his wineglass, leaving a thin trail of melted butter in its wake on the damask cloth. Dortmunder didn't seem to notice that either, but went on staring with hooded eyes at his food a moment longer, while the other three watched. Then he sighed, and lifted his head. Pointing both his eyes and fork at Chauncey, he said, "I got a job for you."

"Oh, yes?"

"Yes," said Dortmunder.

6

Folly Leads Man to Ruin. It was the Veenbes, all right, the original, last seen on the sitting-room wall in New York. Chauncey could have reached out and touched it, but he restrained himself, merely gazing upon it with disguised hunger, plus a wince of pity for the *dreadful* garish frame in which the poor thing now found itself. "I don't believe it," he said, casually, with a dismissing shrug. "Frankly, I just don't believe it's legitimate."

"Well, you *can* believe it," that scoundrel Macdough told him, with a self-satisfied smirk. "That's the genuine article, you can take it from me."

I intend to, Chauncey thought, with no little satisfaction, but all he said aloud was, "I'll be insisting on my own expert valuation, of course."

Leamery, the attentive young twit representing Parkeby-South, simpered diplomatically at them both, saying, "Of course, of course. Under the circumstances, naturally, that's the only thing to do. Everyone agrees."

"Troop your experts through," Macdough challenged, with his whisky-soaked burr. "Troop em up and down and sideways, it's all one to me."

It was at Dortmunder's request that Chauncey was here, in this next-to-the-top-floor value room at Parkeby-South, putting up with Leamery's smarm and Macdough's gloat, gazing helplessly at his own property while feigning disinterest. "You can get in to see the painting," Dortmunder had told him. "You've got a legitimate reason, this picture could cost you four hundred grand to an insurance company. So you'll go in, and you'll look at *everything*, and when you come back here you'll make me a map. I'll want to know where the painting is, what kind of doors and windows, where's the nearest outside wall, what brand is the lock on the door, what else is in the room, do they have closed-circuit TV, security cameras, everything. Is it a regular room or a safe, or a safe inside a room, or a barred cage, or what is it? And how many locks to go through. *Everything.*"

"I'll do my best," Chauncey had promised. "If in fact I can get in at all, which I very much doubt."

"You'll know somebody," Dortmunder had told him, and he'd turned out to be right. The next morning Chauncey had started making phone calls among his acquaintances in town, and damned if a young friend with a local publisher wasn't the nephew of Parkeby-South's head of publicity. The link had been enough to get Chauncey a sympathetic hearing from a vice-manager of the firm, who was certain something could be, as he said, "sorted out."

The sorting out had taken four days, but on Monday afternoon this fellow Leamery had called to say that Chauncey could most certainly view the painting, though "Mr. Macdoo does insist on being present. He's rather a diamond in the rough, you know, our Mr. Macdoo."

"Mac who?"

"Macdoo. The owner of the Veenbes."

"Oh, Macdow, you mean."

"Are you certain?" Leamery sighed, an aspish sound over the phone. "I never seem to get it right."

In any event, the showing was to take place the following afternoon, Tuesday. "I hope you don't mind," Leamery went on, "but we'd much prefer you saw it *in situ*, as it were. That is to say, in our value room."

"That's perfectly all right," Chauncey told him, and here it was Tuesday, and here was Chauncey in the value room, surrounded by the most precious items currently in Parkeby-South's care, memorizing everything in sight, trying his damnedest to be distracted neither by his craving for the Veenbes nor by his loathing for Macdough, a smug sloppy otter of a man smirking like a shop steward. Walls, doors, locks, exterior walls, staircases . . . "I've seen enough," he said at last, reluctantly, and turned away with one last backward glance at Folly and his followers. *I shall return,* he quoted General MacArthur telepathically at the oil, and left the room, pausing to watch with narrowed eyes as the guard locked the locks.

Down the stairs they went, Chauncey ahead of both Leamery and Macdough, his eyes flicking left and right, and on the ground floor Leamery smiled his wet-toothed pale smile and said, "Would you care for tea? We're just serving, in the office."

"Thank you, no."

"Or a peg," Macdough offered, with that *offensive* smile. "You look as though you could stand a bracer."

"I suspect, Mr. Macdow," Chauncey permitted himself to say, "that you should save—"

"Macduff," said Macdough.

"—all the bracers you have in stock. You'll be needing them yourself soon."

"The name is Macduff," Macdough repeated, "and I don't believe I will."

7

"Let's talk about that window again, the one on the staircase."

"*Again?* Dortmunder, I've told you everything I know about that window. I've told you everything I know about *everything.* I've drawn you maps, I've drawn you sketches, I've gone over and over and over—"

"Let's talk about the window."

"Dortmunder, *why?*"

"I want to know about it. Describe it."

"Very well, yet again. It was a window, on the landing half a flight below the value room. That would put it three and a

half levels above the street. It was double hung, with one large
pane of glass on top and six small panes in the bottom. The
wood was painted a grayish-cream color, and it looked out
over Sackville Street."

"What could you see when you looked out through it?"

"I told you. Sackville Street."

"*Exactly* what could you see?"

"Dortmunder, I passed that window twice, once on the way
up and once coming down. I didn't stop and stare out."

"What did you see on the way by?"

"The buildings across Sackville Street."

"Describe them."

"Describe—? Gray stone upper stories, windows, just— No!
By God, now I remember. There was a streetlight!"

"A streetlight."

"I saw it on the way down. It was below window level, of
course. But what possible difference does that make?"

"For one thing, it means that staircase won't be dark. Tell
me more about the window."

"*More?* There isn't any—"

"Lock."

"It didn't have a lock."

"Of course it did. All windows have locks."

"Well, it didn't have that— You know, that catch thing in
the middle. I can remember distinctly, there was— Ah, wait!"

"You're remembering something else."

"Dortmunder, when you're finished with me I'll be fit for
nothing but a sanitarium."

"Tell me."

"It had *two* locks. Sliding bolts on the inside top corners
of the lower half. I suppose the top half must be permanently
fixed in place."

"Sliding bolts? They slide into the frame on both sides?"

"Yes."

"So that's two new things you remembered about the
window."

"No more about the window. *Please,* Dortmunder."

"Fine. Let's talk about the floor in the hall outside the value room."

"Dortmunder, you're driving me crazy."

"Was it wood? Rug? Linoleum?"

"The floor. God help us. Let me think. . . ."

8

"What a country," Kelp said. Trying to shift gears with the stick jutting out on the right side of the steering column, he signaled for a right turn instead, and said, "Damn! Crap! Bastard!" Still signaling for a right turn, he found the *other* stick, jutting out on the *left* side of the steering column, and shifted into second.

"Drive on the left," Dortmunder told him.

"I *am* on the left," Kelp snarled, yanking the wheel hard to the left and thus not hitting that oncoming taxi.

"You weren't before."

"I was."

"You're signaling for a right turn."

"Maybe I'll turn right."

Kelp was in a foul mood, and his first experience driving in London wasn't helping much. Tottering down Sloane Street toward Sloane Square in a maroon Opel, surrounded by coughing black taxis, two-story-high red buses and darting scruffy Minis the size of washing machines and the color of week-old snow, Kelp struggled to deny all his deepest driving instincts. Sitting on the right, driving on the left, shifting with his left hand—and just to compound the confusion, the foot pedals *weren't* reversed.

Not that Kelp had been his usual cheery self even before entering this Opel. Five nights sleeping on the floor in

Chauncey's apartment had already left him stiff, cranky and worn out. His initial alignment, with feet under bed and head under dresser, had quickly proved unacceptable, since both Zane and Dortmunder invariably stepped on his exposed center section if they got up in the middle of the night, and *both* the bastards were *constantly* getting up in the middle of the night. Having Zane's gnarled foot, naked, pressing on one's stomach in the dark, was one of life's least pleasant experiences. The result was, Kelp was sleeping—or trying to sleep—curled up under the dresser, and it was having a very bad effect on both his posture and his personality.

And now Dortmunder wanted to go for a drive. "Where to?" Kelp had asked him. "Around," Dortmunder had said. "What are we looking for?" Kelp had asked him. "I'll know it when I see it," Dortmunder had said. He'll know it when he sees it. Driving around all afternoon in city traffic, on the wrong side of the street, on the wrong side of the car— Kelp signaled for a left turn, swore loudly, shifted into third gear, shifted into fourth gear, and almost ran down two women in tan wool cloaks and high leather boots who stepped out right in front of the car.

"*Christ,* Andy," Dortmunder said, peeling himself off the windshield.

"Those two—those two—" Kelp pointed at the women, more in outright astonishment than rage, while the women in their turn stood in front of the car, giving him reproving looks and pointing to something on the sidewalk. Peering in that direction, Kelp saw a blinking orange globe light over there, atop a pole. "Well, what the hell do you suppose *that* is?" he said.

"Beats me," Dortmunder said.

The women, having shaken their fingers at Kelp, walked on. Kelp sat blinking at the orange globe, which blinked back. "What am I supposed to do now?" he asked. "Wait for it to stay off, or to stay on?"

Peep, said the Mini behind them, and Dortmunder said, "I think you just go now." So Kelp signaled for a right.

"SHIT!"

First gear; tromp the accelerator; *second* gear; tromp the accelerator; *third* goddam gear and there was another one of those orange globes. Tromping the brake, Kelp now saw a similar orange globe directly across the way, and white lines on the street between the two, and as he was himself working out what it meant Dortmunder said, "It's a pedestrian crossing, that's all. Pedestrians got the right of way."

"*I* know it," Kelp snapped, and tromped the accelerator again, and lurched into Sloane Square. "Which way now?"

"Any way you want."

"I wanna go back under the dresser," Kelp said, because Sloane Square was completely full of traffic and people. Kelp inched the Opel along, painfully aware that he didn't know how much car he had on his left, stuck in the whirlpool flowing clockwise around the square, and was practically back where he'd started before he managed to break free, scooting down Kings Road, which turned out narrower than Sloane Street, with more traffic and more pedestrians and more shops and more buses. "And," Kelp cried, "they don't even have MD plates! What if there's an emergency? How you gonna find a doctor?"

"This car's okay," Dortmunder said.

"You try driving it. You try— Oh, shit."

Another pedestrian crossing, this one full of young people wearing carpet remnants. Kelp realized as he was doing it that he was about to shift gears with the wrong stick again, and said, "That's *it*." Depressing the stick, signaling for a right, he just kept on bearing down until the stick said *snap*. "Hold this for me," he said, handed the stick to Dortmunder, shifted into first, and drove on once the carpet sale had reached the sidewalk.

"You're signaling for a right again," Dortmunder told him.

"Tough," said Kelp.

They drove around for another half hour, down through Chelsea and over the Albert Bridge into Battersea, and north again over the Battersea Bridge, and up through Earl's Court and Kensington, with Kelp becoming increasingly adjusted to this weird way of driving, and up in Notting Hill Gate Dort-munder suddenly said, "Stop here."

"Here?"

"No, back there. Circle the block."

So Kelp tried circling the block, and promptly got lost, but after many adventures he got found again, which he didn't realize until Dortmunder suddenly said, "Stop *here*."

This time Kelp stopped, on a dime (or perhaps on a half pence), and the lorry full of metal pipe behind him com-plained loudly and bitterly. Kelp didn't care; he was realizing they'd come to the same spot in Notting Hill Gate from the opposite direction. "Now, how did *that* happen?"

"Pull over to the curb, Andy."

Kelp pulled over to the curb, and the lorry went by, filling the air with Stepney imprecations. "Now what?"

"Now we wait," Dortmunder told him. "You might as well cut the engine."

Notting Hill Gate is the name of a street, not a gate; a commercial street, like a neighborhood in Brooklyn, with movie theaters and supermarkets and dry cleaners. Ahead on the left a storefront was boarded up, with a dumpster at the curb out front and a team of men carrying out basket-loads of rubble. Ahead on the right, a man was working on a street-light, standing in a kind of metal bucket extended way up from the back of a truck parked below; the kind of vehicle known in America as a cherrypicker. Beyond the cherrypicker, a man on a high ladder was replacing the letters on a movie marquee; at the moment it read THE CHARGE OF THE SEVEN DWARFS. On the left, beyond the boarded-up store, a window washer was washing shop windows. The sidewalks were filled with men and women, carrying plastic bags or walking dogs or staring through freshly washed shop windows or muttering to them-selves.

"You're muttering to yourself," Dortmunder said.

"No, I'm not," Kelp said.

"It's the cherrypicker," Dortmunder told him.

"I already figured it out," Kelp said.

9

When a fellow's been sleeping under a dresser for more than a week it's child's play to fall asleep inside a big roomy armoire. Kelp was dreaming of himself as an angel playing a harp on a fluffy soft cloud when the armoire door was pulled open and Dortmunder rudely awakened him by clamping one hand over his mouth for silence' sake and whispering harshly in his ear, *"Wake up!"*

"Mmf!" yelled Kelp, then remembered that he wasn't an angel after all, that he didn't in fact know how to play the harp, and that he was only in this armoire because he was a thief. He and Dortmunder had come into Parkeby-South again late this afternoon, Monday, nearly a week since Chauncey's visit, and had watched and waited and roamed until there'd been opportunities to slip unnoticed into hiding places; Dortmunder into a sheaf of carpets draped over a railing around a stairwell, and Kelp into this armoire. It was slightly after four P.M. when they'd hidden themselves away, and it was slightly before two A.M. now, so Kelp had been asleep for about nine hours. "I'm hungry," he whispered, when Dortmunder released his mouth.

"Food later," Dortmunder whispered, and stepped back so Kelp could clamber quietly out of the armoire. Dortmunder too was hungry, though he wouldn't have admitted it, and at the moment he was less rested than Kelp. An almost overpowering need to sneeze had kept him awake most of the time inside those carpets, and when at last he'd napped for an hour or so an actual sneeze had awakened him. His own sneeze. Fortunately it hadn't alerted any of the guards, so when Dortmunder saw by his luminous watch dial that it was nearly midnight he slipped out of his hiding place. He spent the next two hours dogging the guards' footsteps and at about one-thirty he heard one of them in the ground-floor office say, "Hm. Streetlamp's gone out." So Chauncey was on the job.

Yes, he was. The other day, Kelp and Dortmunder had followed the cherrypicker to its home, a large fenced-in lot in Hammersmith where it was surrounded by other heavy equipment, all painted the same official yellow. Earlier today, Dortmunder and Kelp had dressed in workclothes, armed themselves with a clipboard, and gone back to Hammersmith, where Dortmunder did his unhelpful workman routine while claiming to have been sent "over from the job to get one of those. They were supposed to call from the office." There'd been little difficulty from the pipe-smoking fellow in the little shack by the gate, since they'd been perfectly willing to sign false names to every document he showed them. ("Canadians, are you?" "That's right.") Retiring with the cherrypicker to a quiet cul-de-sac off Holland Road, they'd used black enamel paint to change its ID and license-plate numbers, then parked it quite openly on Pont Street, less than two blocks from Chauncey's maisonette, where Chauncey and Zane had found it waiting at one o'clock this morning. Chauncey, using the key Kelp had given him, had driven the cherrypicker to Sackville Street, where he'd opened the metal plate in the streetlight pole (Dortmunder had shown him how on a streetlight back in Hans Place), and had snipped one wire to put out the light. And now he and Zane were sitting in the cab of the truck, waiting for the signal from inside Parkeby-South.

Within, Kelp stretched and yawned and scratched his head and shook himself all over like a dog in the rain. "You done wriggling?" Dortmunder asked him. "Time we got going."

"Right," Kelp said. Then, patting himself all over, he said, "Wait a minute. Where's my gun?"

Dortmunder frisked him, but Kelp was no longer armed, until they finally found it in the armoire, where it had slipped out of his pocket. A tiny .25 calibre Beretta automatic, it looked like a toy but it was less foolish than the four-inch-barrel custom-made .22 calibre target pistol inside Dortmunder's shirt. Being in a foreign land, away from their normal sources of supply, they'd been limited in armament to whatever Chauncey could come up with, and it had been this: a woman's purse automatic and a target pistol.

"Quietly now," Dortmunder said, unlimbering his own weapon, and the two of them slipped toward the office.

Outside, a complication had developed. Chauncey had been nervous at first—he thought of himself as sophisticated, but armed robbery was rather beyond his experience—but when everything went according to Dortmunder's plan his confidence grew and he found himself quite pleased with the insouciance he was projecting.

Until the bobby came wandering past at about five to two, and stopped to chat. "Out late, are you?" He was a young police officer with a moustache the size and shape and color of a street-sweeper's broom, and he wasn't in the least suspicious of Chauncey and Zane and the cherrypicker. Quite the opposite; a bit bored on these silent empty late-night commercial streets, he'd simply stopped off for human contact, a little shop talk with another pair of night-workers.

Every Englishman, and every American who spends any time at all in England, believes himself capable of imitating a cockney accent, and Chauncey was no exception. Donning his party cockney voice, he said, "Evenin, guvnor. Nice night, innit?"

"Canadian, are you?" asked the bobby.

"Err—yuss," said Chauncey.

Inside, Dortmunder and Kelp, peering out through the eyeholes in the itchy ski masks they were now wearing, entered the cashier's office and told the two guards, "Stick em up."

"Whurr," said one of the guards, and the other clattered his teacup into its saucer, turning to stare with blank astonishment and say, "Ere! Where'd you two come from?"

"Stick em *up*," Dortmunder repeated.

"Stick what up? Me mitts? I'll spill me tea."

"Put the tea *down*," Dortmunder told him, "and *then* stick em up."

"Well, I like that," grumbled the guard, plunking cup and saucer on top of a handy filing cabinet.

"Stickler for ritual, that's what he is," said the other guard, remaining calmly in his chair with his feet up on the desk as in leisurely fashion he stuck em up.

"Trade unionist," agreed the first guard, sticking his own up at last. "Brotherhood a Smash an Grabbers."

Dortmunder pointed the incredibly long barrel of his target pistol at the seated guard—it kept reminding him, unfortunately, of Hansel's stick-finger used to fool the witch about his skinniness—and said, "There's two more guards upstairs. Phone em, call em down here."

The seated guard lowered his feet from the desk and his hands from the air. "Two more upstairs, is it? Where'd you come by that idea?"

"One in an office on the second floor," Dortmunder told him, "one on a chair in a corridor on the fourth."

The guards gave each other impressed looks. "Knows his business," said the first.

"Got the floors wrong, though," commented the second.

"Probably Canadian." The first looked at Dortmunder. "You Canadian?"

"Australian," Dortmunder said. He was tired of being Canadian. "And in a hurry."

"Do like he says, Tom," the second advised. "Get on the blower."

"And be careful what you say," Dortmunder told him.

Outside, Chauncey was being *extremely* careful what he said, in his conversation with the bobby. They'd discussed the weather—was the summertime drought to be an annual event or not, and if so was it a good idea?—and they'd discussed overtime salary, and the bobby's problems with the London Electricity Board which had very nearly shut off his electricity by mistake, and Chauncey was beginning to wish this son of a bitch would drop down dead on the pavement. Beside Chauncey, Zane was fingering something under his jacket and undoubtedly thinking thoughts of a similar, though perhaps more activist, nature.

In the bobby's breast pocket was a miniature walkie-talkie, which occasionally spoke; disconcerting, at first, to be in conversation with a person whose pocket suddenly joins in. The bobby abruptly responded to one of its staccato announcements by looking alert and saying, "Right." Touching his helmet brim in a casual salute, he said, "Duty calls. Ta-ta."

"Ta-ta," Chauncey agreed, and watched in the cherrypicker's rear-view mirror as the bobby hied himself away toward Vigo Street.

"I was about to shoot him," Zane said.

"I was afraid you were." Chauncey glanced over at Parkeby-South. "And what's taking *them* so long?"

Nothing. Things were going very well, in fact. Tom had gotten on the blower and had talked first with Frank and then with Henry, telling them both to pop down to the office a minute, and here they came. Dortmunder and Kelp flanked the door, and in less than no time all four guards were having their hands tied behind their backs by Kelp, while Dortmunder stood well back, pointing the long-barreled gun as though at a slide in a lecture.

"All set," Kelp said at last. "Should I tie their ankles, too?"

This was a previously rehearsed bit of dialogue, and Dortmunder gave the prepared response: "No. We'll bring em with us. I want my eye on em till we're out of here." Meaning, in truth, just the reverse. The guards would be witnesses that neither of the bandits had ever gone upstairs.

Kelp led the way out of the office, followed by the four guards. Dortmunder brought up the rear, pausing first to pull a pocket flash from his jacket and aim it toward the nearest window: on-off, on-off, on-off.

"At last," said Chauncey. Climbing down from the cab, carrying the rolled-up imitation Veenbes in a black vinyl umbrella sheath, he went around to the back while Zane slid over behind the wheel. Chauncey climbed into the cherrypicker's bucket, which contained its own controls, and with some hesitation sent himself upward. He was a bit awkward at first, nearly whacking into the lamp post and then coming within a hair of braining himself on the light, but with practice came assurance, and after only modest adjustments he very quickly

brought himself up to that blessed window that had so fascinated Dortmunder. From his jacket pocket he took a rather
large magnet, which immediately fastened itself inexorably to
the side of the bucket. "Bastard," muttered Chauncey, and pried
the son of a bitch loose. Moving it with difficulty toward the
window—it was like walking an Irish setter puppy on a
short leash—Chauncey went to work.

This part he was already good at. Dortmunder had fixed a
bolt to one of Chauncey's windows, and Chauncey had practiced over and over again the manipulation of that bolt through
the window with this magnet. First the magnet slides *up* the
window, *up* the window, turning the little bolt, freeing its little
handle from the little slot. Then the magnet slides *across* the
window, slowly, gently, and the obedient little bolt slides slowly
and gently out of its nest in the window frame. Repeat with the
second bolt, and the window is unlocked. (Over and over
Dortmunder had returned to the question of this window,
wanting to know if the bolts were brass or iron, and finally
Chauncey had cried, "*Iron,* for the love of God!" "I hope you're
right," Dortmunder had said, "because a magnet won't work on
brass." Which was the first Chauncey had known about the
magnet, and he too had been hoping he was right ever since.
It was quite a relief to discover the bolts really *were* iron—he'd
been guessing.)

Now, Chauncey slid open the window and stepped from
bucket to staircase, carrying the umbrella sheath and pausing
to close the window behind himself. ("We don't want any
guards noticing any unexplained drafts," Dortmunder had
pointed out.) Up the half flight of stairs Chauncey hurried to
the value room, where he took from his pocket the string-tied
bundle of keys given him by Kelp. ("I'm no expert on English
locks," Kelp had said, "but if you got the brand right and the
appearance right, one of these keys should work on each lock."
And he'd shrugged, adding, "If not, the caper's a bust.")

Two locks. Fumbling in the dark, jangling the keys out of
haste and nervousness, Chauncey chose one at random and tried
it in both slots. No. Second one; no. Third one—

The eleventh key worked in the top lock. The seventeenth key—only four from the last—worked in the bottom lock. Chauncey pushed open the value-room door, and entered, as from downstairs there came the sound of glass breaking.

It was Kelp, smashing the front of a display case with the butt of his little Beretta. Reaching through the opening, he scooped up fistfuls of gold rings and transferred them to his pockets. In the background, Dortmunder went on pointing his curtain rod ("It's curtains for you! I brought my rod!"), while glancing from time to time at his watch.

Upstairs, Chauncey was also looking at his watch. Dortmunder had told him he'd have ten minutes from the moment of the flashlight signal, and he'd already used seven just getting into the room. Another time he might have dawdled to admire some of the other beauties in here, but now, shining his flashlight around, he had time for nothing but the Veenbes, which was . . . over there.

Downstairs, Kelp's pockets were full but Dortmunder's watch showed they still had three minutes to stall. "We'll check the next room," he said, and herded the guards ahead of him as Kelp led the way.

Upstairs: Painting off frame, imitation out of umbrella sheath, imitation tacked onto frame, original rolled (carefully, carefully) and inserted into sheath, Chauncey and sheath out of the room with locks snicking into place automatically behind him.

Downstairs: "That's enough," Dortmunder said. "Through that way," he told the guards, leading them to the basement stairs. The four guards went down the staircase, and Dortmunder and Kelp closed and locked the door, then turned and ran for the main exit.

Upstairs: Chauncey and sheath out the window and into the bucket, window closed, magnet out of pocket, magnet stuck to side of bucket, magnet *yanked* off bucket, magnet used to slide the left bolt back into place, the right bolt back into place.

Downstairs: Dortmunder and Kelp running pell-mell out of

the building, Kelp jingling like a Christmas sleigh, and both leaping into the cab of the cherrypicker, one on each side, pushing Zane into the middle, with Kelp behind the wheel. Dortmunder, looking up before entering the cab, saw the bucket descending from the sky, and told Kelp, "He's done. Go."

Kelp went. Throwing the cherrypicker into gear—he was becoming terrific at this looking-glass way of driving by now—he zipped down to Piccadilly and left toward Piccadilly Circus.

In the bucket, Chauncey couldn't believe it when the world suddenly started reeling sideways while he was still descending. "Hey!" he said, releasing the controls—the bucket stopped moving down but continued moving over—and he clutched the rim in both hands as the upper stories of Sackville Street rushed past. "Good God!" said Chauncey, and he didn't at all like the way the cherrypicker swayed when they made the left onto Piccadilly.

"Got to get down," Chauncey told himself. They must be dangerously overbalanced this way. But he couldn't force himself to release either of his handholds so he could operate the controls. Even his toes were making clutching movements, inside his shoes; especially when he looked out and saw Piccadilly Circus dead ahead. "Oh, no," he said.

Oh, yes. *Swayyyyy* to the right went the bucket toward the Eros statue as the truck angled left, then *swayyyyy* to the left as the truck roared around the Circus and shot down the hill of Haymarket. The sharp right turn into Pall Mall at the bottom of the downslope nearly sent them tumbling wheels over bucket down Cockspur Street, but the cherrypicker righted itself and hastened on.

"We were on two wheels!" Kelp cried, in outraged astonishment. "What kind of vehicle is this?"

Dortmunder, looking back through the cab's rear window, said, "He's still up there. Why doesn't he bring it down?"

"He'll tip us over!" Kelp was really angry. "What does he think this is, some kind of joyride?"

Chauncey didn't. Chauncey thought he was in Hell.

St. James's Street; another right turn, this one uphill, and to Chauncey's wondering eyes the traffic lights up on Piccadilly were red. Kelp didn't apply the brakes till the last possible second, which meant the bucket tried to keep going, so the two wheels the truck was on this time were both in front. Briefly the cherrypicker looked like some kind of yellow dinosaur imitating a bucking bronco.

But then it dropped back, and in the sudden cessation of movement Chauncey's hands clutched at the controls and *dowwwwwnn* came the bucket, reaching its bottom position just as the light turned green and Kelp whipped around the left turn into Piccadilly, steaming toward Hyde Park Corner. Midway, another set of traffic lights gleamed red, and no sooner had the cherrypicker shuddered to a halt than Chauncey clambered over the side, gripping tight the umbrella sheath, and ran up to climb into the cab on top of Dortmunder, who said, "What? What?"

"No more," Chauncey said, sitting on Dortmunder. "No more."

"We're being serious up here," Kelp told him angrily, "and you're back there playing games." And while Chauncey gaped at him, speechless, Kelp shifted into first and drove on.

10

When Dortmunder awoke, Zane was already up and out of the room, but Kelp slept on, curled like a collie beneath the dresser. "Wake up," Dortmunder suggested, prodding him gently with a bare toe. "This's the day we go home."

Kelp had learned to awaken cautiously, and not sit bolt upright. Rolling slowly out from under the dresser, he straightened himself with a series of snaps and creaks and moans, while

Dortmunder went off to the bathroom to make himself pretty for the flight. One P.M., leaving Heathrow, due to arrive at four P.M. (eight hours later and five time zones earlier) at Kennedy in New York. Dortmunder actually smiled at his reflection while shaving, and as a result nicked himself pretty badly.

Wearing a patch of toilet paper on the cut, he dressed himself and went downstairs, where he found a cheerful Chauncey, completely recovered from his ride in the bucket, drinking coffee and reading the *Times* in the dining-room window seat. "Good morning," Dortmunder told him.

Chauncey beamed over his paper. "*Good* morning? By God, Dortmunder, this is the sweetest morning of my life! You've made my day, you've turned me into a successful second-story man, and I'm delighted to have been associated with you."

"Sure," Dortmunder said, and reached for the coffeepot.

Edith wandered in, rubbing her hands together in front of her apron and grinning as she asked some sort of question.

"I think we'll have kippers this morning, Edith," Chauncey told her. "Enough for four, there's a good girl."

Edith went off, whickering, as Kelp came in, looking stiff and happy. "Never again under that dresser," he said. "It's like a pardon from the Governor." Seating himself, pouring some coffee, he said to Dortmunder, "Whadawe do with the goods we picked up last night?"

"Well, we don't bring it all through US Customs," Dortmunder said, "that's one thing for sure."

"According to the *Times*," Chauncey said, "you took eighty thousand pounds in merchandise from Parkeby-South last night."

Kelp said, "We're written up in the paper?"

"Right here." Chauncey passed it across.

Dortmunder said, "Eighty thousand pounds? What's that in dollars?"

"Roughly a hundred fifty thousand. How much of that would you get from a fence?"

"Maybe ten per cent."

Chauncey was surprised. "That's all? Fifteen thousand?"

"You don't get top dollar when you're peddling stuff on some police list."

"I'll give you a check myself, right now, for ten thousand dollars," Chauncey suggested. "Is that enough?"

"Not a check," Dortmunder told him.

"Yes, I see." Chauncey frowned, thinking it over. "This cash-only existence of yours can be difficult."

Kelp said, "It says here we were obviously English and well educated and trying to disguise our background with fake Australian accents."

Edith came simpering and bobbing in with four plates of hot buttery filleted kippers with lemon wedges, and they all set to, while Kelp went on reading the *Times*'s exhaustively detailed account of the robbery. He said, "Who's Raffles?"

"Beats me," Dortmunder said.

Chauncey said, "Dortmunder, how about this? I'll phone my accountant this afternoon and tell him to convert ten thousand dollars into cash, for you to pick up next Monday. You'll have a password so he'll know you're the man who should get the money."

"Fine," Dortmunder said.

"If Zane doesn't come down soon," Chauncey said, "his kippers will get cold."

"That's probably the way he likes them," Dortmunder said.

Kelp said, "Can I keep this paper?"

"Of course." Chauncey finished his last mouthful of kipper, swallowed coffee, and got to his feet, saying, "I have to look at it. I have to *see* it again." And he went through into the living room, where the umbrella sheath had been left last night, in the closet by the front door.

Kelp said, "Did I hear right? He'll give us ten grand for that stuff?"

"That's what he says."

"So it didn't turn out so bad after all. With what we got before, that adds up to—" Kelp did some figuring on his fingers. "—twenty-three thousand apiece."

"Twenty-three thousand dollars a year is not good wages,"

Dortmunder said, and from the other room came a sudden cut-off howl, as though somebody had wounded a yak. Dortmunder and Kelp stared toward the doorway, and Chauncey staggered back into the room, his face white, ghastly looking in the frame of yellow hair. From his dangling right hand hung the painting, still partly curled, dragging on the carpet.

"Not something else," Dortmunder said, and went over to take the painting out of Chauncey's lax hand. But when he looked at it, everything was fine: Folly continued to lead man to ruin.

Kelp, coming over, holding in his right hand a fork with kipper impaled on it, said, "What's up?"

"Fake," Chauncey said. His voice was hoarse, as though he'd been punched in the throat.

Dortmunder frowned at him. "This is the fake? This is the one you *brought* there?"

"Different," Chauncey said. "A different fake."

"What?" Dortmunder shook the canvas in irritation. "You saw this damn thing a week ago, why didn't you see *then* it was a fake?"

"That one was real." Chauncey was recovering now, though his face remained bloodless and his eyes unnaturally wide. "It *was* real, Dortmunder."

"You mean there's *two* fakes?"

"Last night," Chauncey said, "I held the real painting in my hands."

"Impossible." Glowering at the painting, Dortmunder said, "You screwed up somewhere, Chauncey, you didn't—" And then he stopped, frowning in a puzzled way at the painting, holding it closer to his face.

Chauncey said, "What is it? Dortmunder?"

Turning back to the dining table, Dortmunder spread the painting on it and pointed at one of the figures behind Folly: a buxom farm girl, carrying a basket of eggs. "Look."

Chauncey and Kelp both leaned over the painting. Chauncey said, "Look? Look at what?"

It was Kelp who answered. "By golly, that's Cleo," he said.

"Cleo? Cleo?"

"Cleo Marlahy," Dortmunder told him. "Porculey's girl friend."

Kelp said, "I *told* you I saw him, that day outside Parkeby-South."

"Porculey?" Chauncey was struggling to catch up. "Porculey did a second fake? But why? How— How did it get *here?*" He stared at Dortmunder, but Dortmunder was looking at something on the far side of the table. Chauncey looked in the same direction, and saw the fourth plate of kippers, untouched, cold. Outside, the sun slid behind a cloud. Rain began to fall. "Zane," said Chauncey.

11

Leo Zane said, "So we have the picture."

"I don't believe you," Ian Macdough said.

"Don't be silly," Zane told him. "Of course you believe us."

Success was within Zane's grasp, and the sense of it was making him expansive, bright eyed, almost warm. He had conceived a complex and daring plan, and he'd succeeded under the very noses of Chauncey and his hired thieves. What would Dortmunder and company think *now* of their cleverness?

The idea had come to Zane in a sudden flash, back in New York, while Dortmunder had been explaining his own painting-switch scheme to Chauncey. The money, the opportunity, everything was right. Porculey had readily agreed to furnish a second fake Veenbes for a quarter of the return, the switch had been made, and now they were here in the Savoy, Zane doing the talking while Porculey ate toast from Macdough's unfinished breakfast. They had come to give the Scotsman their terms.

"Half," Macdough said bitterly. "You think I'll give you half."

Half. Two hundred thousand dollars, more or less; enough to start life all over again. This last year had convinced him;

no more cold wet northern winters. He would live somewhere warm and dry, become healthy, even happy, make friends, perhaps get a dog, a television set. Life would become possible. Two hundred thousand dollars could buy a lot of warmth.

Macdough, this orange-haired red-faced bluff of a man, was wasting everybody's time and his own breath with bad temper. "You're either a pair of filthy liars," he was saying, "or you're despicable thieves."

"Half," Zane said calmly. "If you want the painting back."

"If you even have it. Show it to me, then."

"Oh, no," Zane said. "Not before you sign the agreement."

"How do I know you have it at all?"

"There's an easy way to check," Zane told him, "and you know it yourself. Go to Parkeby-South, look at the painting there, see if it's the right one."

Macdough hesitated, and Zane could see his dark little mind working. The man believed them, all right, and was trying to find some way out. But there was none. Zane had it all sewed up. "Well?" he said.

"All right," Macdough decided. "I'll *go* to Parkeby-South, and I'll look at my painting, and then I'll more than likely have you two arrested for confidence tricksters."

"We'll all go together," Zane said, getting to his feet.

"You'll wait outside," Macdough told him.

"Of course. Come along, Porculey."

"One minute. One minute." Porculey put the last of Macdough's uneaten bacon between the last two slices of Macdough's toast, and the three friends left the suite and took a taxi to Parkeby-South, where Macdough ran grim-faced inside while Zane and Porculey waited in the cab.

Porculey, showing nervousness now that Macdough was out of sight, said, "What if he calls the police?"

"He won't," Zane said. "Not unless he's an even bigger fool than I think. If he calls the police he loses everything, and he knows it."

Macdough was less than five minutes inside, and when he emerged he actually hurled himself like a javelin across the sidewalk and into the cab, where he faced the other two with a glower of helpless rage and said, "All right, you bastards. All right."

"Back to the Savoy, driver," Zane called, and as the cab moved away from the curb he took from his pocket the two-page contract, prepared and typed by himself, and extended it to Macdough, saying, "You'll probably want to read this before you sign it."

"I shouldn't be surprised," Macdough said, and with their concentration on the contract, none of them in the cab noticed the pale blue Vauxhall that started up from the curb half a block behind them and edged forward in their wake.

Zane smiled as he watched Macdough read the contract. In simple clear-cut language, it said Macdough was to pay Zane and Porculey "for their assistance in preparing the said painting for sale," one-half his net return "before taxes" from the painting's disposition.

" ' . . . or paid to the survivor—' " Macdough read aloud, and gave them a bitter look. "Trust each other, do you?"

"Certainly," said Zane, ignoring the startled sidelong look he got from Porculey.

Macdough went on reading, then shook his head and said, "All right. You're a pair of unnatural ghouls, but you have me over a barrel."

"My pen," Zane suggested, extending it, and watched smiling as Macdough scrawled his name at the bottom of the second page.

"Now, give me back my painting," Macdough said, handing over the contract and the pen.

"Of course. But if you have a safe place to hide it, I think you should keep it out of Parkeby-South's hands until just before the sale."

Macdough looked startled, and worried. "Chauncey might try to get it back?"

"Of course he will, and so will the men with him."

"The bastards."

"Do you have a safe place," Zane asked him, "or should we hold it for you?"

"*You* bastards!" Macdough snorted. "I'll hold my own property for my own self, if you *don't* mind."

"Not a bit," Zane said, unruffled. "But if *you* don't mind, Mr. Porculey and I will stay with you while you hide it."

"It's a long way from here," Macdough said doubtfully, "and my car isn't the world's biggest."

"We won't mind at all," Zane said. "Will we, Mr. Porculey?"

Porculey, who looked like a man rampant with second thoughts, vaguely shook his head, saying, "Not at all, no. Don't mind at all."

"So we'll all go for a drive together," Zane said. Putting one cold hand on Macdough's knee and the other cold hand on Porculey's knee, he smiled at both unhappy men in turn. "One for all," he said. "And all, of course, for one."

12

It's difficult to wait unobtrusively in a car on the Strand in the middle of London's horrible traffic jam, but that's what Chauncey was doing, clinging grimly to his bit of curb despite the honking of taxis, the yelling of lorry drivers or the dirty looks of pedestrians. Dortmunder had crossed the street and disappeared into the Savoy, following Zane and Porculey and Macdough, leaving Chauncey and Kelp to wait here in this clogged artery for whatever would happen next.

It was Dortmunder who'd figured it out that Zane would have to go to Macdough, as his only logical customer for the painting, and that Macdough would be bound to check the authenticity of the painting currently held by Parkeby-South. Which was why they'd rented this Vauxhall and taken up a position across the street from the auction gallery. ("By God," Dortmunder had said, with something like awe in his voice, "I'm returning to the scene of the crime.") But even Dortmunder hadn't been able to explain why that despicable trio in the taxi had led them back to the Savoy rather than on to wherever the painting was stashed. Which was why Dortmunder was in there now, trying to find out what was going on without being seen.

Kelp, who had been quietly thinking his own thoughts in the back seat, now leaned forward and said, "You know? I'm getting so I kind of like this town."

"Glad to hear it," Chauncey said. His eye was on the lane leading to the Savoy's entrance.

"It's a lot like New York," Kelp said, "only goofier. You know what I mean?"

"Here comes Dortmunder."

Here came Dortmunder. He trotted across the street, slid in next to Chauncey, and said, "He's checking out, and he ordered his car. A white Mini, license W-A-X three six one A. You owe me five pounds, for bribes."

"Where are they going?" It made no sense to Chauncey that Macdough should suddenly check out of his hotel.

Apparently, it didn't make sense to Dortmunder either. "I suppose they'll go pick up the painting," he said. "After that, I don't know. We'll just stick with them."

"Mini coming," Kelp said.

Out of Savoy Court came an absolutely jam packed white Mini. Macdough was driving, hunched over the steering wheel like a bear riding a tricycle, with Zane a stiff rigor-mortis figure in the passenger seat beside him and Porculey expanding like bread dough all over the back. The Mini's springs were nowhere near able to deal with such a load; *burr-rong,* it bottomed out, as Macdough turned into the viscosity of traffic on the Strand.

"Keep well back," Dortmunder advised.

"I will. I will."

The Strand, Fleet Street, around Ludgate Circus and up Farringdon Street and Farringdon Road and a right turn onto Rosebery Avenue, in the drab disrepair of Finsbury. Just short of St. John Street the Mini stopped and Zane got out to permit Porculey to emerge, panting and wheezing, like a champagne cork out of a bottle that's gone flat. Zane waited on the sidewalk, glancing warily about, while Porculey trotted into a nearby Bed & Breakfast establishment. Chauncey and Dortmunder and Kelp ducked their heads and waited, half a block away.

"There it is!" Chauncey was peeking through his fingers, and his whole body vibrated when he saw Porculey crossing the street toward the Mini, carrying a long tubular object wrapped in brown paper. "Let's get it now! We'll go there right now! What could they do on a public street?"

"Kill us," Dortmunder told him. "I'm sure Zane has a gun, and I know I don't."

Porculey handed the package to Zane while he reinserted himself into the Mini's back seat—exactly like putting a champagne cork *back* into the bottle—then Zane handed the package in to Porculey, settled again in the front passenger seat, pulled the Mini's door shut, and the car moved off, the Vauxhall once again half a block behind.

St. John Street, Upper Street, Holloway Road, Archway Road— "Where are they *going?*" cried Chauncey. Their helplessness was infuriating.

"Beats me," Dortmunder said. "I don't know this town."

"But they're heading *out* of town! They're heading for the M 1!"

"Just stay with them."

Lyttleton Road, the Great North Way, the on-ramp for the M 1. Up on the highway went the Mini, struggling up to sixty miles per hour, bottoming out at every dip, with the Vauxhall nearly a quarter of a mile back.

Dortmunder said, "Where's this road go?"

"Everywhere," Chauncey told him. "Manchester, Liverpool, it's the main road north out of London, it goes up—" He stopped, struck by a sudden realization.

Dortmunder said, "You mean—?"

In a whisper, Chauncey finished his sentence: "—to Scotland," he said.

13

The trip north: The Mini and the Vauxhall both gassed up at a service area near Northampton, then switched from the M 1 to the M 6, and stopped for lunch at another service area above Birmingham. (Macdough and Zane and Porculey ate hot meals at a table in the cafeteria, while Chauncey and Dortmunder and Kelp chewed sandwiches and drank coffee out of plastic cups in the car. Porculey carried the painting with him into the restaurant, to the chagrin of Macdough, Chauncey, Dortmunder and Kelp.) Another stop for gasoline north of Manchester was made by both cars, and yet another just south of Carlisle. (These motorway service areas were large and busy places, where the Vauxhall could keep an unobtrusive distance from the Mini.)

Above Carlisle the motorway ended, and the two cars switched to the A 74 and then the A 73, stopping for gas in Carluke. The Mini chose a small Shell station and the Vauxhall had to go on by, but just ahead there was a Fina station.

East of Glasgow the two cars picked up the M 8 toward Edinburgh, taking the bypass around the city to the Forth Bridge over the Firth of Forth, then the M 90 and the A 90 north to Perth, where the Mini drove around in circles for a while. (Chauncey became convinced Zane had realized he was being followed and was trying to lose them, but in fact Macdough was looking for a particular restaurant of which he had fond memories. He failed to find it.) The occupants of the Mini ate in an Italian restaurant, while the occupants of the Vauxhall filled their gas tank again and ate takeout food from a Wimpy's.

After dinner, with night coming on, Macdough bought more gas for the Mini and led the way farther north, taking the A 9 up into the mountains. The road became increasingly curving and narrow, the distances between towns grew longer, and the Vauxhall had to drive practically on top of the Mini to keep it in sight. Up they went, and north, through the Obney Hills and the Craigvinean Forest and the Pass of Killiecrankie and Dalnacardoch Forest and Glen Truim, till up above Kingussie the Vauxhall made a hairpin climbing turn around the pock-marked stone flank of an ancient barn, and the Mini was gone.

"*Now* what?" Dortmunder said.

Ahead in the Vauxhall's lights the road climbed steeply up a rocky broken slope, angling to the right. The Mini *could not* already have crested the hill. Nevertheless, Chauncey dropped from second gear to first and accelerated at full throttle upward, the back end bouncing and jiggling on the uneven road, the rear tires rattling volleys of stones in their wake.

And at the crest, the view was of a winding descent through hedgerows and stone walls, with three segments of macadam roadway dimly visible, and no vehicle lights at all on any of them.

"They turned off," Dortmunder said.

"But there's no *place* to turn off."

"Lights over there," Kelp said, and when they both turned to look at him (because they had no idea where "over there" was) he was pointing off to the left. Out that way, apparently at some distance in the mountainous dark, what looked to be headlights were flickering. They disappeared, appeared again, disappeared.

"We missed the turnoff," Dortmunder said.

"Damn." Chauncey twisted sideways to look past Kelp's ear at the downslope, easing his foot cautiously on the brake. He was a shaky driver in reverse, oversteering madly, swinging back and forth in abrupt Z's across the road, but he did make it all the way to the bottom before plowing into the front end of a silver Jensen Interceptor III with stereo t/d, AM/FM, a/c, brown int., calfskin uph., electric windows, all power, immaculate cond., private owner, which was just growling at speed around the corner of the stone barn.

"Damn it to hell, I've hit him!"

"The painting," Dortmunder said, and pointed at the faint trail leading upward, next to the barn.

"The painting." Chauncey looked at Dortmunder, at the rear-view mirror, and made his decision. Into first gear, spin the wheel hard left, and *accelerate.*

The initial impact had broken the Vauxhall's left-rear taillight and slightly dented a bit of its rear metalwork, while putting out one of the Jensen's headlights, crumpling its radiator and severely denting both its front fenders. The sudden leap forward by the Vauxhall, just as the Jensen's driver was stepping in horror and astonishment out onto the pavement, jolted the Jensen forward, dumped its driver into the mud and gravel at the verge, and then wrenched the Jensen's front bumper loose. Its gonglike clatter when it hit the pavement served as a kind of announcement for the Department of the Environment highway truck, a big yellow Leyland full of stones and dirt, which at that moment came around the corner of the barn and smacked the Jensen very smartly in the rear.

In the Vauxhall, bucketing up the unpaved side road, Chauncey clung grimly to the steering wheel and Dortmunder hung desperately to everything he could find on the dashboard, while Kelp jounced backwards in the rear seat, gazing down the hill toward the road and saying, "He just got it again. Some truck hit him."

Neither Chauncey nor Dortmunder cared what was going on back there. A half moon and several million stars in a cloudless sky showed even more clearly than their headlights a scrub-filled up-and-down landscape virtually as wild as when Hadrian built his wall. The Picts and Celts might no longer be about (except on football weekends), but the countryside which had formed their rough bad-tempered natures was still as it had been, scarred more by nature than by man. Driving through this scrag, not once did anyone in the Vauxhall see a light, nor any other indication of the Mini, till all at once, as they crawled up over rocks and roots between two gnarled and stumpy pines, Porculey appeared in their headlights, blinking nervously and gesturing for them to turn right.

Chauncey lifted his foot from the accelerator in surprise, and the car, barely moving anyway, promptly stalled.

And now Chauncey's door opened, and Leo Zane's voice said, "Out you come. Dortmunder? Kelp? You weren't silly enough to bring guns, were you?"

No; they were silly enough *not* to bring guns. All three emerged from the Vauxhall, Chauncey looking tense but not frightened, Dortmunder grimly annoyed, Kelp disgusted. Zane said, "Walk up the hill to the right. Griswold, follow with their car. Keep the lights on us."

The three prisoners, followed by Zane, and then by Porculey driving their car, went up the hill, their black shadows long dark charcoal lines lengthening ahead of them. Turning right again at Zane's direction, they found themselves in the battered moss-grown remnant of what had once apparently been a good-sized castle. A few boulderish bits of stone wall, like an early draft for Stonehenge, was all they could see at first, but then Porculey cut the Vauxhall's lights, and in the softer illumination of moon- and starlight they could make out still-standing segments of the building clustered across the way.

Zane now used a flashlight to guide them over a gorse-grown former courtyard to a gray stone wall shielding a flight of worn steps leading down. At the bottom, a heavy door shaped like an inverted shield stood open, and they entered upon a clammy empty stone corridor, its distant end obscured by shadow. Zane's flashlight told them to walk down this corridor and then to enter a doorway on the left, while behind them they could hear the heavy groaning of hinges as Porculey closed the stairway door.

They were now in a large cluttered stone room. Barred windows were spaced along one wall, up near the ceiling. To the left and straight ahead the room was filled with decaying old furniture, piles of wooden boxes and cardboard cartons, stacks of newspapers, bits and pieces of armor and old weaponry, clusters of mugs and jugs and bottles, massed decaying flags, mantel clocks, candlesticks, and in every chink some further bric-a-brac. To the right, an area had been cleared, a kind of

half circle before a huge deep fireplace. Here the stone floor
was covered with a faded old carpet, on which stood a few
massive uncomfortable-looking chairs and tables. Three candles burned on the high mantelpiece, and before the unlit fireplace stood Ian Macdough, looking worried. "So it's true," he
said, as they all walked in.

"As I told you," Zane said, limping to one side while Porculey closed the door.

"Nice place you got here," Kelp said, with his chipper smile.
"Must be tough on the cleaning lady, though."

Dortmunder had turned an accusatory eye on Porculey, saying, "I'm disappointed in you. I knew these other two were no
good, but I thought you were an honest man."

"It's that ten thousand you gave me," Porculey said, avoid-
ing Dortmunder's eye. "Money's a strange thing," he added,
sounding a bit surprised at himself. "As soon as you have
some, it wants you to get more. I never knew I wanted a hundred thousand dollars until I got the ten thousand."

Meanwhile, Macdough was still looking worried, saying to
Zane, "Now we've got them, what do we do with them?"

"Nothing," Chauncey said. "There's a public controversy
over that painting, Macdough, between you and me and the
insurance company. What happens to your sale if I disappear
before it's straightened out?"

Macdough rubbed a knuckle over his lips and cleared his
throat. "You shouldn't have followed us," he said.

"It's my painting," Chauncey said, "and you're going to
have to deal with me."

"Split the take *six* ways? Man, man, that doesn't pay my
hotel bill!"

"These two were already paid," Chauncey said, with a gesture toward Dortmunder and Kelp so casual, so dismissing,
that Dortmunder understood at once the teams had regrouped,
leaving himself and Kelp out in the cold.

So, speaking just as casually, Dortmunder said, "That's
right. We just came along to help Chauncey, so now we'll leave
you people to dicker without a lot of outsid rs—"

"No, no, Dortmunder," Zane interrupted, smiling behind his gun. "Don't you hurry away."

Irritably, Chauncey said, "Why not, Zane? They don't want anything, let them leave."

"With what they know?" Zane shook his head. "They could still make money, Chauncey. From your insurance company, for instance."

Chauncey gave Dortmunder a sudden sharp look, and Dortmunder told him, "You know better than that. All we want is our airfare, and we're quits."

"I can't think about you now, Dortmunder," Chauncey said, shaking his head like a man pestered by gnats.

"Mr. Chauncey," Kelp said, "I didn't sleep under your dresser for a week and a half to be treated like this."

But Chauncey wasn't listening. He'd turned back to Macdough, saying, "I want my painting."

"Buy it at the auction."

"I've already paid for it. It's *mine*."

"I won't give it to you," Macdough said, "and that's that. And I won't give up the lion's share of the money either."

Dortmunder said, "Why not pull the insurance game again?"

Everybody looked at him. Macdough said, "What insurance game?"

"You go back to Parkeby-South," Dortmunder told him, "and say you're worried because of the robbery, you want the same experts to come back and look at the painting. They do, they see it's a fake, you claim the original was stolen during the robbery—"

"Which is what happened," Macdough pointed out, sounding bitter.

"So you aren't even lying. The gallery's insurance company pays you, so you've got your money. You sell Chauncey the original for a few dollars and everybody's happy."

There was interest in Macdough's face, and also in Chauncey's, but then Zane had to stick his two cents in, saying, "That's cute, Dortmunder, but it won't work."

"Sure it will."

"Insurance companies won't pay twice for the same painting," Zane said.

Which was the flaw in Dortmunder's argument, as Dortmunder had already known, but he could only do his best with the materials at hand. "They'll have to pay," he insisted. "How can the gallery's insurance company refuse to pay Macdough for a painting everybody says is real?"

"By stalling," Zane said. "That's the way insurance companies operate anyway. There's already a lawsuit between Chauncey and *his* insurers in the states. The insurance company here would just tell Macdough they won't settle his claim until the lawsuit on the other side is settled. *One* of those two might get some insurance money, but not both."

Chauncey's already had his," Macdough grumbled, and from the lowering expression on his face Dortmunder knew the ploy had failed.

"I'll give you a hundred thousand for the painting," Chauncey told Macdough. "I can't afford it, but we have to break this deadlock somehow."

"Not enough," Macdough said. "I signed a paper with these two for half. I'd only get fifty thousand pounds out of it."

Chauncey shook his head with a rueful smile. "I'm sorry, it's worse than you think," he said. "I meant a hundred thousand dollars."

"What? Sixty thousand pounds? With *thirty* for me?"

"Keep all sixty," Chauncey told him. "Tax free. It's under the table, you don't have to declare it and these two can't take you to court."

"I wouldn't take him to court," Zane said dryly. "Forget it, Chauncey. Macdough and I—and Porculey, of course—intend to split four hundred thousand dollars. If we get it from you, fine. If not, we'll get it at the auction."

Dortmunder said, "Not if Chauncey makes an anonymous call and tells the London police to check the copy in Parkeby-South. You don't dare stop Chauncey, but he can stop you. Once the cops know the original was stolen, Macdough doesn't dare show up with it. And you're right back with only one buyer: Chauncey."

Chauncey smiled at Zane. "He's right, you know."

"He's not in this conversation," Zane said, angrily.

"I'm the one took the painting away," Dortmunder told Macdough. "I could put it back."

"*I* can put it back!" Zane yelled, glaring at Dortmunder. To the others he said, "We won't talk in front of these people any more. They're out of it."

Chauncey said, "You can't let them go, and nobody wants you shooting them."

Kelp said, "I'd just like to mention, today's my birthday."

"There are rooms here with doors that lock," Zane said mildly. "We'll put them away till the discussion's over."

Dortmunder said to Macdough, "I could be useful to you."

But it wasn't enough; not against Zane's gun. Macdough glanced away, biting the insides of his cheeks, and Zane gestured with the gun barrel, saying, "Come on, you two."

There wasn't any choice. Dortmunder and Kelp went, out the door and farther down the hall to a closed door with a thick wooden bar across it. "Take off the bar and lean it against the wall," Zane ordered, standing back too far for Dortmunder to swing it at him. Then he had them enter the room, which they saw in the flashlight's beam to be filled with the same massed clutter as the room they'd just left.

"There's no light in here," Kelp said, crossing the threshold.

"There's nothing interesting to see," Zane assured him. "Step back from the door." When Dortmunder stood facing him, just barely inside the room, Zane smiled at him and said, "Relax. You know they won't let me shoot you."

"They'll let you leave us here. Is that a better way to die?"

Zane shrugged. "Where there's life, I understand," he said, "there's hope." And he shut and barred the door.

14

"He's crazy, you know," Chauncey told Macdough, the instant Zane had led his prisoners out the door. "He wants *all* the money, and he'll kill every one of us before he's done."

"He's my partner," Macdough said. "You're just trying to split us up."

"He's a killer. That's what attracted me to him in the first place."

Porculey, stepping toward the two men, said, "Mr. Chauncey, I agree with you, and I want you to know I am heartily sorry I ever got involved with the man."

"I can handle myself with Zane," Macdough insisted, rather too forcefully. "And with you." Both he and Chauncey ignored Porculey, as though he hadn't spoken, as though he weren't there.

"You're out of your depth," Chauncey said. "I *will* queer your pitch, Macdough, and even Zane knows he doesn't dare stop me."

"We'll find another buyer. We'll get just as much on the black market. Some Arab sheikh."

Porculey, seeing he'd get cold comfort from both these two, and also seeing how absorbed they were in their argument, sidled as unobtrusively as a stout terrified man *can* sidle toward the door, picking up the still-wrapped painting on the way by. Quietly, without fuss, he departed the room.

Meanwhile, Chauncey pointed out Macdough's lack of expertise in selling paintings on the black market, and Macdough stated he had nothing but time and could probably sell the painting *and* collect on Parkeby-South's insurance, and Chauncey said, "And the minute you get your hands on the money, you're a dead man."

Which was when Zane entered, saying, "Talking against me, Chauncey?"

"Telling him the truth."

"Macdough knows better than that," Zane said, though from the way Macdough looked at Zane maybe he *didn't* know better than that. Still, Zane went blithely on, saying, "Porculey and I have no—" Then he stopped, frowned, looked left and right. "Where *is* my little friend?"

"Porculey?"

"The painting!" Macdough pointed at the table on which it had lain.

"He—he wouldn't dare!"

The three men turned toward the door, about to race in pursuit, Zane already waving his pistol over his head, when Porculey himself came backing in and turned to give their astonished faces a sheepish smile. The tubular package was held at port arms across his chest.

"*You!*" Macdough shrieked, and led the charge, closely followed by Chauncey and Zane. Porculey, his smile panicky, yelped and ran away into the piles of junk, the other three pursuing, Zane actually firing a shot in the air, a vast blast of explosion which deafened them all in that confined stone room, so that nobody, not even Zane himself, heard his own voice shout, "Stop!"

Porculey wouldn't have stopped anyway. He was climbing an upended mohair sofa, scrambling over pillows and library tables and candelabra up toward the ceiling, with half a dozen hands clutching at his ankles. They were dragging him back, dragging him down, and Porculey was shrieking a babble of absurd explanation, when all at once a voice from behind them all said:

"*Ul*-lo ullo ullo, what's this; then?"

They looked back, all of them draped on the stored goods like a quartet of mountain climbers who've just heard a rumble, and coming through the doorway was a tall-helmeted young police constable in uniform, pushing his bicycle.

15

The fact was, the driver of that Jensen Interceptor III was locally a Very Important Person. Sir Francis Monvich, his name was, he was fifty-six and very rich, and when his eighty-three-year-old father died he would become the 14th Viscount Glengorm, which in that neighborhood was pretty good. When Sir Francis Monvich's Jensen was hit both front *and* rear, and when the hooligan who hit it in front promptly ran away into the surrounding countryside, the local constabulary could be expected to take a very serious view of the situation. They would consider their position. They would proceed at *once* to find some individuals who would assist the police in their enquiries.

"*That* way," Sir Francis informed the first pair of constables to arrive on the scene, and pointed dramatically toward the winding track leading uphill next to the barn. These constables were on bicycles, which were more a hindrance than a help on the path they were now required to take, though they did get the odd terrifying downhill plunge between the uphill plods. They had reached Castle Macdough, and were studying the empty Vauxhall and Mini, when another pair of constables arrived, these in a white police car. All four spread out, shining their flashlights this way and that, the first two keeping their bicycles with them to prevent their being stolen by concealed miscreants, and thus it was that Porculey, having been forced to hide in another doorway while Zane walked back to the main room from locking up Dortmunder and Kelp, stepped out of his hiding place to see a police officer with a bicycle coming this way, flashing his light from side to side. In panic,

Porculey ran on tippy-toe back to the room with the others, and realized just one second too late what a mistake he'd made.

The constable—PC Quillin by name—failed to see Porculey run ahead of him down the corridor, but he did hear the yelling that followed, and he *certainly* heard the shot. So did the other three constables searching the vicinity, and so did two more constables, just arriving in another police car.

PC Quillin entered the room. Zane thought briefly of shooting him, shooting everybody else, taking the painting, and starting all over again in a new location with an entirely different crowd.

Three more constables entered the room. Zane decided not to shoot anybody. In fact, he tucked his pistol away in among the hassocks and halberds.

Macdough and Chauncey started telling different lies to the constables.

More constables entered the room.

Porculey started telling every truth he could think of.

Zane didn't speak at all, but smiled amiably (as he thought) at all the constables.

PC Quillin, having noticed that the long tubular package seemed to be of general interest to these babbling crooks, took it from Porculey's willing hands and opened it.

Chauncey tried to bribe a constable.

The constable—PC Baligil—gave him a rough unfriendly glower. "American, are you?"

"Canadian," said Chauncey.

"We'll sort this out at the station," PC Baligil decided. "And which of you has the firearm?"

Firearm? Firearm? After the general denials, PC Quillin made a quick search and within thirty seconds found the thing hanging from a halberd. "Careful about fingerprints," PC Baligil told him.

Macdough turned an embittered eye on Chauncey. "I blame you for this entire thing," he said.

"And *I* blame *you*," Chauncey responded. "You cheap opportunist crook."

"Blame each other at the station," PC Baligil suggested, "where we can take it all down. Come along."

They were reluctant, but they went along, complaining at one another and trying out new lies on the constables, who paid very little attention. "We might as well see are there any more," PC Baligil said to a young constable called PC Tarvy. "We'll just have a look at these other rooms along here."

So PC Tarvy took one side of the corridor and PC Baligil the other, flashing their lights around one debris-packed interior after another. "It's nothin but lumber rooms," PC Tarvy said.

"Oh, they'll have a deal to tell us, that lot," PC Baligil answered. "All stolen goods, this, I shouldn't be surprised." And he turned to see PC Tarvy removing the bar from a locked room. "Now, then," he said. "Who'd be in a room locked on the outside?"

"I just thought I'd look." And PC Tarvy pulled open the door and shone his light on nothing but more of the same: furniture, old trunks, a cluttered pile of armor on the floor. (In truth, there was no reason these days to keep that door barred; but where else would you keep the bar?)

"Come along, Tarvy," said PC Baligil, and PC Tarvy turned away, leaving that door not only unbarred but open (which is how bars get lost), as he and PC Baligil went up to join the other constables and their prisoners.

Dawn comes early in the highlands in the summer. It had been well after midnight when the Mini had turned off the A 9 and the Vauxhall had ricocheted off that Jensen, and now it was after two in the morning, and the first faint lines of color outlined the mountains to the east as the constables distributed themselves and their bicycles and their prisoners into the four cars and went away.

For several minutes, there was only silence in the moonlit ruin of Castle Macdough. The orange line defining the eastern mountains grew a bit broader, lightening toward a pinkish yellow. Then a kind of clanking sound was heard from deep within the bowels of the castle, and heavily, thud by thud, a suit of armor came up the steps. It stopped when it reached the courtyard, looking left and right, creaking and squeaking with every movement. Then it called, in Dortmunder's voice, "They're gone."

And up came a second suit of armor, slow and clanking like the first. (These two complete sets had been lying on the floor, sprinkled over with stray additional bits and pieces of armor, when PC Tarvy had shone his light into the room.) The second suit of armor, speaking in Kelp's voice, said, "That was a close one."

"It was more than close," the first suit said. "There goes Chauncey *with* the ten grand he promised us, *and* the jewels and stuff still in his house, and *us* with no money for airplane tickets."

"I was thinking about that," the second suit said. "While we were lying on the floor down there. And I think I got a terrific idea."

"Oh?"

"Listen to this. We fake a skyjacking, but what we *really* do—" And at that point the eager voice faltered to a stop, because the first suit had turned its blank metal face and was gazing fixedly at the second suit. "Dortmunder?" said the second suit. "Something wrong?"

Instead of answering, the first suit raised a mailed fist and swung it in a great half circle, but the second suit jumped (*clank!*) backward out of the way, so that the first, following the momentum around, nearly but not quite fell down the steps. Balance regained, it advanced on the second suit, which backed away, saying, "Dortmunder? Don't *be* like this. You'll regret it when you're calm."

The first suit kept moving forward, swinging the right arm again and this time striking a spark from a slight *knick* against the second suit's nose.

"No! cried the second suit. "Dortmunder!" But then it turned and ran, out of the courtyard and down the steep stony hill in the moonlight, the first suit blundering and thundering after, both yelling now, up crag and down glen, clanking and crashing eastward toward the sunrise, one suit of armor chasing another, a thing that hasn't been seen in that neighborhood for years and years. And years.